ALIEN BELIEVE TOO!
TRILOGY SPECIAL EDITION

Written by Brian Hiller

All Rights Reserved ©2017 Hiller Creations Ltd.© Any use in any manner of this material without the expressed written consent of Brian Hiller of Hiller Creations Ltd.© is prohibited by law. Any similarities of the content of this material is purely coincidental, and the above party, or parties are not liable for any action taken against the party, or parties listed above. Warning: copyright infringement is illegal and punishable by law.

About the Author:

Brian was born in Long Island N.Y by his beloved mother Paulette F. Munn, and late father Robert N. Hiller Sr. His father being an aviation machinist, developed and ran an Academy of Aeronautical Machinery located in Long Island N.Y. Brian's late grandfather Alfred Hiller, was as well a pioneer in the early years as an Aerospace Designer.

Like his father and grandfather before him, Brian was also fascinated with the field of aviation, and space exploration...yet in a different perspective. All of his life, he's enjoyed writing about his own thoughts and ideas about space travel, and the endless boundaries of the Universe, for the most part in fictional characteristics. His first publication is ALIENS BELIEVE TOO! His second publication is ALIENS BELIEVE TOO! 2 The Dark Swarm. His third publication is ALIENS BELIEVE TOO! 3 Return Of The Akkinuu.

Illustration Info:

The front and rear cover illustrations were performed by the amazing artist Mark Taylor from the U.K. His ability to deliver such incredible graphic visions, is to me an amazing achievement! Mark also performed the front and rear illustrations for my 2nd book in the Aliens Believe Too! trilogy The Dark Swarm, and the 3rd book in the trilogy Return Of The Akkinuu. I thank and owe Mark a great debt of gratitude for his truly amazing illustration art! Below, are the illustrations he performed for books 2 and 3 in the trilogy:

Special Thanks:

First and foremost, my beloved mother Paulette Francis Croley, for giving me life, loving me, and the opportunity to be able to write. My loving Fiancé Theresa Stevens, who encouraged me with my writing. My father Robert Norman Hiller, grandfather Alfred Hiller, brother Robert Hiller Jr., my wonderful son Brian Hiller Jr., my wonderful sister Theresa Hiller, once again the amazing artist and dear friend Mark Taylor for his truly amazing illustration art, the amazing actor/director/producer Mark Hamill, the amazingly talented Cartoonist Roger Phillips, amazing actor/author Dee Wallace, amazing recording artist Marcus Hernandez, Lucy Esposito, the wonderful Becky Escasmilla, my dear friend Theresa Caldwell AKA The Arizona Sky Watcher, one of my biggest fans Johnny Stevens, Debbie Sekula Sistare, Stefan Johansson, Annie Rutledge Herbin, Bubee and Jennifer Cloutier, Mathew Cloutier, and the rest of my family, friends and fans that have made a wonderful difference in my life. Thank you all!

ALIENS BELIEVE TOO!
Written by
Brian Hiller

Introduction

Outer space…what locked secrets does it hold in its depths? The many unanswered questions from the past to present, in mankind's will and devotion to discover all of its mysteries?
Perhaps the biggest question of all…are, or are we not alone in the Universe?

With all of the endless strange and bizarre accounts of UFO sightings, and alien abductions, we are only to wonder…what could be extra terrestrial's motives, and why Earth? Without any real concrete evidence…we shall continue to believe in the possibility of other life forms existing in our great Universe.

Brian Hiller

ALIENS BELIEVE TOO!

Table of Contents:

Chapter One. Visitation *pg. 8*

Chapter Two. Observation *pg. 16*

Chapter Three. Abduction *pg. 24*

Chapter Four. Violation *pg. 32*

Chapter Five. Intrusion *pg. 43*

Chapter Six. Transition *pg. 51*

Chapter Seven. Extraction *pg. 62*

Chapter Eight. Elevation *pg. 74*

Chapter Nine. Invasion *pg. 80*

Chapter Ten. Annihilation *pg. 95*

CHAPTER 1
VISITATION

The time is about seven thirty pm. and very dark in a backyard somewhere in Arizona, as a young man in his late thirties, James Lowery, Caucasian, dressed in slacks, a loosely buttoned shirt, holding a full glass of wine and crouched over a telescope views the clear starlit heavens. Suddenly what resembles a slow shooting star, streaks across the sky. "Well hello there," says James as he tracks its course intently. The so-called shooting star suddenly stops briefly, then descends out of sight. "What the hell," says James as he quickly raises his head with a look of amazement at the dark desert horizon. He then grabs the front of the telescope and spins it around for an observation of any debris on the lens. The lens appearing spotless, he looks at the horizon again, then his glass of wine. "Good stuff." He downs the entire drink then exhales, "Ahhhh." Suddenly a young woman's glistening voice from behind James asks, "Any signs of life yet?" James instantly wears a grin as he turns around to reply, "As a matter of fact." He then walks up to a beautiful young woman, his wife Debbie,
Caucasian, blonde, green eyes, curvy, dressed in a sheer nightgown, and holding a glass of wine. They softly embrace each other and James continues,
"My little green friends were thinking about coming over for dinner tonight." Debbie smiles while saying, "In that case, I'll see what I can whip up." With no delay, they kiss passionately. James sets his glass down on the edge of a table, but it falls to the ground and shatters. He then swoops Debbie up into his arms. She moans a little as they continue kissing. James then carries her into the house via the French doors. Meanwhile, viewing the dark horizon,

James and Debbie's moans, and the sound of Debbie's wine glass shattering on the floor are heard, as a brief flicker of blue light appears on the horizon.

  Located at the base of several desert hills in the moonlit night, exists a ranch with your traditional red barn, an old pickup, various animals, and a mobile home adorned with wooden plaques and wind brushed wind chimes singing their own melody. The front door of the mobile home suddenly swings open, and an old man, Jessie Taylor, Caucasian, gray hair and beard, wearing overalls and a straw cowboy hat steps outside. An old woman's voice, Jessie's wife Kate, blares over the sound of the television, "And don't furget to feed Lila!"
"Yeah yeah yeah," Jessie replies as he slams the door and walks away toward the barn. He strolls up to the right front side of the barn, picks up an old bucket, and begins to fill it with oats from a dispenser located on the corner of the barn. In the pitch-black barn, several horses in stalls begin to act spooked, and begin to buck and kick. Jessie still filling up the bucket shouts, "Oh quit your whining! I'm a feedin yeas!" The rest of the animals also begin to act restless as Jessie finishes filling the bucket, and walks up to the front entrance of the barn. Gust's of wind suddenly begin blowing all around. The sound of wood breaking, and the horse's yowling as Jessie is almost trampled by the horses running out of the barn. He quickly steps back and shouts at them, "Git back here! Ya durn blasted no good varmints!"

The horses continue to run away, as a bright blue light
shines from behind on Jessie. His eyes widen
and roll side to side as he slowly turns around
towards it. Once fully turned, his eyes widen even
more as his jaw drops along with the bucket of oats.
The light intensifies, as a swift wind removes
Jessie's hat. A moment later, the front door of the
mobile opens and Kate, Caucasian, wearing a dress
with an apron steps out and shouts, "Jessie?"
Suddenly the bright blue light shines down on her.
She looks up and screams with a deafening shriek.

   The light of day now shines through the curtains
of James and Debbie's room, as James lay half naked, and
half covered with a sheet, hugging a
pillow. A clock radio time reads seven thirty am.
The minutes suddenly flip over to eight o'clock in a
matter of seconds. The radio comes on playing
rock'n roll, then James rolls over still hugging the
pillow, and starts kissing it. "Oh baby," James softly
moans. He suddenly realizes his foolishness, opens his eyes
and tosses the pillow away. He sits up and yawns aloud and
long, then smacks the top of the clock radio, shutting it off.
He grabs a television remote, points it at his television
located at the foot of his bed and clicks it on. He then leans
back on the
headboard. On the television, a news anchor, Bob
Spencer, Caucasian, in his early fifties doing the
morning news, "Good morning, and welcome back to the
eight o'clock report. And now with a further update on the
strange sightings of lights that have been
reoccurring for the past month, I turn your attention
to my colleague Debbie Lowery."

Debbie appears brisk and gleaming. "Hello beautiful," says James in an introductory voice. "Thank you Bob. Yes, that's right folks. The strange unidentified lights in the night skies are at it again. Several people have reported sightings of the lights at all hours of the night last night. We spoke with local police and government officials about the sightings, but neither of them could give an explanation as to what they are, or where they come from." Debbie turns to Bob. "What do you think
Bob? Possibly UFOs? Or someone playing a
practical joke?" Debbie smiles and lifts a cup of coffee to sip. Bob replies, "Well, you know what they say Debbie? Seeing is believing." James lifts the television remote and clicks off the television. "A believer, you're not." He then jumps out of bed with the sheet around him, and walks toward his master bathroom. His cell phone on the dresser rings with a cosmic tone. He answers it. "Hello, the one and only James Lowery speaking. How might I be of service to
you?" An older man's raspy voice on the phone...
"You can start by setting your alarm clock. It's past eight Lowery."
"Oh, hello sir. Sorry! It won't happen again."
"I'll let it slide, on account of it's your Anniversary."
 "Thank you Sir."
"Yeah. Now get your ass down here!"
"Right away sir."
James hangs up and begins mocking the man's
voice on the phone, as he walks to the bathroom.
"It's past eight Lowery. I'll let it slide. Now get
your ass down here."

   In an elevator, James stands alone wearing a brown leather sport jacket, blue jeans and dress

shirt, with snake skin boots as he grooms his hair. The elevator doors open and James steps out. Dozens of people, working in dozens of cubicles, mulling around. A coworker, Todd Barker, Caucasian, late twenties and a little on the heavy side, approaches James. "Hey look everyone! Lowery's just in time for lunch!" Everyone looks briefly, as James crosses his arms and sighs. "What is it this time Barker... lose your bone?"
"Ha ha. Just wanted to wish you a Happy Second Lowery."
"I'm touched. You really mean that?"
"Not," replies Todd with a smile.
Todd turns and takes a few steps, then turns to James again. "Oh by the way, I see your wife's more on top of things these days."
Todd turns and walks away, as James smiles and pats his chest briefly.
"Ho ho ho! You're so funny Barker. Next time I'll equip myself with an extra pair of underwear just for you!" James quickly points toward Todd briefly. The man from James' phone call, his boss Dan Olsen, Caucasian, half-bald and gray with a beer gut stands in an office doorway and shouts, "Lowery!" James smiles and walks towards him. "Coming Sir." They both enter the office, the walls lined with awards, trophies, etc...and Olsen sits in his chair behind a large mahogany desk, James stands.
"Shut the door and have a seat Lowery." James closes the door, then takes a seat in front of Olsen. Olsen lights a cigar and opens the conversation. "I'm under the assumption you've seen the news this morning?"
"Just a glimpse."

"A glimpse of the ongoing decline of this paper."
"How do you mean Sir?"
"Never mind. What's more important…is that we get the ball rolling again. Like this strange light stuff going on. As stupid as it sounds, that stories getting a lot of attention…and more attention means what Lowery?"
"More publicity?"
"No Lowery. More papers sold."
"Right, right."
"Lowery?"
"Yes Sir?"
"This paper was here, long before radio or television was even invented! You know that?"
"True Sir?"
"Which brings us to a solution."
"A solution sir?"
"Yes."
Olsen stands up, walks around to the front of the desk and sits in front of James. Olsen continues, "You're gonna get your rear end out there, and get to the bottom, or top of this deal with those lights. This time you're going to do it my way, and my rules. You've cost this paper way too much in the past! Understand me?"
"Completely."
"Good. There's one more thing."
"What's that Sir?"
"I don't want, and don't care to here about any of your theories of aliens, or any other shit like it. Facts Lowery. Capiche?"
"Well Sir." Olsen quickly points his finger at James. "I'm warning you Lowery! Don't even think about it!"

James mimics a hand drill on his head briefly, then replies,
"Nothing. Clean as a whistle." James
briefly whistles. Olsen returns to his seat.
"Amusing. Now get out of here, and bring me
something back I can print on the front page, to
crank things up." James nods and stands up, then
walks to the door, opens it and looks at Olsen.
"I'll try, not to let you down Sir."
"You'd better not, for your own sake."
"Right Sir."
James briefly waves with half a smile and exits the
office, shutting the door hard at the last second.
James looks at everyone watching, as Olsen shouts
his name. James smiles and adjusts his shirt collar,
then walks away while whistling.

CHAPTER 2
OBSERVATION

Inside the local police department, a policewoman, Dixie, black, forties, sitting at the dispatch desk takes a call. "Hello, police department. How may I help you sir?" A brief moment. "Did you say the Taylor Ranch sir. OK. Thank you very much sir." She hangs up, then gets up and walks over to a door that reads: Chief Miles Davis. She knocks. A man's voice replies, "YES!"
She opens the door and enters. Once inside, she approaches a black man in uniform, Chief Miles Davis, mid-forties, sitting back in his chair, spinning the wheels on a toy police car.
"Sir, a man just reported horses roaming loose near the Taylor Ranch." Davis puts the toy car down and replies, "That's twice this month now."
He stands up and puts on his hat while saying, "I'll go myself this time and check it out."

In front of the Chronicle James walks out and approaches his white mini-van. He presses his unlock button on his key chain. Suddenly two men, appearing to be Caucasian, mid aged, wearing plain clothes, and dark shades approach James. James goes to open his door when one of the men asks, "Mr. Lowery?" James turns to them and replies, "Yes, who are you gentleman?"
"Who we are is of no importance. But as a matter of National Security, it is."
"Let me guess? Was it something I said, or wrote about in my columns?"
"No Sir. It's of another nature."
"Like what?"
"Mr. Lowery, we know of your past surveillance schemes near our facilities. And we're here to

inform you, that we'll be watching your every move." James smiles and replies, "Oh no, you guys have mistaken me for someone else. I can assure you of that." "Never the less Mr. Lowery. We'll be watching. Have a good day." The men turn and walk away. James says aloud, "You too!" Then under his breath "Moron's," as he opens his door and gets in his van. He starts it up, revs the engine, then throws it in gear peeling away... Smoke everywhere.

  On a dirt road just out of town, Davis is driving his squad car. On the side of the road some seventy yards ahead of him, a horse stands alone eating grass. Davis slows down and pulls up near the horse, keeping a safe distance so not to frighten it. He shuts the car off and exits ever so calmly. He slowly walks over to the horse.
"Easy boy." The horse looks at him, as he continues to approach it. "No one's gonna hurt ya." Davis stops just a foot away, and gently pets the horse's forehead. "That a boy."

  At the Taylor Ranch, the front gates are wide open as Davis walks up with the horse led by a leash he fabricated from his T-shirt. He leads the horse in through the gates, and removes the leash. The horse trots away as Davis walks up to the mobile home. The front door of the mobile still wide open, as Davis draws his gun. "Jessie? Kate?" He shouts aloud. With no reply, Davis continues to approach the mobile home. He cautiously looks all around, seeing the old pickup and the spilled bucket of oats in front of the barn. He reaches the entrance of the

mobile home and says aloud, "Hello? Anyone in there?" Still no reply, he enters. Inside he looks around a little, and then steps back outside and holsters his gun. He uses his shoulder radio. "Nelson?" A man's voice, Nelson's, replies.
"Yes sir?"
"I want you and Barnes to come out and meet me here at the Taylor's ranch."
"We're both eating lunch right now sir. We can be there." Davis interrupts,
"Now Nelson!"
"Right away sir."
"And bring a horse trailer."
"Did you say a horse trailer?"
"Yes! A horse trailer Nelson!"
"Understood sir."
Davis takes off his hat and wipes the sweat away from his forehead. "What in the world could have happened here?" He looks in wonder all around.

In front of the local television news station, James' van pulls in and parks. He steps out and shuts the door, but the engine suffers pre-ignition knock briefly, stopping with a loud backfire. James imitates a gun with his finger pointed at the van, then blows on his finger and pretends to holster it, as he walks towards the station entrance.
Inside the news station, James walks down a hallway past several personnel, finally stopping at a door that reads: News Anchor Debbie Lowery.
He knocks with a ratter tat tat. "Who's there" Debbie asks out loud. James comically replies, "Just your average secret admire!" Inside Debbie stands by the door with a smile. "A secret admire? My husband

would be insanely jealous if he heard about this!"
"I'm willing to keep a secret, if you are?"
"I guess it's all right." Debbie opens the door and James wraps his arms around her and kisses her as he pulls her into the office, then kicks the door shut with his foot. They kiss until they both run out of breath, and gasp in each other's face. "Not, now James."
"Just five baby?" Debbie nod's, "Ok, just five."
They kiss passionately again and fall backwards out of view with a thud noise. "Ow!" James shouts.

Back at the Taylor ranch, Davis watching a marked suburban backing a horse trailer up to the barn opening. It stops and two policeman, both Caucasian, Randy Nelson, thirties, and Jeff Barnes, late twenties, exit the vehicle and walk to the back of the trailer. They lower the trailer ramp and two horses walk out into the barn. "Whelp, that's the last of them," says Nelson. Davis walks up to the trailer, takes off his hat and leans on the trailer.
"I need not remind you men of the circumstances we'll face if this gets out to the media. So I expect you two to keep this under wraps. That is until we find out what happened."
"We understand Chief," says Nelson.
"Good! You boys can go now. I'll catch up with yea's at the station later." Davis takes a step away from the trailer, as Nelson and Barnes get back in the suburban, start it up and pull away... trailer ramp still down dragging the ground. Davis shouts, "Hey!" The suburban stops and Barnes jumps out of the passenger side and runs to the back of the trailer, lifts and closes the ramp, then looks at Davis

and shrugs his shoulders as he returns to the vehicle. Davis shakes his head as they pull away.

   Returning to Debbie's office at the television station, James eats a candy bar while looking through Debbie's file drawers. The door opens and James slams the drawer shut, and turns quickly to see Debbie standing with a small box in her hands staring at him curiously. She asks, "Find what you were looking for?" James replies, "I just uh, dropped my candy bar." James nods toward the file cabinet then continues, "How did it go?" She sighs then shuts the door and sets the box on her desk. James takes the box and opens it, while finishing with his candy bar. "You got it." He closes the box and takes it, then stands in front of Debbie smiling.
"Don't get caught with it, Ok? I could lose my job if you do," says Debbie. James replies, "Don't you worry about a thing sweetness." They lean in and kiss for a moment. "I'll be home around eight, Ok ," says James.
"Ok," replies Debbie. They kiss briefly and James exits the office quickly.

   Outside in the station parking lot, James gets in his van and starts it up. He adjusts his rear view mirror, and notices the two men from earlier sitting in a black SUV across the Street watching him. He starts to whistle as he puts it in gear and pulls out of the parking lot towards the two men. As James passes right next to them, he smiles and waves. "Hey! How's it hanging," he shouts, as they pull out and follow him. James looks in the rear view mirror and says, "So you boys wanna play huh?"

James turns on the radio full blast playing Heavy Metal music, then floors it. The SUV floors it right through a red light almost hitting two cars, honking from all directions. James runs through another red light, zig zagging through cross traffic. The SUV approaches the intersection and partially locks up the brakes, sliding sideways then regaining control in pursuit of James...more horns honking.
James looks in his rear view and says,
"Not bad, lets see how you handle this?"
James whips into an alley. An old bum sits in the alley wearing an old trench coat and a cap, drinking a bottle of whiskey. James speeds by him and just misses him. "Sorry!" Shouts James. The bum ignores him and puts the bottle to his mouth, when suddenly the SUV whips into the alley and also just misses the
bum, causing the bum to drop the bottle and break. The bum looks in their direction and drunkenly shouts, "Somoma bitches!" James passes a dumpster on wheels and locks up the brakes to a screeching halt. He jumps out of the van and runs up to the dumpster, then pushes the dumpster into the middle of the alley. Finishing, he runs back into the van and peels away. The SUV locks up the brakes and stops just tapping the dumpster. The man driving pounds the steering wheel and growls aloud, "Arrrr!"
James still speeding away and jamming the radio, looks once more in the rear view and says, "Mess with the best...burn like the rest." He speeds away. Meanwhile, the two men move the dumpster out of the way and hear the sound of metal scraping the ground. They look behind them and see the bum dragging a trashcan, walking towards them. The bum picks up the can over his head, and staggers

backwards falling to the ground, with the can knocking him out. After seeing the bum knock himself out, they look at each other blankly.

CHAPTER 3
ABDUCTION

At a local gas station, James pulls in and stops at the pumps. An elderly man, Max, Caucasian, 60's, wearing overalls and a baseball cap, wiping his hands with a rag approaches James.
"How much today Mr. Lowery?" James replies, "Filler up Max." James hands Max his credit card, and Max begins to fill up the tank. James opens the box Debbie gave him, and pulls out a digital police scanner. He turns it on and flips through the channels. After a moment, he finds a live channel and tunes it in. Nelson's voice, "We're almost back from the Taylor ranch now... over." Dixie's voice replies, "Affirmative." James turns off the scanner and stares forward for a moment. He then leans out the window towards Max. "Say Max?" Max Replies, "Yes Mr. Lowery?" "How would I get to the Taylor ranch from here?" Max finishes with the gas pump, and approaches James, handing him his credit card back.
"You talkin bout Jessie's Place?"
"Yeah, Jessie's place."
"Well, just take Main here due East as fur as you can go, then take a right. Yea can't miss it."
"Thanks Max." James smiles and starts up the van, then flips a quarter to Max. Max catches it as James pulls away.
"Thanks," shouts Max as he waves to James.

On the dirt road leading to the Taylor ranch, James speeds down the road jamming to the music with a long dust cloud behind him. Davis's car approaches from ahead of him. They finally pass each other, and Davis looks in his rear view mirror, "Lowery! Shit!"

Davis whips his car around, turns on the lights and
sirens, and pursues James. James still speeding
down the road and jamming to the radio doesn't
notice Davis pursuing him. Davis on the bull horn,
"Lowery! Pull over! Now!" James still doesn't notice or
hear Davis as he pulls into the Taylor's driveway and stops
just eight yards from the mobile home. He turns off the
radio then the van. The pre-ignition kicks in briefly, then
stops with a bang. Davis stops right behind him and shuts
off his car, then steps out and walks up towards James.
James exits the van with a camera around his neck, and a
pad and pencil in hand. "Lowery," Davis says aloud. James
turns to
Davis and says, "Oh hi Chief. What brings you out
this way?"
"That's funny Lowery. I was just about to ask
you the same thing."
"Well, you know…just doing my job as a public
servant."
"Is that so? Well let me be the first to inform you,
you're not going to find anything out here. In fact…
why don't you tell me what led you out here in the
first place?"
"Look Chief. I'm not looking for any trouble.
I'm just going on a hunch is all."
The sun begins to set, as the stars become more and
more visible. "Well your hunch was wrong Lowery. So
pack it up and move it on out." Davis looks towards the
horizon behind the ranch, and his eyes widen.
James turns and looks, and his eyes widen as well.
Both their jaws drop at the same time, as they just
stare in awe at a bright metallic UFO, hovering
slowly towards them measuring approximately
twenty-five yards across, twelve yards in height,

and fifty yards off the ground.

"Are you seeing what I'm seeing," asks Davis.

"Yeah, incredible isn't it?" James drops his pad and pencil, then begins taking pictures. Davis slowly puts his hands on James' shoulder and says, "Lowery? We've gotta get out of here, now."

"Are you kidding? This is my ticket to Stardom. I wouldn't miss this for the World!" James continues snapping away, as the UFO gets closer. Davis tugs on James' arm. "Come on Lowery! Now!"

James doesn't budge as he continues snapping pictures. Davis angrily shouts, "Damn you Lowery!" He runs away to his car, gets in it and tries to start it, but no power source what so ever. The gates of the entrance and both vehicles begin to shake and shutter. Davis tries his shoulder radio, "Nelson! Come in!" A brief moment and no reply. Heavy winds suddenly all around. Davis gets out of his car and shouts at James, "Lowery! Come on!" James quickly turns to run towards Davis, and in doing so drops his camera, as a blue beam of light suddenly shines down on him, freezing his movement. James just stares at Davis with widened eyes and slurs,

"Chief?" Davis pulls out his gun and begins shooting at the UFO and yelling, "Ahhhhh! Ahhhhh!" The UFO now completely over James, shoots a small blue laser beam at Davis's gun, shooting it clean out of his hand some fifty yards away. Davis stops yelling and stares for the moment, as James is lifted up into the UFO by the blue beam. With James clearly out of sight, the blue beam disappears and Davis turns and runs away as fast as he can. He suddenly trips on a rock in the

middle of the driveway, and falls to his stomach, then covers his face as the UFO dives downward towards

him. He lies still as if dead. Just ten feet off the ground, the UFO right over Davis, suddenly climbs upward at an incredible speed and out of sight. Davis stands up and looks around for a moment, and his car lights suddenly come on. He looks carefully at his car, then slowly gets in and tries the ignition. It starts.
"Yeah," he shouts as he puts it in gear and does a one eighty peeling away from the ranch.

  Inside the police department, Nelson, Barnes, and the two men in shades are sitting down at the desk in the lobby. The entrance door opens and Davis walks in, face and clothes dirty. He stops and faces everyone. "Sir? These gentlemen are with the government, and they've been waiting to see you," says Nelson. Davis takes off his hat and addresses the two men. "What part of the government do you men represent?" The leader of the two speaks, "The one which is considered of the utmost priority."
"National Security. So… what are you men of utmost priority looking for?"
"We're interested in a certain individual by the name of James Lowery." Davis briefly laughs then replies, "You're not gonna find him. Least not anytime soon." The two men briefly look at each other, then the man asks, "And why is that Chief Davis?"
Davis takes a few steps to the water cooler and turns his back to fill a glass of water, and a long wide burn mark from his buttocks to the top of his head is present, along with a missing patch of his hair. Everyone stands to stare at Davis, and the two men take off their sunglasses to see Davis's backside more closely. Davis continues, " Because he's

gone…far gone. And where to, I wouldn't know where to begin." Davis turns around with the glass of water and sips, then stops to see everyone staring at him. "Chief?" Nelson slowly and briefly directs his finger at Davis's back.
"What?" Davis asks as silence fills the room. He briefly looks behind him and says aloud, "Well? What is it?" The two men look at each other, nod their heads, and then look at Davis again.

  A strange humming noise fills the interior of the UFO, as James lays unconscious only wearing his boxers, on a table tucked away in one of the UFOs compartments. Both of his wrists and ankles bound by metal restraints. An alien, approximately five feet tall, bluish gray skin tone wearing a light gray body suit, a very slender build with a large pear shape head, large upward slanted eyes, a tiny slit for a mouth, and tiny holes for both nose and ears gracefully approaches James. The alien holding a small cylindrical chrome type of device gently places it on James' forehead. The device lights up brightly, but briefly. The alien removes it and James wakes up suddenly, startled with fear and gasping. He looks at the alien and starts to panic. "Who are you? What have you done to me? Where am I?" The alien replies in English, with a style and voice that sounds like a four-year-old on a sugar high, "Do not be frightened. We mean no harm to you." James refrains from his panic and stares at the alien. "If that were the case…why am I strapped to this table? Hey…you speak English." The alien smiles and says, "Yes. For many of your centuries we have adapted the use of your culture

with our own. Necessary for communicable relations."
James in awe just staring at the alien asks, "Who are you?"
The alien smiles again and addresses himself, "I am Deek."
Deek addresses James, "And you?"
"Scared shitless. That's what I am."
"Do not worry Mr. Shitless." James responds quickly, "No no no. Lowery. My name is James Lowery."
"A pleasure it is to have you with us Mr. Lowery. We have long searched for a subject of your nature to conduct non extinction process." James' eyes glare at Deek with total curiosity and worry. "What do you mean by subject, and extinction?" Deek replies, "Your genetic culture is of one among billions. Harness it we shall, to save life."
"What your saying, is I'm gonna be some sort of experiment, to save what life?"
"Your world Mr. Lowery."
James' eyes widen as he asks, "My world? What's wrong with my world…Earth?"
"The race known as the Tre'toan, a virus they have released. Soon spread it will, until your kind exist no more."
"Your serious, aren't you?" Deek simply gestures with a nod. "I've a lot of questions for you, Deek. But first, could you let me up off this damn table, and bring me my clothes?"
Deek smiles again and waves the little cylindrical device over the restraints, and they receded into the table. "Apologize we do Mr. Lowery."
James sits up and rubs his wrist, as another alien approaches with James' clothes.
James briefly bows to the alien, and the alien returns his gesture, then sets James' clothes on the table and walks away. James grabs his clothes and

29

begins dressing. "This is so unreal...any second now I'm gonna wake up." Suddenly the faint sound of a cow mooing. James briefly stops dressing and listens, then shakes his head and continues dressing.

CHAPTER 4
VIOLATION

Back at the police station, Davis now with a change of clothes and cleaned up with a shaved head, covered with a baseball cap, exits his office and walks up to Nelson and Barnes playing cards and drinking soda's. They look at Davis, and Barnes comments, "Hey Chief… that cap looks swell on ya." Nelson kicks Barnes in the leg and Barnes looks at Nelson as Davis responds,
"As soon as you two are finished sitting around on your butts, drinking soda's and making like the streets are gonna patrol themselves?"
Nelson and Barnes both stand up quickly.
"Right away sir," says Nelson as he looks at Barnes and they both walk away. Davis turns to them. "Nelson?" Nelson and Barnes stop and turn to him. "Yes Chief?" Replies Nelson. "Did you get a good look at those men's identification?"
"Well… come to think of it sir...not really."
Davis moves his hands from his hips and crosses his arms. "What do you mean not really Nelson?" Davis's tone strengthens by the second. "Either you did…or you didn't." Nelson removes his hat and replies,
"Well…no sir." Davis instantly showing the frustration of Nelson and Barnes' incompetence, points his finger at both of them. "You mean to tell me…that I just told two men that no one knows who in the hell they actually were…how to get to Lowery's house to do who knows what to, to his wife possibly?"
Nelson and Barnes look at the floor with disgust, as Davis continues, "And all because you two idiots didn't check their Id's?" Davis quickly walks past them to the entrance door, then turns to them and says aloud, "Don't just stand their dipsticks!" Come on! "Davis opens the door and exits, as Nelson and

Barnes follow. Davis's voice, "It's amazing you two even graduated kindergarten!"

  A grandfather clock in James and Debbie's house presents the only sound heard with its hands reading eight fifty five. A sudden knocking on the door. Wearing jeans and a halter top, Debbie arrives in the foyer and immediately opens the door and says, "Where have," she stops and there stand the two yet unidentified men. "Mrs. Lowery I presume," asks the leader. "Yes. Who are you gentlemen? What do you want?"
"May we come in and talk with you Mrs. Lowery? It's a matter of national security." Debbie wears a look of curiosity as she asks, "First you tell me who you really are, and what this is about. Otherwise, I'm shutting the door." The men look at each other briefly, then the leader says, "I'm afraid I can't tell you just who we are, or discuss what needs to be discussed out here in the open of your dwelling." Debbie places her hand on the door and says, "Then I'm afraid I can't help
you." She tries to close the door and the leader quickly stops her with his hand. "Hey! Who do you think you are?" Debbie tries one more time to close the door, buy can't. "Help! Help! Somebody help me," she shouts aloud with fright as the men force the door open, covering Debbie's mouth and nose with a cloth, and Debbie passes out as they quickly shut the door.
Aboard Alien Deek's ship, James fully dressed walks alongside Deek towards what appears to be the control bridge, filled with triangular shaped holographic monitors, displaying star systems, planets, and strange alien charts with shapes and

number sequences. James in total awe as he looks all around. "My God...unbelievable," says James as he continues his exploration of the incredibly advanced technology. Four more aliens present working touch activated control panels. There are also several luxurious chairs located around the center of the bridge. James stops walking and rests his hands on the backrest of one.
"So this is how they work. For that matter... evade all proof of existence man has ever so tried to reveal." Deek has a seat next to James still standing. Deek then nods to his alien companions, and they touch a panel, then small portions of the bridge wall approximately six feet wide by three feet tall, begin to slide side to side slowly revealing outer space, and stars streaking by traveling forward. James' eyes widen as he slowly walks towards the window. "No. It can't be." James arrives at their edge and just stares in disbelief. "Deek, just how far, and fast are we going?" Deek replies, "What is known to your people as light speed. Ten light years of travel we shall." Suddenly a man's voice with an English accent behind James, "So, what do you think?" James quickly turns to face a man about sixty years of age, clean cut gray hair, neatly trimmed beard, and wearing a white jumpsuit with his hands rested behind his back.
"Who in the hell are you? You look a little familiar." James tries to make him out. The man replies, "Landin Burke. It's a pleasure to meet you James." They briefly shake hands.
"Now I remember. Professor Landin Burke of the European Study for Aviation and Exploration. But...you suddenly turned up missing for no

apparent reason some twenty years ago. Wow, it's a small Universe after all."

"I'd have to disagree with you on that comment." James briefly waves his hand and says, "Well yeah. So tell me professor… how did you come about… all of this?"

"It's quite a long story, one that I don't care to discuss. But I can tell you…that mine, and Deek's people's intentions are truly sincere…and if all goes well, we'll be able to put a stop to the Tre'toans dark plan to wipe out all mankind on Earth." James crosses his arms and says, "You know…you could've made my arrival here a little less, we'll, terrifying."

"What…and deny you the right of the total alien abduction experience? You should thank me." Burke looks at Deek and winks. Deek smiles. "Crap," says James. "What," asks Burke.

"I didn't get a chance to tell my wife I loved her."
"Don't worry James. I assure you, you'll be seeing her again soon. Why…she's probably cooking your dinner as we speak."

In front of James and Debbie's house in the darkness, Davis pulls up with his lights off and parks. Nelson and Barnes pull up in the Suburban and park with their headlights still on. Davis on his shoulder radio whispers coarsely, "Turn off your damn lights, now." Nelson's lights go off. Davis slowly gets out of his car and draws his gun, then jesters for Nelson and Barnes to come over to him. They exit the suburban and jog over to Davis. Davis whispers, "Listen close, and listen real good. I'm going to the front door, and then make my way in as quickly as possible. You two clowns are

gonna come in from the back on my signal. Got it?"
They nod and Davis goes towards the front door,
Nelson and Barnes to the back. At the front door,
Davis whispers into his shoulder radio, "I'm going in now."
Davis kicks the door open busting the door jam, and
running into the house with his gun pointed. In the back of
the house, Nelson and Barnes standing by the French doors
both counting, "One, two, three!" They both run and jump
into the French doors, knocking the doors down then
landing on top of them. Davis walks up to them and
holsters his gun. Nelson and Barnes stand up in pain,
rubbing their arms and heads. "At least you two can do one
thing right. Mrs.
Lowery's not here. No sign of struggle or
anything."
"Where do you suppose she is Chief," asks
Nelson. "We need to make some phone calls. I'll start
with the news station, while you two clean up this
damn mess."

  In the back seat of the two men's SUV, Debbie
lays bound in ropes and unconscious…the leader in
the passenger side, and the other driving on a
deserted highway. "She will prove vital to the
cause," say's the leader.
"Yes…she shall." The SUV speeds off into the
distance.

  Back aboard Deek's ship, James and Burke are
sitting down in the luxurious bridge chairs.
"So how did you know where to find me…out of
a billion people for that matter," asks James.
Burke smiles and replies, "You could say that
ninety nine percent of it was pure good old fashion

luck." Deek walks up to them and takes a seat, as
another alien enters and stops in front of them, with
a tray of what looks like a white glowing substance
in clear glasses. The alien serves them.
"What is this Professor," asks James as he slowly takes one
and carefully smells it. Burke and Deek drinking, Burke
replies, "Just a little concoction I developed, to strengthen
ones senses of inner well being." James sips it a little, then
tastes. "Tastes like…a White Russian?"
Burke smiles and says, "Yes…good isn't it?"
"First alien abduction…then I find out about
man's possible extinction, and me being a lab rat.
And now, I'm drinking White Russians traveling at
light speed to god knows where with a mad
Scientist, no offense…and you want my opinion
about a drink?"
"Think of this as a vacation…with a twist of
mystery and adventure."
"I get enough of that back home, thank you."
Burke sets his drink into a holder on a table between
them, then stands facing James. "Come…I'd like to
show you something?"
"Great. More surprises."
James sets down his drink and stands up to follow
Burke. They walk down a ramp into the lower half
of the ship. Once there, James looks at the Taylor's
laying down unconscious, fully clothed and
restrained. Overhead lights dimly light the room,
and alien medical equipment hangs from the ceiling
and walls. James walks up to the Taylor's.
"Who are these folks Professor?"
"As of right now, their contained evidence. I was
only borrowing," Suddenly a clear sound of a cow

mooing. James turns and takes a few steps and sees
a cow behind a set of bars, with suction cups
attached to its utters and eating hay. Burke finishes, "Their
cow."
"Now that's," James points at the cow, "Gotta
be a first!"
"Actually…it's not."
James turns to Burke and asks, "Tell me Professor… just
what sort of technique, was used on me…to find out about
my genetic cell structure,
as you would refer to?"
Burke briefly looks at the floor, then James, then
upwards at a series of long needles, long curved
shaft probes, and binding equipment, then back at
James. James looks upwards at the equipment and
passes out. "Now that's, a first, and the conclusion
of our tour."

  Davis driving his car in town pulls up to a stop
sign and puts his car in park, then stares forward for
a brief moment. He then uses his shoulder radio,
"Nelson? Come in Nelson." Nelson's voice,
"Yes Chief?"
"I've scoured every inch of this side of Town.
You boys find anything yet?"
"No Sir."
"All right. Keep looking. I'm gonna try out by
the dumps." Davis puts his car in gear and pulls away.

  With the time now being midnight, the black
SUV is parked at the City dump in front of a
portable trailer. Only one light on in the trailer,
visible all around the entire area as well. Inside the
dimly lit trailer, in an office with a bookshelf, three

chairs and a table, Debbie sits in one of the chairs across from the two men. Her arms crossed, and eyes squinting at them with a piercing stare.
"Do you realize who I am…and the shit that's gonna hit the fan when I turn up missing,"
says Debbie with an authoritative tone. The leader takes off his glasses and leans forward in her face.
"You should realize, that your petty words are a waste of your final breaths. Soon you will bare witness to the birth of a more deserving race than of your own…as we Tre'toans anticipate the annihilation of you discussing, and foul excuse of beings unworthy of inheriting this world."
Debbie's eyes widen as the Tre'toan's eyes begin to glow red.

  On the bridge of Deek's ship, Deek and his companions at the controls, as Burke stands over James who is sitting down unconscious. Burke lightly slapping James' face. "James…come on son. Snap out of it." James starts to come to, slowly opening his eyes.
"What…what happened,"
says James with a groggy voice. Burke hands him a glass of water and a couple of pills. "Here you go. This will help you." James takes the water and the pills then asks, "What are these?"
"Simple ordinary aspirin. Don't you trust me?"
"Have I got a choice?"
James pops the aspirins in his mouth and gulps down the whole glass of water. He sets down the glass and sits up straight as Burke takes a seat next to him and says, "I had no idea a Supreme specimen of our race would be…how shall I put it…squeamish?"

"For your information Professor…it just so happens…that I earned every metal possible…in my Boy Scout Troop. It's just a little phobia I have about needles…and such."

"When and if we return safely to Silus, I'll be sure to administer a non…appalling approach upon the extraction process." James quickly looks at Burke with suspicion. "Wo wo wo! Lets back up to the part where you said…if we return. Just what are you, not telling me Professor?"

Burke sighs and replies, "Well…not to intentionally frighten you James, but judging by our previous location, I'd say we were smack dab in the middle of Tre'toan Space."

"Why in the hell of all places are we here?"

James awaits an immediate response. "Relax James, we travel this route quite often. It's the quickest and safest route for that matter. And besides…the Tre'toans never pose as a threat at the speed we're traveling now."

Suddenly an eerie deep pulsating alarm sounds all over the ship. James' eyes widen, as Burke stands and looks at Deek. Deek says aloud to Burke, "Three vessels of Tre'toan origin approach in quadrant Alta!" James stands up and says aloud to Burke over the repetitive alarm, "I guess you could say you stand corrected!" Burke looks at James with haste as the ship suddenly shakes from a laser blast from the Tre'toan vessels. Burke and James both fall to the ground, James on his back, and Burke lying directly on top of James. James says while barely breathing, "Not my idea…of a good time."

"Don't worry…you're not my type."

Burke rolls off of James and stands up, then jogs over to Deek's side, as James sits up and re-gains his breath. "Strap yourself in James! We're about to engage in an intergalactic game of chess," shouts Burke. James quickly gets up and sits down strapping him-self in while saying, "Maybe they'd settle their differences over a White Russian!" Burke making trajectory adjustments with Deek replies, "Actually, their drink of choice, is blood!" James' eyes widen and brow's lift, as suddenly a small portion of the ceiling descends downward, revealing a gunnery station . The alarms finally stop sounding, as Burke runs towards the gunnery, when suddenly another hit from the Tre'toan's rocks the ship. Maintaining his balance, Burke gets into the seat of the gunnery station and straps himself in. Suddenly small blue beams from the ceiling shine down on Deek and his fellow Silustrians…a source of stationary support. Burke touches some shapes on the instrument panel, which light up upon doing so, and a hologram of the Tre'toan vessels appears…triangular in shape, slender in height, and deep black in color.

CHAPTER 5
INTRUSION

In space, Burke's and the Tre'toan's vessels still traveling at light speed, shifting in patterns side to side, and top to bottom in a cat and mouse chase, as laser fire exchange runs continuously. On the bridge of Burke's ship, Burke intently aiming and firing with the whole gunnery station pivoting back and fourth. "Hang tight James! I'm getting warmed up!" "We're gonna die," says James while leaning over covering his eyes. "Faith James! Have a little faith!"

On board one of the Tre'toan vessels, several Tre'toans dressed in black, sit at odd digital control panels, and one sits in a chair high above the rest. The interior resembles that of octagon shaped panels with lighted symbols flashing randomly. The Tre'toan Captain points forward. "Closer! We must destroy them before we enter Silustrian Space!"

Back on the bridge of Burke's ship, Burke still using the gunnery station, and James now with his fingers in his ears rocking back and forth repeating, "La la la la la." Burke carefully aiming on one of the Tre'toan vessels, "Come on...just a little bit more. Gotcha!" Burke fires and hits the center of the Tre'toan vessel's hull, blowing it to pieces. "Yes," shouts Burke.

Back at the dumps, Davis pulls up slowly and turns off his headlights, while stopping his car approximately fifty yards away from the SUV parked at the trailer. Noticing the SUV, Davis uses

his shoulder radio, "Nelson? Come in Nelson."
Nelson's voice, "Yes Chief?"
"I'm down at the dumps, and I found the SUV we've been looking for."
"We're on our way Chief."
"Good. Just keep your damn lights off when you get here."
"Yes Sir. Be there in about ten."
"Make it five Nelson."
"We'll try. Over and out."
Davis opens his glove compartment and pulls out a box of shotgun shells, then grabs a shotgun off his seat and begins loading the magazine chamber.

Inside the trailer, Debbie still forced to sit in the chair, watching the Tre'toans holding an octagon shaped tray, with refractions of alien letters rising upward and vaporizing at their eye level. She leans forward. "How do I fit in to your evil scheme?" A moment, and no reply. She continues, "Hey…I'm talking to you bozo!" The leader looks at Debbie with his eyes glowing again and with a deep scratchy tone says, "Silence!" His eye's glow even brighter as Debbie begins to feel dizzy then suddenly passes out on to the table. He looks at his companion and his companion says,
"The element exists within her womb."
"Send the coordinates for our departure. Soon… we shall finally be rid of these humans, and ruling this new world along-side the Lord Zemious himself." He smiles.

Davis sitting in his car tapping his fingers on the barrel of the shotgun impatiently. He looks at his

watch and sighs, then says, "Screw it." He opens his door and exits quietly, then cautiously walks toward the trailer with his shotgun aimed. He reaches the trailer and looks in the windows, and sees movement…the Tre'toan's shadows. He then quietly walks up the steps and suddenly one of the steps creak. Davis freezes. Inside the trailer, the Tre'toans both turn their heads toward the door.
Outside the door, Davis tries the handle and it's unlocked. He slowly opens the door with a bit of door hinge creaking. The door fully open, Davis quickly jumps into the trailer with his shotgun drawn. He sees no one or thing yet, so he walks towards the back room, where the light escapes from under the door. He stops at the door when suddenly he is hit on the head from behind, his shotgun going off and falling to the ground, but not unconscious. He quickly turns towards the two Tre'toans and shouts, "Hey you son of bitches! Who do you think you are?"
The leader speaks, "We are the beginning, of your glorious ending…and you Chief Davis will further bare witness as well." Both their eyes begin to glow brightly as Davis briefly displays a frightful facial expression, then passes out.

   Returning to our friends battling it out with the Tre'toans somewhere light years away from Earth, the cat and mouse chase continues with the two Tre'toan vessels pursuing. On the bridge of Deek's ship, James is slumped in his chair, eyes closed, squinting, and hands over his ears. Burke still firing at the Tre'toans, while Deek and companions control the ship. Suddenly another hit rocks the

ship, and Deek says aloud to Burke, "A fifty percent loss of shielding, suffered we have."
"We should be close enough to alarm the guardian fleet of our situation!" Deek nods and touches alien letters to alert their guardian fleet for help. James opens his eyes and removes his hands from his ears, then looks at Burke, "Did you say fleet?" Burke still hard at it with the shooting replies, "That you did!"
"Well in that case…is there anything I can do to help?"
"Yes…you can stay put, and stay alive! If your Dead, this entire venture would be for nothing!"
"Sounds good to me! You're doing just fine!"
Burke briefly looks at James with a sigh, and continues his fighting. "Deek? When I say…go up left down!"
Deek nods as Burke focuses. "Now!"
Viewing the battle in space, Deek maneuvers the ship quickly to Burke's request and Burke fires rapidly at one of the Tre'toan vessels, directly hitting their bridge.

  On the bridge of the Tre'toan
vessel, the crew screams as a tremendous explosion destroys the entire ship, and flaming debris flies away revealing Burke's ship.

  Back aboard Burkes ship, Burke shouts, "Yes! One more to go!"
"Yeah! Kicking some alien, I mean Tre'toan butt," shouts James as the Silustrian crew members look at James, and he smiles widely then waves to them.

  It's nearly one am now at the trailer location, as

Nelson and Burke finally arrive with their lights off. They stop behind Davis's car and shut off the engine. Nelson uses his shoulder radio, "Chief?" A moment and no reply. Nelson tries again, "Chief …Come in Chief." Still no reply. "I don't see him in his car, and he's not answering," says Nelson.
"Where do you suppose he is," asks Barnes.
"He must be in there." Nelson and Barnes both looking at the trailer.

  Inside the trailer, Davis still lays on the floor unconscious. The Tre'toans finish with the strange octagon tray device, and the leader folds it up and inserts it down the front of his pants. The grunt Tre'toan then lifts up Debbie, who still lays unconscious slumped over the table, onto his shoulder. The leader turns then walks out of the office, and the grunt carrying Debbie follows. Just outside the door of the trailer, Nelson and Barnes standing near the foot of the steps hear the Tre'toans walking towards the door. "There's two people," says Nelson.
"What if it's the Chief and Mrs. Lowery?"
"What if it's not?"
"What if it is?"
"But what if it isn't?"
"Is."
"Isn't."
"Is."
"Isn't"
Suddenly they see the doorknob begin to turn. Nelson and Barnes run away to the corner of the trailer and peek around the corner. The Tre'toans step out of the door with Debbie still on the grunt's

shoulder. They stop and turn facing Nelson and Barnes. Nelson and Barnes keep tucked behind the corner and look at each other while drawing their guns and counting to three. On three they jump out with their guns drawn, and the doors on the SUV shut as it starts up and peels away. "Shoot! They're getting away," says Barnes as they holster their guns. "The Chief," says Nelson as they run up the steps and quickly push the door open. A thud noise and Davis's voice, "Damn it!"
In the trailer on the floor, Davis sits up holding his nose and looks at Nelson and Barnes.
"Before this is over, remind me to pull my boots out of your asses!" Nelson and Barnes rush to his aid, but Davis holds up his hand to stop them.
"Stop! Nelson, give me your gun?"
Nelson briefly looks at Barnes and back to Davis.
"Why do you need my gun Sir?" Davis stands up. "So I can shoot your dumb asses!"

   Returning to the galactic chess game, the zig zagging and laser fire continues. On Burke's bridge, Deek and crew remain at their posts, as Burke remains in the gunnery firing, and James seated watching the hologram, as the Tre'toan vessel fires directly towards the bridge. Laser fire hit's them, breaking through the shields and damaging the gunnery station as sparks and smoke emit all around Burke. Electricity out of the console suddenly shocks Burke, and knocks him out. James looks at Deek and Deek says, "Worry not Mr. Lowery… fleet arrived it has!" James turns and looks toward the windows to see dozens of UFOs approaching from all directions.

In space, the Tre'toan vessel alters its course quickly, but is destroyed by several of the Silustrian ships laser fire. The Silustrian ships then assume an escort position around Burke's ship, as they slow to mach speed. On Deek's bridge, the blue overhead containment beams disappear, and one of the crew walks over to Deek and takes over the controls. Deek quickly walks over to Burke who is still knocked out. James struggles briefly with his seat belt, freeing himself and running over to Burke. James unbuckles Burke, and Deek helps James lift him out of the gunnery and lay him down on the floor of the ship. Another Silustrian crew member walks up with a small round shiny disk, and slowly waves it over Burke's head. Everyone kneeling beside Burke, as his eyes suddenly open.
"That was a close one," says Burke as he slowly rises while rubbing the back of his neck.
"We're safe now Professor. Their fleet's here," says James with a look of relief. "I see what you mean now…by enough of this entertainment back home," says Burke with a grin. James lends Burke his hand and helps him to his feet while saying, "But this, is way off the charts!"

CHAPTER 6
TRANSITION

Speeding down the dark desert highway, are Nelson and Barnes' Suburban. Nelson driving, Davis riding shotgun with a shotgun, and Barnes in the back seat leaning forward between them.
"How do ya know they didn't double back to Town Chief," Nelson asks.
"Ok Nelson…here's an IQ test for ya. If you kidnapped a woman, and zapped a police officer with your eyes, where would you most preferably high tale it to?" Nelson thinking as Barnes says, "I know the," Davis interrupts, "Shut up Barnes!" Barnes' eyes widen as he slowly leans back in his seat. Davis continues with Nelson, "Well…come on Sherlock! You don't know do ya?" After a moment of Nelson trying his hardest to answer Davis, Davis adds,
"That's why I'm a Chief…and both of you two clowns, are clowns!"

   Also on the dark desert road miles ahead of Davis's posse, the black SUV driven by the Tre'toans also speeds down the road. The grunt at the wheel, the leader riding shotgun, and Debbie in the backseat laying down unconscious. She begins to wake up, slowly opening her eyes, and careful not to make any sudden movements. She slowly slides her legs off the seat and onto the floorboard. The leader briefly looks back at Debbie, and she closes her eyes remaining still. After a moment, she opens her eyes again, and slowly rises up behind the driver seat. She suddenly starts choking the grunt and the SUV weaves all over the road as him and the leader struggle with Debbie.
"Stop the vehicle!" Shouts the leader, and the

grunt slams on the brakes, sliding all over the road for a moment, then finally coming to a stop sideways. Debbie quickly releases the grunt, opens the door, then jumps out and runs into the desert hills. Both the Tre'toans exit the SUV, then walk toward Debbie's direction. Their eye's light up red like flashlights, scanning the hillside as they walk.

Returning to deep space ten light years away, Deek and the rest of his fellow Silustrian's UFOs approach a planet that looks similar to Earth, but three moons of different proportion and color exist among the planet's outer origin. An orange sun burns brightly in the distance.
Aboard Burke's ship on the bridge, James and Burke stand by the bridge window viewing the totally new and fascinating world in James' eyes for the first time. James in complete and total disbelief, leans against the windowsill and says, "Wow...I never knew such another world like this could exist."
"Besides having three moons instead of just one... Silus is also four times the mass that of Earth."
James turns with excitement to Burke,
"Plenty of elbow room...hey Professor?"
James performs a little elbow routine, then returns to the view of Silus as they draw closer to the illustrious beautiful New World.
Just a quarter of a mile high above a city on Silus looking down, dozens of beautifully crafted architectural buildings and sculptures similar to Earth's ancient architecture, fill seventy percent of the landscape. The rest of the surroundings compiled with lush green trees, water fountains,

hillsides as far as the eyes can see, and dozens of
UFOs of all different shapes and sizes flying
around. Burke's ship and the fleet fly downward towards an enormous round landing platform, located in the center of the city atop a round spiral building.
Landing indicator lights that flash into lighted rings
appear all over the landing port. Still looking out the window of Burke's ship, James and Burke remain leaning on the sill next to one another. James looks all around in amazement and says, "It's the most beautiful thing I've ever seen." James looks at Burke to add, "Besides my wife that is." James turns back to the window as the ship stops and begins to land.
"Silus has many things more beneficial than
Earth. One of them, being its pollution free air.
Wait till you get a breath of that in your carbonated lungs."
"What a story this could be," James whispers as Burke looks at him. "Did you say story," Burke asks with curiosity. "Just talking to myself is all," James replies as Burke nods and pats James on the shoulder. "Come on lad. We've got fish to fry."
Burke and James walk away.

  Back on the desert road, Davis and posse pull up to the stranded SUV parked in the middle of the road. Everyone exits quickly to positions behind their doors, guns drawn.
"Go ahead Nelson, say I told ya so." Says Davis sarcastically.
"Barnes, you watch our six while we move in.
And remember one thing, no matter what…do not look into their eyes. Understand?" They answer, "Understand."

"Good, lets do this."
Davis looks at Nelson, Nelson appearing nervous as all hell, and gestures to move in. They both ease out from behind the doors, guns aimed at the SUV, and slowly approach it. Making it all the way up to the SUV safe so far, Davis whips the barrel of his shotgun into the driver side only to see it empty. He lowers his shotgun and turns around to see Nelson shaking so much, his gun could drop at any second. "Boy…you look like a wet dog on a cold winters night." Davis begins to laugh, and then Barnes laughs for a moment. They finish laughing as Nelson lowers his gun and calms down.
"All right you two, time to get down to business. I'm gonna head up over that way,"
Davis points in Debbie's last known direction,
"And you two head over that way. If you spot our Suspects, or Mrs. Lowery, stay put and radio Me, quietly. Can you handle that?"
They both nod. "If you screw this up, you boys are gonna either get yourselves killed, or end up flippin burgers down at the burger ranch." Davis slings his shotgun over his shoulder and walks away. Nelson and Barnes shut the doors to the Suburban and walk away.

   Deep in the desert hills of the pitch black night, Debbie about out of breath and struggling to keep a steady pace through the rugged terrain, stops to look behind her gasping with a look of fear, and sees the red beams of light from the Tre'toan's eyes getting closer. She turns and continues her quest to safety. The Tre'toans keep tracking her steadily.

Back on Silus in the lower deck of Burke's ship, James looks at the floor in fear of looking up and seeing the needles and probes again. Burke is packing a satchel with medical and chemical items. James glances over at the Taylors and says, "What's gonna happen to those old folks Professor?"
"They'll be just fine. They're in a bit of a hibernation sleep for the moment. They'll be returning to Earth as well." The cow moos.
"What about our furry companion?"
The cow chomping on hay.
"I suppose, that it would be of her own decision." James briefly wears a curious look, as Burke finishes with packing his satchel and turns to James. "Are you ready to take that big step for Mankind," says Burke as he gestures with his Hand, and a large portion of the floor begins to descend, forming an entrance ramp.
"After you, I insist," Replies James with a brief hand gesture of his own. "All right …as you wish." Burke begins to walk down the ramp, and James follows. Just outside the ship, the fleet ships docked, entrance ramps down and all aliens exiting the ships as Burke and James exit and stop at the foot of the ramp. James looking around taking a deep breath through his nose then exhales slowly, "Ahhhhh." Burke looks at James with a smile, "Well?" James takes another deep breath and exhales then looks at Burke, "Yeah!"
"Exactly my thoughts as well, upon my first arriving."
"It's so…pure. You could market it!"
"The only problem with that idea, is your ten light years away."

"That would be a bit of a problem."
Deek casually walks down the ramp, as the dozens of other UFO crewman walk by James and Burke, smiling and briefly waving to them. James notices in the distance, women Silustrians approaching while smiling, but are dressed in different color skin tight suits...and to his surprise, he can't help but notice a distinct difference in the proportion of their groins. James looks curiously at Deek, then Burke. "Professor...is Deek...well...you know," he asks in a low tone. Burke looks at James with a grin, "A bit obvious, isn't it?"
Burke chuckles briefly and adds with a low tone, "Believe it or not, of the male gender he is...just the opposite biologically." James' eyes briefly widen. "Wow, bizarre. But hey, each to his...or her own." Burke takes a step and turns to James. "Come, I'll introduce you to the Queen."
James' eyes widen again briefly as he answers, "Queen? All right." James, Burke and Deek begin walking away and Burke places his hand on James' shoulder and says, "The Queen is going to enjoy making your acquaintance." James looks at Burke inquisitively.

Back in the dark hills of the Arizona desert, Davis now deep in the hills, uses his shoulder radio, whispering, "Nelson?"
"Yes Sir," Nelson speaks aloud.
"Damn it Nelson... keep it down," Davis whispers coarsely. Nelson responds, "Yes Sir. Sorry Sir," Nelson whispers.
"You two find anything yet?"
"No Sir."

"Well, keep at it…over and out." Davis continues his search, pressing forward to save Debbie.

  Debbie strung out and about to collapse suddenly slips and falls down a slope of small rocks, sliding and screaming as she goes. She finally stops sliding and screaming, only to come face to face with a black scorpion. She freezes still and just stares with a look of fright, then ever so slowly begins to back away from it. The red lights of the persistent Tre'toans eyes, are again visible to Debbie from above her location. She quickly rises to her feet and continues to trek her way to safety. The Tre'toans Stop and turn off their glowing red eyes, then the leader takes out the octagon tray. He holds it level in the center of his hands, and it folds itself out to full size. It suddenly lights up brightly, and the strange refractive letters and shapes begin to rise from it. Davis only about a hundred yards away, notices the light beam produced by the Tre'toan device. He stops in his tracks and uses his shoulder radio.
"Nelson? Come in!"
"Yes Chief," Nelson whispers.
"Work your way back over towards me. And hurry! I think I found our suspects."
"We're on our way Chief."
Davis aims his shotgun and walks toward the beam of light.

  Back on Silus in a long and narrow glass tunnel, James, Burke and Deek stand in place as they are escalated to their first destination, the Queen's

Temple. Across from them, James can't help but notice a human couple. While staring at them James asks, "Are they from, Earth?"
"If I said no...I'd be lying."
"How many more of us are here Professor?"
"Oh...about a million...give or take a few."
James looks at Burke, "How is that possible?"
"Simple...we humans have been coming to Silus for centuries. So if you did your homework correctly...you would assume the same equation."
"You're the scientist."
"Yes...so nice of you to remind me."
They finally arrive at the opening of an ovular shaped hall. They all walk into the hall, a beautiful tall structure, with pillars about its walls. Dozens of Silustrians standing, turn and face James, Burke and Deek. They all bow briefly, as James, Burke and Deek stop and bow in return. They continue walking forward, and just ahead of them, the Queen, Mirla...appearing to look half Silustrian and half human with beautiful big blue eyes, proportioned like a model, wearing a silver tiara, and dressed in a purple gown. She sits on a luxurious throne comprised of a velvet type of material. Two Silustrian woman also in dresses stand on each side of her. James, Burke and Deek stop before her and bow briefly. Mirla displays an instant interests for James upon seeing him. Burke begins the introductions, "Your Highness...always a pleasure to be in your presence." Burke takes her hand and briefly kisses it. James just standing still holding his hands, and noticing the way Mirla stares at him with a smile. He tries to avoid her stare without being rude at the same time. Mirla stands while smiling at James,

and her height is five foot eight. She approaches
James with her hand out. "Your Highness, I present to
you…James Lowery." Burke finishes with the introduction.
James looks at Burke, and Burke signals James to take her
hand and kiss it. James briefly tightens his lips, then looks
at Mirla still smiling, and takes her hand and quickly
kissing, then releasing it.
"I am Mirla, and you must be the supreme human
the professor has long been searching for. It's quite
an honor to meet you James." Mirla's voice as of a
humans, and very soft. James responds, "My pleasure as
well your Highness. You'll have
to pardon any rudeness I may present…this is all so
new to me." Mirla looks at James with a seductive
smile, as she ever so slowly walks around James,
observing him, and lightly caressing his shoulders
and back. James looks at Burke with the widest
eyes ever, as a plea for help. Burke tries his hardest
to contain a smile and refrain from laughing. Mirla
finishes her observation of James, standing in front
of him. "Yes…indeed you are a supreme
specimen."
"Me? Na," says James while shaking his head.
"Tell me James…have you a companion back
Home," she asks with a sexy wink. James instantly
holds his hand up to show his wedding ring.
Pointing at it with a smile he replies, "Happily married,
see?" Mirla smiles and says, "She's quite a fortunate
woman." Mirla sits back down and adds,
"I would be as well. I look forward to having
you…for dinner this evening." James' eyes widen again, as
he swallows hard and says, "For dinner…swell."
Burke takes a step forward, " If you'll excuse us

now your Highness…we've a lot of work to get started on." Burke briefly bows, then James and Deek as well. They turn and walk away.
James addresses Burke quietly, "Why didn't you warn me?"
"I thought you handled the situation rather well… don't you?"
"No thanks to your silence."
They continue walking away.

CHAPTER 7
EXTRACTION

Still in the dark desert ravine, Debbie now strung out and dehydrated, struggles on her feet to evade the Tre'toans. She suddenly drops to her knees from exhaustion, and looks behind her. She sees nothing but the dark ravine, and its illuminated shadows cast from the setting moon. She then decides to sit down and rest for a while.
Davis crouched down and walking slowly with his shotgun aimed, approaches the Tre'toans from approximately forty feet away. He stops and takes cover behind a boulder, watching the Tre'toans holding the strange device. He looks carefully all around them, but doesn't notice Debbie anywhere. The Tre'toans suddenly stop with the device and the leader puts it away again down his pants.
Davis uses his shoulder radio, "Nelson, come in," he whispers.
"Yes Chief," Nelson whispers.
"I found them…but Mrs. Lowery's not with them. What's your location?"
"We're approaching the vehicles just now."
"Oh hell, I need you two to put it in gear and get your asses up here ASAP."
"You mean as soon as possible Chief?"
"Yes Nelson!"
Davis realizing he may have been heard, looks around the edge of the rock and notices the Tre'toans walking his way. Davis quickly leans his back against the rock, and exhales long while hugging his shotgun, then looks up to the sky.
"Don't fail me now Lord…please don't fail me now." Davis takes several deep breaths quickly, psyching himself up to confront them, then with lightening speed whips out from behind the rock,

positioning the shotgun dead aimed at the two.
"Freeze you son of a bitches!" They freeze.
"And don't you think about pulling any of that red eye shit with me either…or the Coyotes'll be lickin your brains up off the ground. Ya dig?"
The leader smiles and replies, "The simple truth being somewhat of a disappointment for you to digest Chief Davis…is even if you were to end our lives…nothing can save yours, or any of your people from the inevitable deaths you so truly deserve."
Davis switching aim from head to head, "I'll be the judge of that! Now tell me where Mrs. Lowery is! You've got five seconds!" A brief moment goes by as the Tre'toans just smile. "This is your last warning! Where is she?"
Suddenly a large rock hits the grunt Tre'toan in the back of the head, and he goes down to the ground unconscious. The leader jerks his head to look behind him, and sees Debbie holding another one. Debbie stands still with an angry stare, as the
leader grits his teeth with anger. Davis still aiming his shotgun and Debbie says, "I've had about all I'm gonna take from you assholes anymore." Davis shouts to Debbie, "Mrs. Lowery, it's Ok now! Come on over to me! He so even twitches, he's road kill!"
Debbie runs over to Davis and stands behind him. The leader staring at them with intense anger. Says, "You're making the last mistake you ever will." While no one pays attention to the grunt on the ground, he opens his eyes and looks at Davis and Debbie as his eyes begin to glow red. Davis catches it in time and takes aim at him, then pulls the trigger, blowing off the top of his head. The grunt squeals with a shrieking sound for one moment then dies. "I warned em about that red shit,"

says Davis, still aimed at the leader.
"Now you've done it, says the leader, and suddenly seeing something the size of a fist, tries to force its way out of the rear end of the grunts pants. It punches and hisses at the same time. Davis and Debbie watching it and the leader is smiling again.
Debbie appearing frightened again as Davis asks the leader, "What is that!" The leader replies,
"Why don't you ask it yourself, Chief Davis?"
Suddenly the strange creature busts upward out of the grunt's rear end, resembling a long slimy slug, with legs like a centipede, horns like a beetle, teeth like a piranha, and glowing red. It flexes like a King Cobra and screeches. Debbie screams, as Davis keeps his aim on the leader. The creature then begins to move towards Davis and Debbie, and just before it comes within four yards of them, Davis shoots a round into it, blowing it in half, as it screeches briefly to its death. Davis quickly cocks the shotgun and aims it at the leader, as he tries to take a step forward with his teeth gritting stare again. "From what I've just seen…you must be from the planet hemorrhoid," says Davis to the leader.
"You fail to amuse me with your lame and meaningless insinuations!"
"Your ass is fixin to be lame, just like your slimy friend, if you don't start talking and tell me where the hell your space ship took this ladies husband!"
Debbie looks at Davis with question,
"Space ship, James? What are you talking about Chief?"

Somewhere around the location of the scene, Nelson and Barnes are jogging, tired and gasping.

They stop and lean over to catch their breaths.
"I'm telling ya… it came from that direction,"
says Nelson as he briefly points.
"I sure hope your right. The Chief's going to have our butt's…cookin burgers if you're wrong."

   Davis finishing his explanation to Debbie, while still aimed at the leader.
"And that's the way it went down…didn't it snake ass?"
"Enough of this," The leader says aloud as he reaches into his pants.
"Stop, or I'll blow your damn head off," shouts Davis as the Leader's eyes light up red, and he pulls out the device. Davis shoots and blows a huge hole through his head. The leader drops to the ground like a side of beef. Davis looks at Debbie, "Run!"
"Why, you've got a gun." Suddenly another creature begins to work its way out of the leader's rear end.
"I'm out of ammo," says Davis.
"That's a good reason."
They both run away as the creature exits the leader.

   Returning to Silus, James, Burke, and Deek walk through the illustrious City streets filled with aliens and humans, strolling along, working in shops, shopping and etc.
"It looks like everyone's, one big happy family," says James while observing his entire surroundings. "Yes, and you'll also notice, no policeman patrolling the streets…no hustle and bustle of congested traffic or crowd's of people. And most importantly…no crime what so ever. Hard to

believe isn't it?"
"Not from what I've seen so far. In fact we could use a huge dose of this back home."
Burke laughs briefly and says, "Yes…quite a difference it would make." Deek looks at James and says, "A sadness however, several Earthlings understand not the importance of peace, and tranquility." Burke responds, "In due time Deek…in due time." They come to a three story building round in structure, white in color, with domes extruding upwards from its roof. Burke steps up to a chrome doorway and stops, then turns facing James and Deek. The door opens upward and Burke gestures to James, "You first this time James…I insist."
James checking the place out asks, "What is this place?"
"My home," replies Burke with a proud smile.
"Your home…looks more like an observatory."
"Well, to a degree…thus also being the truth. Shall we?" Burke gestures again, then James and Deek walk in with Burke following them.

  Back home, Debbie and Davis run through the dark hills, as the Tre'toan creature still glowing with its illumines red color and hissing, snakes its way along the ground at a comparable speed to Debbie and Davis's. Davis right behind Debbie uses his shoulder radio, "Nelson, Barnes, we're being chased by…something…I can't explain! Are you their Nelson?" Nelson and Barnes standing on top of a ridge, listening to Davis panic for help. Nelson on his shoulder radio replies while looking at Barnes, "We hear you Chief! Where are you?"

"We're headed back to the road, hurry up,"
Davis's voice replies gasping for air.
"We can't screw this up Barnes. Let's go!"
They both take out their pistols and run towards the road.

   While Debbie and Davis still run from the Tre'toan creature, she stumbles and falls face first to the ground. Davis quickly stops and kneels down to help her back up, and suddenly a long and eerie hiss is heard behind them. Debbie sits up as Davis slowly turns his head and sees the creature just seven feet behind them, coiled up like a cobra ready to attack. Debbie and Davis remain calm, as Davis slowly grabs his shotgun, then suddenly slings it at the creature, hitting the creature in the side of the head, but doing no damage what so ever. The creature shrieks loudly as Debbie picks up her rock again and secretly gives it to Davis from behind him. He chucks it as hard as he possibly can right at the creatures face, and the creature opens its mouth wide and catches it in its mouth. The rock begins to glow. The creature then chomps down on the rock, and it shatters into pieces. The creature then smiles.
"Oh shit," says Davis. They quickly get to their feet and run like hell.

   Back on Silus In Burke's lavishly furnished home, adorned with ancient art, tapestries, and photos of man's historic discoveries in space, Burke stands behind a bar of what appears to consist of black marble. He pours drinks, as James looks at the photographs. Deek then walks up to Burke and stops.

Burke looks at Deek and quietly says, "Prepare for the extraction. We'll be along shortly." Deek nods and walks behind the bar, where an exit ramp going downward awaits him. Deek enters the exit ramp, and the exit ramp closes into the floor. Burke walks over to James and holds out a drink to give him. "Drink?" James turns around and curiously takes the drink while replying, "Is this another one of your homemade concoctions?" James smells it briefly and Burke replies, "Actually it isn't, It's Silustrian Ale." James sips it and says, "Hmm. Not bad, not too bad at all. So Professor...I presume that since we're in no immediate danger, you'll tell me about this virus, that's threatening Earth as we speak?"

"Let's have a seat, shall we?" Burke gestures James to sit on a round luxurious black leather couch. They both sit down and Burke opens the conversation, "It started some thousand years ago...War between Silus and Tre'toa. Strangely, the Tre'toans idea of peace and harmony, was to have complete control of Silus' activity's with other worlds." Burke takes a drink
and continues, "But of course, Silus wouldn't comply to such an outrageous, and mad request. So...the war began, and now...Earth is the Tre'toan's prime source of showing Silus its devilish capabilities. Ending all human life on Earth, and posing more of a threat by inhabiting it...for further empowering forces of evil." James just staring blankly at Burke, takes a
big gulp of his drink then asks, "Where on Earth... the location, did they release the virus Professor? And how are we gonna stop it in time?"

"Sadly, we don't know the exact location of its Release, but as for stopping it...an entire coverage of Earth's atmosphere with evaporative dispensing of a neutralizing serum, should prove successful enough to stop it in its tracks." James suddenly begins to feel dizzy. He looks at Burke with sleepy eyes, holding out his glass with a groggy tone and says, "What…drink?" Burke takes James' drink and says, "Night, night son." James passes out on the couch.

Back on Earth In the dark and now windy desert hills, Debbie and Davis still run from the Tre'toan creature. Closely by, Nelson and Barnes run on top of a cliff's edge towards Davis and Debbie's location.
Nelson looking down, sees in the distance brief segments of the Tre'toan creature's movement through the rocks. He suddenly stops, and Barnes stops, both of them panting. Nelson points,
"Look! What is that?"
"It sure ain't no firefly, I'll tell ya that!"
"Come on, let's go!"
Nelson and Barnes continue running towards the direction of the creature. Debbie and Davis now exhausted, jogging along with every ounce of energy they can possibly muster. They see the road up ahead of them in the distance. "Look, the road's up ahead," says Davis as he begins to hold his chest, and panting heavily with total perspiration. Right
behind them, the creature begins closing in on them. They finally reach the road where the two vehicles still sit unattained. "Hurry…get in," shouts Davis as they pull on the door handles to Nelson's Suburban, but the doors are locked.
"Shit," shouts Davis as he turns to see the creature approaching them. "Come on, get on top of the truck,"

Davis shouts to Debbie as they both quickly climb on to the hood, then over the windshield onto the roof. They look at the front of the Suburban and all around, but can't see the creature anywhere. Suddenly its hissing sound is heard.

"Where is it Chief," asks Debbie as she hides behind him, shaking with fear.

"I don't know." Suddenly one of the rear tires blows out. They look down at the ground by the blown tire, but see nothing, as the other rear tire blows out. Debbie screams briefly with fright and says, "What is it doing?" Davis uses his shoulder radio, "Nelson? Where in the hell are you?" Nelson and Barnes standing with their guns aimed about fifty feet away from the Suburban, and Nelson shouts, "Right here! Get off the truck, now!" Davis and Debbie stand up quickly and jump off the back of the Suburban and hit the ground hard, then get back to their feet, and run like hell as Nelson and Barnes spray the entire side of the Suburban with bullets trying to kill the creature on the side of it. The creature lets out a long and eerie screech as a bullet pierces the gas tank, and the suburban blows up twenty feet skyward into the air, then returning to the ground in a smashing inferno of flames. Davis and Debbie hit the deck, as Nelson and Barnes lower their guns. "Wooo hooo! That critter's toast," Shouts Nelson. Barnes comment's, "I think the Chief's gonna be upset…his ride?"

Davis and Debbie get to their feet and look at the remains of the Suburban, and smoldering blob of Tre'toan flesh. Davis approaches Nelson and Barnes with a serious face and says,

"You just wasted taxpayer's money! But well spent men. Well spent."
Davis holds out his hand for a shake, and Nelson and Barnes smile and shake hands. Debbie looks at Davis and asks, "What about my husband Chief? Where is he?" Davis faces her with a look of comfort, and holds her shoulders. "Don't worry Mrs. Lowery. I'm sure he's gonna be all right, Ok? Where ever he is…I'm sure his thoughts are with you." Debbie smiles with sorrow and lowers her head, "Yes, I'm sure they are."

  Back on Silus in Burke's underground laboratory, James lays restrained on an operation table again, only in his boxers. A fish net of wires covers his entire body from the neck down, and round cylinder probes extrude out of the table and stop at the sides of his ears. Burke sits at a control panel pushing buttons and turning knobs. He signals to Deek standing at a power lever to turn on the juice. Deek pulls down on the lever and suddenly a humming noise fills the laboratory. On the operation table, the fish net wiring begins to glow bright blue, as electricity current travels along the probes next to James' ears. James begins to shake like a fish out of water, and mumbling repetitively. Burke and Deek remain still during the DNA extraction process. Suddenly James opens his eyes and screams briefly, then passes out.

  Moments later, James now lays on the couch in Burke's living room again…fully dressed, sleeping with his mouth wide open, and snoring. Burke sitting across from him is enjoying a Silustrian ale.

71

James begins to mumble in his sleep, then suddenly wakes up, and sits straight up with a terrifying look while gasping. He feels his head, then his chest while looking at Burke, "Did you…drug me Professor?"
"You appear to be in good health."
"You did."
"No need to worry James…we now have the final ingredients for the serum."
"Easy for you to say. You didn't just have a nightmare from hell!"
"For that, I sincerely apologize. And I can promise you…It doesn't have to happen again."
Burke takes a drink then smiles at James. James begins to wear a smile and points his finger at Burke while saying, "Your quite the clever old dog."
"They don't consider me, a cunning Professor for nothing you know."

CHAPTER 8
ELEVATION

Driving down the dark desert road, is the Tre'toan's SUV. Davis driving, Debbie riding shotgun, and Nelson and Barnes in the back seat. "I still don't think it's a good idea to have that thing in our presence Mrs. Lowery," says Davis as he briefly looks at Debbie's lap. Debbie holds up the Tre'toan device concealed in a zip lock bag. Nelson leans forward and says, "Yeah, that thing could be a bomb or something. For all we know…more of those things could be looking for it." Debbie briefly looks at nelson and Davis while saying, "And that's one reason I'm keeping it. Maybe somehow or someway it'll bring James back. So don't thing about taking it away from me…that is if you want to keep this information from the public."
Davis looks in the rear view at Nelson and Barnes, "We wouldn't dare think of it Mrs. Lowery… would we boys?" Nelson and Barnes look at each other quickly and both answer, "No Sir." Davis staring forward at the road says, "See Mrs. Lowery, nothing to worry about." Debbie continues to stare at the device, as they drive away.

   Returning to Burke's home on Silus, James and Burk stand by the door ready to exit. Burke tugs a little on the collar of James' jacket while saying, "You can't go to the Queen's dinner hall looking like this."
"What's wrong with my duds Professor? Do I not fit shall we say, the Queen's criteria?" Burke crosses his arms and says, "No…it's just they, well, smell poorly." James smells his underarms and replies," Ok, I can agree with you on that note."

Next we see James and Burke in a Silustrian clothing store…Burke standing with his arms crossed watching James enter a changing room with a stack of clothing. Other Silustrians and Humans present shopping. After a moment, James exits the change room wearing a super tight alien spandex suit, so tight that he can barely breath. He looks at Burke who is about to bust out laughing and says, "Hey, I could get use to this. Ya think my wife would like it?" James walks like a toy wooden soldier back into the change room, and Burke bust's out laughing.

   Back on Earth in front of the local Police department, the black SUV pulls up and parks. Everyone including Debbie holding the Tre'toan device, exits the vehicle and walks up the steps into the department. Once inside, Davis says to Debbie, "One moment, I'll be right with ya." Debbie nods as Davis takes Nelson to the side, "I want you to call up Dixie and ask her to come on down. And don't tell her anything yet, Ok?" "Sure Chief." Nelson and Barnes walk away as Davis walks over to Debbie, and gestures her to enter his office. They enter his office and Davis closes the door, then they sit down…Davis sitting behind his desk, and Debbie in front of the desk. Debbie still holding the Tre'toan device in her lap. "I still can't believe it. Murderous Aliens from, Tre'token, or whatever. UFOs snatching up my husband. And they said we're all gonna die some how. What are we gonna do Chief?"
"We just need to relax for a little while first, Ok? I'm sure there's a logical explanation for all of this."

Debbie just looks down at the Tre'toan device and caresses it with her thumb.
"You gonna be alright," asks Davis, as Debbie doesn't reply. "Mrs. Lowery?"
"Yes," says Debbie with a saddened tone. Davis stands up and walks to the door, opens it, then asks Debbie, "Would you care for some coffee or donuts ?" Debbie slowly shakes her head and replies, "Thanks, but no thanks."
"I'll be right back." Davis exits the office, closing the door behind him. "Where are you James?" Says Debbie in her time of sadness, and concerned thoughts for James.

Returning to Silus, in a large hallway leading to Queen Mirla's dinner hall on Silus, several humans, Silustrians and other Alien species walk towards the entrance. James wearing a hefty sized white jumpsuit, Burke wearing a formal gray suit, and Deek as himself walk along together towards the entrance. A faint sound of strange alien rhythmic music gets louder, as they approach the entrance. Also, flashes of light emanating from within the dinner hall. As James, Burke and Deek enter the hall, the music sounds intrinsic, as dozens of Humans and Silustrians dance around the hall in a display of grace and culture. James looks up at the ceiling and to his surprise, sees dozens of multi colored orbs flying all around, and forming various shapes to the beat of the music. James once again in total awe asks Burke, "Are those what I think they are Professor?"
"Yes...the ever so mysterious, and elusive orbs."
"Wow...more truth around every corner."
Mirla dressed in a skin-tight bodysuit, wearing a

jewel fashioned belt and her tiara, walks up to them while smiling at James...and her gender appearing to be normal.
"Good evening," she says softly.
James peels his eyes away from the orbs to see Mirla standing right in front of him, making eyes at him. James with a surprising look says,
"Oh, hello there your majesty."
"You can call me Mirla."
She instantly takes James by the arm and leads him into the hall. James looks back at Burke following them, and gives him an eye-widening plea for help. Burke trying to contain his laughter, simply shrugs his shoulders. James then glares at Burke, and turns his head. After they walk through the choreography of dancers, James and Mirla come to a series of floor couches. Mirla forces James to sit next to her on a couch. James scoots away from her a little, as she continues to hold his arm, as Burke and Deek sit down next to them.

   In another remote part of the Universe, is a planet, Tre'toa, dark in color, and two small suns with no moons in the distance. A Tre'toan ship suddenly fly's by toward the planet. On the planet surface, dark low lying constructed buildings of various proportion outline the perimeter of a massive, tall structure with large openings, with red lights shimmering all about them. The Tre'toan ship approaches one of the openings at idle speed.

   Inside the structure, the Tre'toan ship lands inside a triangular docking port, surrounded by dozens of other ships docked. Deep inside the structure, the

Lord Zemious, leader of the evil Tre'toan, dressed in a deep red hooded cloak, wearing large chrome inscribed bracelet's sits on a dark granite throne…in a large chamber constructed of a dark composite type steel, with one large octagon light located in the center of the ceiling. Two Tre'toan guards dressed in gloss black uniforms similar to military issue, stand on each side of Zemious, and hold in their hands chrome laser rifles. A Tre'toan soldier also in a gloss black uniform enters and takes a knee before Zemious.
"My Lord Zemious, I regret to inform you of a change in events on our mission to Earth."
Zemious removes his hood quickly, and he appears to look mid-aged.
"Change in events," Zemious asks with an already angered tone.
"The Silustrians my Lord. Again, they have interrupted our plans to fore go the elimination of the Earthlings." Zemious stands quickly as his eyes glow with fire. "The virus, released it you have?"
"Yes my Lord…but." Zemious interrupts,
"But what?"
"We failed to retrieve the Human specimen. The Silustrians managed to grab him before we could." Zemious' eyes suddenly shoot fire at the soldier, the soldier shrieking and burning to a cinder. Zemious' eyes return to their normal state, as the soldier's corpse smolders.
"Fetch me the fleet commander, now," Zemious shouts as the two guards jog away. Zemious squints as he says,
"Now…the long awaited war of wars will begin." His eyes briefly flash with fire.

CHAPTER 9
INVASION

    The light of day now pierces through the blinds of Davis' office windows, as Debbie sleeps in the chair, still grasping the Tre'toan device. Davis can be seen through his interior office window talking to Nelson and Barnes. They finish talking, then Nelson and Barnes walk away, as Dixie approaches Davis. They talk for a moment, then Davis points at Debbie. Dixie nods her head and walks to the door, opening and entering the office. Dixie places her hands ever so gently on Debbie's shoulders. Debbie suddenly wakes up shouting, "James! James!"
"It's Ok mam. Your safe," says Dixie as Debbie looks at Dixie with sadness. Dixie hugs her and softly says, "Oh you poor dear."
After a moment of Dixie's comforting Debbie, they draw away from the hugging and Debbie has tears in her eyes slowly running down her cheeks. Dixie takes out a tissue and wipes her tears away while saying, "There there…it's gonna be alright. Dixie's here to take care of ya honey." Debbie begins to show a little smile. "That's more like it." Dixie stands up and extends her hand to Debbie. "Come on. You can stay with me, Ok?" Debbie nods and replies, "Ok", as she takes Dixie's hand and stands up. They both turn and exit the office.

    At Queen Mirla's dinner hall on Silus, everyone has left but Deek who lays asleep on the couch with his legs stretched out over Burke's lap. Burke passed out with an empty bottle in one hand, and in the other an empty glass…while James barely sits up drunk and singing, as Mirla is wide awake and slightly clinging on James' arm. James singing,

"God bless America…my home sweet," James suddenly passes out on to the couch. Mirla shakes her head and stands up. She then leans over and amazingly picks up James in her arms with ease, then walks away with him.

   In Mirla's chambers, a large round bed with several exotic pillows, and fine silky curtains hang from the ceiling all around. She enters with James in her arms and proceeds to the bed. She then gently lays James on the bed. He rolls over and hugs a pillow. She then turns and walks away.

   Back in the evil Lord Zemious' lair on Tre'toa, he paces slowly around another soldier. "A surprise attack from our entire fleet, shall put an end to their
further interference with our goals. What else of
further use do you recommend commander?"
"Perhaps a campaign of fusion missile bombardment, to severely fracture they're Capital City installations… rendering their main communications weak."
Zemious stops and faces the commander.
"Yes…a brilliant idea. Assemble the fleet and
all the missiles we can possibly carry. We'll give
them such a war…they'll fear our very existence.
And the moment victory is near…invade them we
will. This moment has gone unanswered far too
long. See to it Commander."
"Yes my Lord."
The commander bows briefly and walks away.
Zemious wears an evil grin.

   Returning to Queen Mirla's chambers on Silus, James now lays under the covers still fully

dressed, and Mirla lays under the covers in a skimpy nightgown, on the opposite side of the bed. Both of them sleeping. James rolls over towards Mirla, and his hand touches Mirla's shoulder. James dreaming of Debbie and him rolling around in bed. James now lightly caressing Mirla's shoulder. She smiles and moans a little. James still dreaming of Debbie's face in the heat of passion. Now James kissing Mirla's shoulder… Mirla moans a little and rolls over towards James. James suddenly opens his eyes and they widen to the extreme. He screams and Mirla opens her eyes as James jumps up and rolls out of bed hitting the floor hard. "Owwww," he shouts.
Mirla pulls herself to the side of the bed to see James sitting up rubbing his head. She laughs briefly, and James suddenly looks at her again with the widest eyes, and shakes is hand briefly in her face. "Stay there," says James as he quickly gets to his feet and adds, "Your Majesty… goodnight." James walks away quickly while shaking his head as Mirla rests her head on her hands and says, "Why is it always the cute ones?"

   Back home on Earth in Dixie's house, Dixie sits on the bed next to Debbie lying down under the covers. "You rest as long as you need to, Ok?" Debbie nods and replies, "Thank you."
"Don't mention it Honey. I'll be home later on."
They both smile as Dixie stands up and walks away. Debbie pulls out the Tre'toan device and looks at it, as she dozes off. Debbie now holding the device in the palm of her hand, the device begins to open up, until fully opened. The strange refractive

letters and shapes begin to rise up into the air. Debbie begins to dream of the evil Tre'toan's plans to eliminate the entire inhabitance of Earth's population…People choking and dying at homes, in cars, office buildings and City streets…by the millions.
The Tre'toan device slips out of her hands and falls onto the floor, shattering into pieces. Debbie still dreaming, as tears run down her cheeks.

  Looking at the exterior of Lord Zemious' towering complex of darkness on Tre'toa, Zemious stands at the entrance of a landing bay, watching the Tre'toan fleet vessels exiting dozens of bays by the dozens. He briefly throws up his hands to them, turns and walks towards an enormous ship awaiting his presence aboard. Next, the huge command ship exits the bay and fly's skyward towards the Tre'toan fleet.

  In Burke's house on Silus, the front door opens, and James helps Burke into the house who is still drunk , and Deek staggering a little enters as well. James helps Burke to one of the couches, and Burke falls onto the couch and quickly dozes off. "The doctor has left the building," says James as he falls backwards onto one of the couches. Deek staggers up to the center table, drops to his knees and passes out face first onto the table. James looking up at the ceiling closes his eyes, when suddenly a super loud fart sounds throughout the house. James sits up quickly with a disgusted look, and notices Deek smiling.
"I've the perfect house warming gift for you...a cork!" James quickly lays back down face first into a

83

couch cushion.

Light years away Aboard the Command Bridge of Zemious' ship, he sits on a throne type chair accompanied by his personal guards, and about ten crewmen controlling the ship. He presses a lighted symbol on his armrest. "How long Commander, before we can make the jump?" In a lower section of the ship, the Commander standing at a voice console on the wall replies,"
"Just a short while longer my Lord."
The Commander then turns to view dozens of crewmen loading dozens of slender liquid filled missiles into missile batteries located in the deck of the ship. Back on Zemious' bridge, he says aloud to a crewman in front of him at a console,
"Alert the fleet of our readiness for light-speed!"
"Yes my Lord."
In space, the entire Tre'toan fleet of at least a hundred or so vessels, fly's by and away, with Zemious' ship bringing up the rear.

Back home In Olsen's office, he sits back in his chair, smoking a cigar while on the phone. He speaks harshly on the phone.
"No, I don't know where his wife is either! And I don't need you TV buffs nosing around here as well! Good day!" Olsen slams down the phone, stands up quickly and storms out of his office and demands loudly,
"Anyone seen, or heard from Lowery?"
Everyone present working shakes their heads no.
A moment goes by and Olsen shouts,
"What are yea staring at! Get back to work!"
Everybody quickly gets busy as Olsen re-enters his

office, slamming the door behind him and shouting, "Damn that Lowery! He's finished!"

  Back in Dixie's house, Debbie with wet hair in just a towel is talking on the phone in Dixie's kitchen, "I appreciate you filling in for me Laura. I just need a little time to sort some things out. Thanks Laura, goodbye." She hangs up and sits at the kitchen table in front of her. She sips a cup of coffee, then suddenly set's it down and picks up a newspaper. The paper reads: Unidentified virus claims forty-three lives in South America. After a moment of reading the newspaper, She slowly sets down the paper as she lifts her head and thinks to herself.

  Nine light years from Earth, Zemious and his dark fleet prepare to jump to light speed. All the ships assume a divided formation on each side of Zemious' Ship. On Zemious' bridge, Zemious gives the order to jump to light speed. "Ready commander!" The Commander walks up to a seat just below Zemious, and sits while saying towards the crewmen at the flight control console, "All ships to engage on my mark!" Watching the ships from behind their location, all of the ships starting from the ones most forward, jump to light speed, gone in a fraction of a second.

  In the dark stillness of night on Silus, the Capital City Streets lay empty of any signs of life. Only the strangely shaped lights that adorn the buildings, provide any light what so ever. Suddenly the deep and loud sound of pulsating Sirens fill the entire city with the fearful warning of the incoming threat of the Tre'toans arrival. Dozens of Silustrian UFO crewmen exit several buildings, running in one direction, towards the UFO landing ports. Dozens of more Silustrians dressed in dark blue battle gear, holding slender chrome laser guns and rifles, also exit buildings. Humans and Silustrians also exit quickly from their dwellings, curious of the alarm and actions of the crewmen and soldiers.

In Burke's house, James, Burke and Deek all suddenly wake up. Burke and Deek run to the door, it opens quickly, and they step outside. James sits up and says, "What's all the fuss about?"

On Zemious' bridge, him and the entire crew can see the Capital City through their bridge windows. "Move the fleet into flank position and fire your missiles Commander!"
The Commander briefly bows to Zemious and faces the crew captain sitting in a revolving chair and orders, "Signal the fleet and begin missile bombardment!" The Captain swivels to his control panel. Looking at the Tre'toan ships, the fleet ships fly down over the City in a V formation, as Zemious' ship flies forward towards the City.

Burke and Deek still standing outside of the doorway, watching all the Silustrian and Human civilians frantically running around and screaming, as the Tre'toans quickly descend on the City, and begin firing their lasers and fusion missiles all over. The Silustrian soldiers begin firing back at the Tre'toan ships, as Tre'toan lasers hit buildings and civilians, and missiles exploding all over in liquid embers, instantly dissolving their targets. Burke runs back into his house and towards the lab entrance behind the bar. "Don't move James," shouts Burke, as he runs down into the Lab. With the sound of the events taking place just outside and watching Burke, James stands up and runs over to the door.

At the UFO landing port, the Silustrian fleet quickly board their ships. One of the UFOs is suddenly fired upon heavily and explodes, sending debris everywhere, as the UFOs begin to take off. Laser cannons pop up atop the Cities buildings and begin firing at the Tre'toan ships. James leaning on the doorway looking out at the battle, sees Mirla running down a corridor in fear for her life. A fusion missile hits one of the columns supporting the roof of the corridor, dissolving the lower portion, and causing the roof to collapse just in front of her. James quickly looks at Deek and says, "I'm gonna help her!" James runs to Mirla's rescue.

Above the City, Silustrian UFOs battling Tre'toan UFOs. Aboard Zemious' bridge, Zemious remains in his chair, While the Commander stands and says aloud to the Captain, "Prepare the second approach of missile bombardment!" The Captain nods and turns to his console.

Back to the battle scene in the streets of the

Capital City, James dodging laser fire runs his Fastest to reach the Queen's location. Just about to her, a laser hits the ground next to his feet, igniting his boots on fire, as he screams and dives over the rubble pile from the corridor. He land's next to Mirla who is ok and kneeling down behind the rubble. James quickly begins stomping his feet and blowing on them hard to put out the flames. James decides to pull off his boots quickly. Burke jogs up and out of the lab carrying a medium size chrome briefcase, and two laser pistols. He runs out the door and stops facing Deek while gasping.
"Where's James?"
Deek points to James and Mirla's location while replying, "There, to save the Queen."
Burke hands Deek a laser pistol.
"Take this…follow me!"
Burke runs towards James and Mirla, and Deek follows hot on his heels.

Above the City, Zemious' ship flies above making another run with the fusion missiles, as the UFOs continue their fighting.

In a remote area a hundred miles away from the Silustrian Capital City, on the dark horizon some five miles away, little specks of bright lights moving in various patterns, become larger by the second. After a moment it becomes clear the lights are orbs, traveling hundreds of miles per hour. They pass and fly away quickly towards the Capital City.

Burke and Deek reach James and Mirla, both

hiding behind the rubble. James putting on his now soaking wet boots. "Are you all right your Highness," asks Burke.
"Yes, I'm fine."
Burke then sniffs the air and asks, "What is that smell?" James finishing with his boots replies, "Don't ask." A brief moment later, James adds, "I guess the Tre'toans found out about our little secret."
"Yes, it would appear so," says Burke as the battling from all directions continues.

   Inside the Police station, Dixie sitting back in a chair and reading a book. The phone rings and Dixie pushes a button on the switchboard.
"Hello?" A brief moment goes by.
"Oh, hey girl. How ya doing?"
In Dixie's kitchen, Debbie on the phone.
"Alright. Say Dixie, is the Chief available?"
Dixie's voice answers, "Sure, hang on a minute, I'll fetch him."
"Thanks."
In the station, Dixie stands up and walks over to Davis's door, opens it and leans into see Davis holding up a mirror, looking at his bald head.
"Chief?" Davis suddenly hides the mirror while looking at Dixie. "What ever happened to knocking?" Replies Davis, as Dixie wears a smile.
"Mrs. Lowery's on line two."
"Here we go." Says Davis, as Dixie still smiling closes the door and walks away. Davis picks up the phone. "Hello Mrs. Lowery, is everything alright?"
Debbie on the phone in Dixie's kitchen. "I don't

think so Chief. It's already started." Davis's asks, "What's all ready started?"
"The alien's plans to kill us off. It's started already in South America, a virus…an unknown virus… growing and killing people." Davis on the phone, "And how do you know what your saying's true?"
Debbie on the phone, "It's right on the front page of the Chronicle. Don't you read the paper?"
Davis on the phone, "Not really. Look Mrs. Lowery…we don't need to jump to any conclusions here. There's always diseases, killing people all the time. So what makes this one any different from all the rest?"
Debbie on the phone with a serious look, "And what if I'm right, and we all die because we didn't do anything about it? Don't you care about that possibility Chief?"
Davis on the phone, "Well of course I would," It's just that I don't see", Davis here's the phone click. "Mrs. Lowery?" After no reply, Davis sighs and hangs up the phone, then leans back in his chair thinking to himself.

Returning to the battle in the Capital City on Silus, James, Burke, Deek and Mirla still seek shelter behind The pile of rubble, as the laser fire from the war continues to pose a threat to anyone caught in its crossfire. "We've gotta get you out of here James, and back to Earth with the Serum."
"I couldn't agree with you more," replies James as they see Zemious' ship flying overhead, firing missiles and laser shots forward and ahead of their position.
Burke peeks out from behind the rubble and

notices the fighting has decreased near their own position. He looks at James and Mirla, "Alright, this it. Follow my lead, and stay close as you can." James nods as Burke peeks one more time, then rises to his feet and runs away with everyone closely following behind him.

　Approximately a half a mile away from the cities outskirts, the orbs in the distance spread out and fly in all directions. A Tre'toan ship giving chase to a Silustrian ship, is chased itself suddenly by two of the orbs.
Aboard the Tre'toan ship's bridge, a crewman scanning an octagon shaped radar screen sees the orbs presence behind them and quickly turns to his Captain and shouts, "Energy mites approaching!" Suddenly orbs enter the Ship's Bridge and the Captain and crew tense up as orbs penetrate the ship's control consoles, creating massive sparks, intense explosions and panic for the entire crew.
Just outside of the ship, the orbs quickly exit it and fly away, as the ship begins to blow up and disintegrate.

　Still continuing their trek, Burke, James, Deek and Mirla run into a long one-story building. Once inside they see a couple of Silustrian soldiers, walking towards them, one helping the other due to injury. Everyone quickly jogs up to them and they all stop, then one of the soldiers says,
"Penetrated the compound they have."
"How many," asks Burke.
"Don't know. Turn back you must."

"I think we'd better take their advice and turn back Professor, don't you," asks James as suddenly laser fire barely wings the wounded soldier's back, sending him to the floor, and everyone else ducking. Half a dozen Tre'toan foot soldiers run towards them, firing their weapons as they approach. James quickly bends over and picks up the injured soldier, and holds him over his shoulder and runs away with everyone else running away as well.

  On the bridge of a Silustrian UFO, the crew witnesses through their bridge window, their orb friends penetrating the Tre'toan ships and destroying them. The crew smiling and cheering for the moment. From a distance above the city up in the sky, the orbs can be seen flying everywhere, attributing to the many explosions all over the sky from the disintegrating Tre'toan ships.
On Zemious' control bridge, the Captain quickly turns toward Zemious and the Commander, "We've lost communications with most of the fleet!" Zemious' eyes begin to glow red as he quickly stands and says with anger, "How can that be! A view of the remaining ships, now!"
Another crewman pushes a button and a hologram appears, showing several of the Tre'toan ships being invaded by the orbs, and being destroyed.
The Captain says, "Energy mites my Lord!"
Zemious responds fiercely, "Who is responsible for this lack of information?"
Zemious looks at the Commander, then the Captain, and the Captain looking at Zemious briefly glances at the Commander. Zemious' eyes

begin to burn with fire as he looks at the Commander. The Commander suddenly takes a knee and pleads with Zemious, "Please my Lord…I swear I did not know of their presence upon our arrival." Two fire beams suddenly exit Zemious' eyes and hit the Commander's, blowing him back against the bridge wall in a brief fireball…the remains of the Commander but a smoldering shell. Zemious sits down and looks at the entire crew whom all bow briefly from their fear of the moment.
"Recall the remaining ships and troops Captain…and set a holding pattern away from the planet!"
"Yes my Lord." The Captain bows briefly and turns to his console. "They'll pay fiercely for this," says Zemious with determination.

CHAPTER 10
ANNHILATION

In Dixie's living room, Debbie now dried off and fully dressed in a pair of jeans and a T-shirt, sits down on the couch in front of the television and uses the remote. The television comes on and Debbie flips through a couple of channels and stops on her news channel. Her co-anchor Bob Spencer telling the news, "With the death toll now rising to approximately one hundred and seventy three, all airports, trains, bus lines and shipping of any kind, have been suspended in South America, due to the sudden and increasing risk of the still unidentified virus. Their government forces have quarantined a four hundred square mile perimeter, in hopes of
stopping the virus from possibly spreading any further. In other news, the stock market," Debbie turns off the television and leaves the couch. She walks into the kitchen and uses the phone. She dials a number. "Yes, I need a cab please."
Debbie now at the front door, opens it and exits the house. On the kitchen table she has left a thank you note for Dixie.

   At the police department in Davis's office, he sits in his chair and leans forward, then uses the phone. After a moment of no reply, he gets up and walks quickly out of his office.

   Back in the compound on Silus, our friend's run and take shelter around a corner from the intense laser fire from the Tre'toan foot soldiers. Our friends now being trapped at a dead end. Burke and Deek exchanging laser fire, as everyone else stays low and close to the wall. "I don't know how much longer we can hold them off," shouts

Burke while firing his gun. James looking all around for a way out of their situation. He notices a square outline on the floor. He faces the soldier and points at it, "Where does that lead to?"
"Vast subterranean cavities…lead to port terminals they do." James quickly gets to his knees and tries to open the hatch with his bare fingers, but can't. He turns to Mirla?
"Might I borrow your belt Mirla?"
She smiles and replies, "Certainly." She unbuckles it and hands it to James. Burke and Deek still firing at the Tre'toan soldiers. One of the Tre'toan soldiers ducked down and holding a small gold octagon shaped disk in his hand, speaks into it, "We have the Queen and her conspirators sieged! Requesting more troops!"

On Zemious' bridge, he sits in his chair listening to the soldier's request. Zemious replies, "We cannot afford to lose any more ships! Order them to continue, and if the Queen and her conspirators resist…kill them all!" An octagon shaped radar scope displays several incoming Silustrian UFOs. The crewman at the scope turns quickly to Zemious, "Silustrian vessels approaching from our port side my Lord!" In space at a distance of approximately one kilometer, the Silustrian ships close in quickly for a counter attack against the Tre'toans. Ships from both sides engaging each other with massive laser fire exchange.

Returning to the inside of the compound on Silus, James now with the lid off the shaft, hands

Mirla her belt and crawls down onto a ladder attached to the shaft wall. He looks at Burke and Deek who are still firing at the Tre'toans, and shouts, "Professor! Come on!"
"I'll provide us enough time to get everyone out…go," shouts Burke. James gestures the seriously wounded soldier to get on his back. "Don't worry, I won't drop ya. Just hang on tight." Mirla and the other soldier help him on to James' back. The soldier wraps his arms around James' neck too tightly, and James begins to choke, then trying to speak but can't. He suddenly loses his footing, and slides down the ladder with the soldier…both yelling all the way down. James finally tightening his grip good, and using his boots to slow them down…coming to a complete stop and James still yelling briefly. James' boots just inches from the floor of a narrow tunnel carved out of the Earth, and dimly lit by small flat and circular overhead lights. He helps the soldier off his back and assists him to the ground against the wall out of harms-way. Mirla looking down at them shouts, "Are you Ok down there?" James looks up and shouts back, "We're still alive, if that's what you mean!"

Near the outskirts on the opposite side of the city, several Silustrian soldiers tucked tightly behind an enormous statue that resembles an Alien Sun God, exchange laser fire with Tre'toan foot soldiers. Suddenly in the near distance, two dozen or more orbs approach rapidly, and assume a position over the Tre'toan foot soldiers location. They suddenly descend on them, in a spiraling and fast motion…entering them as the soldiers begin to shriek, then blowing them into pieces as the Silustrian soldiers jump up and cheer with their hands held high in celebration. After the orbs finish destroying the remaining Tre'toans…they form an alien's face that smiles.

   As Burke and Deek exchange laser fire with the Tre'toans, Deek shoots and hits one of them in the chest, blowing him back several feet…and the Tre'toan shrieks to his death. A creature instantly exits, but only half way out, it screeches its last breath…falling to the ground with its tongue hanging out dead. Mirla and the other Silustrian soldier carefully enter the shaft and proceed downward, as Burke hands the briefcase to Deek, "Go Deek…go now!"
"But Professor." Burke interrupts,
"Trust me, I'll be just fine…now go!"
Deek takes one last shot, then runs over to the shaft and enters it, climbing downward quickly.

   Back on Earth in front of James and Debbie's house, a cab pulls into the driveway. Debbie exits from the rear left passenger side, closes the door quickly and hands the cabby a twenty, then turns and proceeds to the front door as the cabby backs out and pulls away. At the front door, Debbie places her hand on the knob and twists, but the door doesn't open. She puts her shoulder into it and the door jam breaks off while it opens. She looks closely at the jam…and it reveals globs of chewing gum.
"Gum," Debbie questions as she enters the house.

At Dixie's house, Davis driving a Police cruiser, and Dixie riding shotgun pull into the driveway quickly and park. Davis and Dixie exit the car quickly with their guns drawn…Dixie behind Davis. They make their way quickly to the front door and stop. Davis looks at Dixie and nods, then opens the door quickly…running into the house with their guns aimed.

"Mrs. Lowery," shouts Davis, as they both cautiously spread out… Dixie towards the kitchen area, and Davis towards the bedrooms.

"Are you here Mrs. Lowery?" Still with no reply, Davis approaches the guest room where Debbie slept, and opens the door quickly with his gun drawn in front of him. He notices the broken pieces of the Tre'toan device on the floor. He starts to walk towards them and they suddenly burst into red-hot lava…and after a moment turn cold and explode into a powder sort of ash. Davis jumps back and almost falls backwards. His face full of curiosity as he regains his composure… looking at the mysterious dust cloud engulfing the entire room. He holsters his gun and walks back to the living room, where Dixie stands holding the brief note left by Debbie on the kitchen table. Davis stops in front of Dixie and takes the note and looks at it. It reads: Thank you Dixie, love Debbie.

"What was that noise back there Chief," asks Dixie. "Just another clue that Mrs. Lowery isn't here," replies Davis as he walks to the front door, then turns to Dixie, "Come on, I need you back at the station." Davis turns and walks out the door, and Dixie asks while following him Outside the house,

"You wanna tell me what's really going on here Chief?"
Davis hesitates to answer her, as he opens his car door.
Dixie walking over to her door asks, "Well?"
"Trust me when I tell you…that the less you
know…the better off you'll be." Davis gets in the
car, shuts the door and starts the engine, as Dixie
opens her door and enters the car. She asks him
one more question, "So where do you suppose she
went?" Davis backs out, then pulls away and
replies, " Not far...I'll find her."

  Returning to the battle in space over Silus, the
full scale battle continues…Silustrian ships
chasing Tre'toan ships, and visa versa…as large
cannons on Zemious' ship fire at several Silustrian
ships trying to get in closer for a more effective
hit. One of Zemious' cannons fires repetitively on
a Silustrian ship, blowing it to pieces.
On Zemious' control bridge, he remains seated
and calm for the moment, as the massive battling
is seen through the bridge window. The Captain
turns to Zemious, "They're attempting to take out our Aft
Thruster systems!"
"I trust you'll handle the situation without failure Captain?"
"Yes my Lord."
The Captain turns to his console and speaks,
"All ships draw their fire away from our Aft
position!" In all directions around Zemious' ship the
fighting continues…ships from both sides being destroyed.

  Returning to our friends on Silus, Burke still

firing at the Tre'toan soldiers, hits one dead center in the gut, blowing him back several feet. The soldier screeches to his death. Burke decides it's a good time to flee the scene, so he runs to the shaft while tucking his laser pistol down his pants, climbs into the shaft and straddles the ladder, then slides quickly all the way down to the bottom. At the bottom, everyone looking at Burke and James asks, "What took you so long?"
Burke grins while replying, "Target practice...let's go." James once more helps the wounded soldier onto his back, and everyone jogs away down the long and narrow cavity. Just above the shaft, the four remaining Tre'toan foot soldiers stop, and one of them pulls a dark round sphere off his belt clip and says, "This will slow them down."
He presses a button inward, then drops it down the shaft. At the bottom of the shaft, the dark sphere now having four red laser sights stops three feet from impacting the floor. Suddenly four little laser barrels pop out as it begins to make a distinct humming noise, like the sound of a powerful transformer. It begins to move in on our friend's direction. Our friends still jogging along and Burke suddenly slows down. The seeking sphere continues to move faster and faster. Burke stops in his tracks, and everyone else as well. They turn and look at him. "What is it Professor," asks James. "Shhh," replies Burke with his finger up. The seeking sphere still moving fastly towards them, as Burke speaks quickly, "Everyone down on the ground, now!"
Burke and everyone quickly lay down, including the wounded soldier still on James' back.

"Don't move a muscle…or breathe heavy for that matter," whispers Burke. The seeking sphere now moving slower and slower arrives at their location, probing the entire area for any movement with its infrared sights. Everyone with fear in their eyes, watches the sphere as it begins to hover over them, turning and searching for them.
Suddenly a green bug that resembles a small crab with suction cup antennas, crawls out from a crack in the floor and towards Mirla's face. Her eyes widen as she wears the most terrifying look. Only James, the wounded soldier on his back, and the other soldier sees the bug approaching Mirla's face. The seeking sphere slowly moves beyond their position, as the soldier looks at the other soldier on James' back, then Mirla and whispers, "For your honor my Majesty."
The soldier suddenly gets to his feet and runs as quickly as he can back towards the access shaft. The seeking sphere turns quickly and pursues the soldier…speeding over everyone and firing bright but thin lasers at the soldier. The soldier on James' back shouts, "Sim, no!" Burke and Deek begin firing at the sphere, but having a hard time hitting it. Sim now some thirty feet away takes a direct hit to the back, the laser beam cutting clean through him…he falls to the ground and dies. Burke and Deek finally hitting the sphere, and the sphere explodes with the power of a stick of dynamite… and the entire tunnel begins to shake with the area of the spheres destruction, collapsing in. Everyone quickly gets up and runs away as the tunnel caves in behind them…and the alien bug squashed in the process. The soldier on James'

back with tears in his eyes sadly says, "Sim," as they continue to run away.

  Back home on Earth in front of the Police Station, Davis walks out with Nelson and Barnes following him. "We've gotta find her before anything else can go wrong." Davis stops by his car door, opens it and turns while resting his hands on the door, as Nelson and Barnes stop in front of the black SUV facing Davis. "You boys follow me…but not too closely."
Davis gets in his car and shuts the door, starting his car and backing out, as Nelson and Barnes get in the SUV. Davis peels away.

  In front of James and Debbie's house, Debbie exits the front door wearing a white halter-top, and matching overalls…and she carries a little black purse. She closes the front door and walks over to the garage then takes a remote for the garage out of her purse, aims it at the door and presses. The door opens all the way up, revealing a brand new top of the line midnight blue SUV. Debbie gets in, starts it up, then backs out as the garage door closes. Backed up all the way out of the drive, she peels away. Davis and posse pull up to Debbie's and park, just missing her.

  Debbie in her SUV driving down the road, places a picture of James and her posing together at an Amusement Park on the center console. In the back ground of the photo, a man maid UFO sits perched on a wide pole. Debbie looking at the photo smiles out of sadness, as a single tear rolls down her cheek.

Returning to space over Silus, the battle yet remains in full swing. Aboard one of the Silustrian ships, a crew of six stands at their controls…as the blue containment beams shine down on them from above. One of the crew in the gunnery station, firing and speaking quickly to himself in Silustrian dialect. On his hologram, a Tre'toan ship in his sights. He fires with precision aim and blows it up. He cheers loudly, "Yahaaa!"

Returning to our friends in the long tunnel, they approach another ladder leading upwards and stop. James panting heavier than everyone else, decides to take a short breather, setting the wounded soldier down against the wall.
"If I'm not mistaken, this should lead up to the landing port terminals," says Burke while looking up. Mirla comforts the wounded soldier, as James, Burke, and Deek watch them talking.
"My brother not die in vein your Majesty. Fool was he, but brave as well."
Mirla gently holds his face and replies, "Yes, he shall be honored in the halls of Rue Silus." She softly kisses his forehead, and he smiles a little. Mirla looks at everyone watching. Burke places his hands on the ladder and says, "Sorry folks…but we must be moving on." Burke starts up the ladder as James sighs heavily then helps the wounded and heart broken soldier onto his back again. James and the soldier start up the ladder behind Burke, then Mirla, and Deek left to bring up the rear.

In a room dimly lit by sconce lighting, with silver crates stacked on one another, and two doors

located opposite of each other, a floor hatch slowly opens up and it's Burke's face peeking to see if the coast is clear to exit. Seeing that it is, he quickly lifts the hatch lid all the way back and softly lays it down. He then climbs out and helps with James and the soldier first. James panting again says, "Is this the last flight?"
Burke helps him and the soldier all the way out and replies, "We'll know that as soon as we reach the landing port." Burke continues to help Mirla, then Deek. Finished, Burke steps up to one of the doors, where a lighted button on the wall blinks continuously. Burke signals Deek to stand on the opposite side of the door. Deek does so, while they both hold their guns aimed, Burke nods to Deek, then pushes the lighted button, and the door opens upwards swiftly, revealing a long hallway with many openings. Parts of the ceiling and walls appear to have been hit with Zemious' fusion missiles…hundred square foot areas completely gone, and portions of the flooring dissolved.
Burke thinking the coast is clear, steps out a few feet and suddenly laser fire from three different guns hits the door jam next to him, as he quickly runs back into the room and seeks shelter behind the wall. "Blasted! They must have been tracking us the whole time," loudly says Burke, as everyone also assumes shelter along the wall. James looking at Burke says, "From the looks of things…I'd say we're right back where we started."
The laser fire suddenly stops and a Tre'toan's voice shouts, "Give us the Queen, and we'll spare the rest of you! And if you refuse, you all will be annihilated! You have but a few moments to

decide!" Burke looks at the chrome crates and notices a particular symbol on its side, resembling an atom. "I've an idea," says Burke.

   Back on earth in front of James and Debbie's house, Davis, Nelson and Barnes approach their vehicles and stop. Davis takes off his baseball cap, takes out a rag from his back pocket and wipes his sweaty bald head while saying, "You two go ahead and resume your patrol. If I need your assistance later for any reason, I'll contact yea's." Nelson and Barnes Nod and say, "Yes Sir," as they open their doors. Davis already turned with his cap back on, turns to them again and points his finger while saying aloud, "And remember…you know nothing when it comes to you know what!" They respond with a nod, then get in the SUV, start it up and pull away past Davis. They all wave briefly as Davis gets in his car. He shuts the door and rests his arms on the steering wheel…wondering where Debbie could be. After a moment, he starts his car and pulls away.

   Debbie driving down the road, she pulls into Max's gas station, up to the pumps and shuts off the engine. She gets out and is greeted by Max. "Hello there Mrs. Lowery. What can I do ya fur?" Debbie replies, "Hi Max. You can fill it up."
"Will do."
Debbie walks towards the store entrance, as Max fills her tank. Davis pulls into the station and to the pumps on the opposite side of Debbie's SUV. He gets out and shuts the door, then walks around

the pumps past Max, towards the store entrance.
"Hey Chief! Filler up,"
says Max aloud. Davis replies aloud,
"You got it!"
"Alrighty", says Max has he begins to fill up
Davis's tank as well. In the store, Davis walks in
and a young man, Tommy, Caucasian, nineteen or
so years old greets Davis, "Hi Chief."
Debbie nowhere in sight, as Davis stops at the
magazine rack and replies,
"Staying out of trouble these days Tommy?"
Davis picks out a magazine and opens it, while
Tommy replies, "Oh yeah…my days of partying
are over."
"That's good to hear Tommy."
Davis places the magazine back and walks toward
the restrooms. Once there, he opens the door and
enters, and at the same time, Debbie exits the
ladies restroom and walks up to the counter.
"That'll be thirty five twenty nine mam,"
says Tommy as Debbie hands him fifty. He works
the register and gives her the change and a receipt.
"Thank You," says Debbie as she walks away
out of the store.
"You're Welcome!"
Outside at the pumps, Debbie gets in her SUV
and Max says aloud, "Bye Mrs. Lowery!"
"Bye Max!"
Debbie shuts the door and starts the engine, then
pulls away. Inside the store in front of the men's restroom
door, the sound of the toilet flushing. A brief
moment later, Davis exits and walks up to the
register. "How much ," asks Davis.
"Twenty five even Sir," replies Tommy.

Davis hands him twenty-five even, then walks towards, and out the door.
"Keep up the good work Tommy!"

   Returning to the battle in space above Silus, only a few ships from each fleet remain in the survival of the fittest…still fighting it out, away from, and around Zemious' ship.
On board Zemious' bridge, he gives an order to the Captain, "Speed us up Captain, and set a safer course in orbit over the Capitol!"
The Captain turns to Zemious,
"But my Lord, our remaining ships." Zemious eyes briefly flicker of fire as he interrupts, "Do not question my authority Captain…ever!"
"Forgive me my Lord."
The Captain bows briefly and adds, "As you wish." He turns to his console.
Viewing Zemious' ship in space, it quickly fly's away from the now diminishing battle.

   Back on Silus in the storage room, where our friends plot to rid themselves of the Tre'toan foot soldiers, Burke holds what looks like a small nuclear bomb, with one handle on its upper end. A Tre'toan's voice shouts, "Your time is over! Give us the Queen…or you all die!" Burke shout's back, "Just a moment…we're getting her prepared!"
"You have twenty seconds!"
Burke hands the device to James, and he carefully takes it while asking,
"Is this thing nuclear Professor?"
"Heavens no…it's just an atomic switch."

James' eyes widen as he says,
"Just, atomic?"
"Now remember…throw it high in their direction. Got it," says Burke. James replies, "Got it."
Burke turns to see Mirla still standing against the wall, the soldier sitting against the wall, and Deek standing in an empty chrome crate, with an attached lid that stands open like a jewelry box. Deek holding a laser pistol. Burke looks at Deek and says, "You sure about this Deek?"
"Sure I am."
"Alright." The Tre'toan's voice shouts, "The Queen! Now!"
"Here she comes," shouts Burke, as James assumes his position, and Deek squats down in the crate. Burke assumes a position behind the crate with his laser pistol in one hand, closes the lid over Deek, then leans on the crate while saying,
"One Deek in the box, coming right up."
Burke pushes with all his might on the crate, and releases it just at the doorway…the crate sliding across the floor some twenty-five feet to a dead stop, as laser fire sprays the crate, but doing no damage what so ever. Seeing the direction of the laser fire, James tosses the device high and far, as Burke fires at it just before impact, blowing it up, into an explosion so powerful, the entire complex shakes, as debris fly's everywhere, and the sound of Tre'toans shrieking to their deaths.
Suddenly Deek pops up with his laser pistol, just as the last Tre'toan comes hobbling out and shooting his laser rifle. Deek fires several rounds into the Tre'toan soldier killing him. Burke leans over and picks up the chrome briefcase off the

ground, then grins and says to James,
"Jolly good throwing James."
"Horse Shoe's Captain of the Boy Scouts."
Burke smiles and says, "A dead ringer you are at that. Let's go." James picks up the soldier onto his back again and asks him as everyone exits the storage room. "Since we've met, I don't know your name."
"Jim is my name," replies Jim.
"Jim? I had no idea that…well…it's a pleasure to meet you, Jim. I'm James."
"Likewise James."
Our friends continue their trek to the landing port.

  Back home on Earth, Debbie driving down the road and looking at a piece of paper, decides to pull over and look around her present location. After observing the area, she looks forward and pulls back onto the road in the direction of the Taylor's Ranch.

  Davis driving through the City Streets at about thirty miles an hour looks at a white mini van exactly like James' driven by an elderly couple. As he drives past them, his eyes suddenly widen as he says, "Shit!" He whips his car around, tires screeching, then burns the tires off into the direction of the Mini Van. He speeds passed the Mini Van at about fifty five M.P.H. scaring the hell out of the elderly couple, as they veer off the road…horn
honking, and crash into a newspaper stand. One of the papers lands on the windshield, and it reads: Unidentified virus still growing!

Back above Silus in space, Zemious' ship remains

Unscathed, alone and the last of the Tre'toan ships posing a serious threat. On Zemious' Bridge, the Captain and crew now display a look of concern and worry as the Captain turns to Zemious, "My Lord, shouldn't we at least," Zemious interrupts fiercely, "No Captain! Again you question my authority! We will remain here…until I say otherwise!"
The Captain tips his head a little while looking at Zemious and says, "Once again My Lord…forgive me." The Captain turns to his console, and the entire crew watching the conversation, return to their duties as well.

Looking at a large entrance with a catwalk that leads upwards to the Silustrian Capital's landing port…our friend's walk through the entrance, and up the catwalk. Upon reaching the top of the catwalk, the sound of at least a thousand or more voices are heard cheering and celebrating the victory of the evil Tre'toan's failed attempt of annihilation. Our friends look in the direction of the landing area, and see a half dozen UFOs landing…and one already grounded, it being Burke's ship. His crew exits, waving with smiles. Deek and Burke wave to them. Burke then says to James, him still with Jim on his back,
"Whelp…I guess there's one more flight after all." James looking relieved and smiling replies, "And I'm looking forward to it, more than you know." Mirla walks over to the edge of the platform and begins waving her hands to the cheering crowd below. Suddenly four Silustrian men with a strange looking gurney that hovers, approach

James and Jim, stopping next to them with
smiles, and one of them says, "Take him we will,
help him now." James immediately helps Jim onto the
gurney, and Jim lying down says to James, "A true friend,
and brave you are." Jim smiles as James replies, "Thank
you Jim, and you take care, ok?"
James smiles as Jim adds, "Take care I
will, goodbye." James says, "Goodbye," as they take Jim
away. Burke, James and Deek join Mirla at the edge of the
landing platform, she still waving.
They stand next to her and look down to see
dozens of orbs flying all around, over the thousand
or more soldiers and citizens of Silus, cheering
and applauding in their celebration. Burke and
Deek wave to them, and James quickly holds his
hands up high, displaying peace signs.
The crowd cheering briefly increases. Burke and
Deek finishing waving, and Burke turns to James, and
James puts his hands down and looks
at Burke, while Burke then says, "Well…you'd better be
going now." James wears a curious look, as Burke hands
Deek the briefcase containing the serum.
"What are you saying Professor?"
Deek nods to Burke, and Burke nods back, as
Deek walks away. Burke continues,
"Don't worry James, Deek knows what to do…
and I assure you he'll take good care of you as
well." Mirla turns towards Burke and James…
thinking of what to say, or do upon James'
departure. "Why aren't you coming with us,"
asks James with a look of concern.
"My services are needed here…to be of
assistance in any further threat the Tre'toans may
have up their sleeves."

James smiles briefly then says, "I understand."
Burke wears a look of curiosity and asks,
"Tell me James…just what is your occupation
back home?"
James' eyes widen briefly as he sighs heavily and
tilts his head a little while replying,
"A News paper reporter…would you believe
that?" Burke still with a curious look asks,
"You don't say?"
James smiles and replies, "Don't worry
Professor, your secret's safe with me."
Burke grins and says, "I'd be more worried about
everyone's reactions back home, upon hearing such a
farfetched, and unbelievable story."
James chuckles and says, "Good point Professor."
Burke grins and says, "Yes."
Mirla wearing a smile walks up to James and briefly bows
to him and says, "I and the people of Silus, owe you our
complete gratitude. And we shall all miss you James
Lowery." She leans in, closes her eyes and kisses James on
the cheek. James remains smiling for the moment, as she
finishes kissing his cheek with
thankfulness.
"Thank you your majesty," says James as Burke
pulls out a Silustrian currency coin and hands it to
James. He takes it and Burke says, "Wouldn't
want you to go home empty handed now." James
nods and smiles, then extends his hand to Burke,
and they shake. "Thanks Professor."
"No…Thank you."

  Back home at the Taylor Ranch, James' Mini
Van is still parked where he left it, as Debbie
spots it and pulls up quickly, locks up the brakes,

and exit's her SUV quickly, running up to James' van. She reaches it, looks in and sees the digital scanner, then looks around the area in front of the van and sees James' camera, and his notepad and pencil on the ground. She picks them up and looks at them for a moment…then with tears running down her face, she looks up to the stars that slowly become visible as the sun begins to set.

Davis speeds down the highway, and finally reaches the dirt portion of road, as a dust cloud blocks the rear view of his car, disappearing from sight.

Back at the landing platform on Silus, Burke and Mirla wave goodbye, as Burke's ship begins to take off. On the bridge of the ship, James stands at the window and waves for a moment, then turns to Deek and says, "Alright Deek, take me home, safely." James sits down in the center of the bridge, and straps himself in, as the rest of the five-crew members assume their positions at their control stations. Just above the atmosphere of Silus, the ship approaches quickly, and zips by and away.

Aboard Zemious' bridge, the Captain turns quickly to Zemious and says with urgency, "My Lord, our scanners have picked up a Silustrian vessel approaching !"
"Lay in that course Captain, and pursue them Now," demandingly says Zemious. Zemious' ship suddenly zips away after Deek's.

Back aboard the bridge of the UFO, the deep pulsating alarms begin, as James looks at Deek and shouts, "What is it Deek?"
"Tre'toan ship fastly pursuing… a Command ship it is." James' eyes grow with fear, as one of the crew quickly runs to the gunnery station, now unfolding out of the ceiling. The crewman gets in it quickly and straps himself in…his hologram appearing, displaying Zemious' ship closing in.
The blue containment beams suddenly kick in, as James says, "Round two, here we go."

In space, Deek's ship zips by, as Zemious' ship fly's closely behind firing his huge laser cannons. Back aboard the UFO, the crewman at the gunnery aims ever so carefully and fires a direct hit to Zemious' ship, but does no damage.
Wearing a worried look he says, "Uh oh."
In space almost at light speed, the chase persists.

Back on Earth on the now dark desert road, Davis still driving fastly suddenly sees a coyote in his headlights so he turns the wheel to avoid it and spins out into a ditch. "Oh hell! Not now!"
Davis frustrated floors the gas, but only digs himself in deeper. "Come on," he shouts as he tries reverse, and digs himself in so deep, that he bottoms out. He slams his hands on the steering wheel, and shouts, "Damn Coyote!"
He then uses his shoulder radio. "Nelson!"
After a brief moment, Nelson responds, "Yes Sir?"

At the Taylor's Ranch, Debbie sits in her SUV

looking at the stars through her rolled back
sunroof. "I know your somewhere out there James. And
I'm right here...waiting for you." She begins to
breakdown.

  Back in deep space, the chase still in full swing,
with constant laser fire exchange.
Aboard the UFO, Deek touching several
lighted controls says to James,
"Hold tight Mr. Lowery, shortcut we will take!"
"Shortcut? What do you mean shortcut Deek,"
says James loudly, as he watches Deek nod
towards the bridge window. James quickly turns
his head toward the bridge window, and his eyes
widen with fear, as his jaw drops while looking at
a black hole getting closer. James slowly points at
it, then says, "D,d,d Deek? Is that a black hole?"
"No worry Mr. Lowery! Safe we will be!"
"Won't we be ripped apart,"
asks James as he begins to grip his chair ever so
tightly. Outside the UFO, a fluorescent blue
shielding system suddenly surrounds the entire
ship. Behind them, Zemious still pursues with massive laser
firing.

  On the bridge of Zemious' ship, the crew still at
their posts, and Zemious still sitting in his chair
shouts, "Get us closer Captain!" The Captain replies, "My
Lord, they're attempting to enter the vortex just ahead of
our location!"
"They will not escape me!" The Captain looks at Zemious
with question and says, "My Lord...we can't," Zemious
quickly stands and his eyes glow with fire fiercely as he
says aloud, "You will Captain!"

After a brief moment, the Captain just turns
around to his console, then exchanges glances with
a couple of other crewmen...doubt in their eyes.

   Looking at the entrance to the black hole, the UFO dives
in quickly, and the front of the ship
begins to stretch. On the bridge, everyone, and everything
begins to slow down and stretch from the black hole's
effects. James tries to speak as his eyes, nose, and mouth
stretch forward about five inches. He slowly crosses his
huge eyes to look at his nose.

   Zemious' ship begins to enter the black hole, it
too stretching forward. On Zemious' bridge,
Zemious and crew also suffer the same effect, but
his ship begins to shake with tremendous
vibration. An alarm begins sounding. The crew
slowly falls to the floor, as the effects from the
black holes gravity are too unbearable.
Zemious screams "Noooooo!" As fire exits from
his eyes.

   Inside the black hole, Zemious' ship begins to
disintegrate and explode from the stern to aft.
After just a moment, he, his crew and the ship are
but granules of small debris.

   Looking downward at the UFO in the black hole, it holds
together well, as it is stretched to the shape of a cigar. On
the bridge, James still stretched rolls his big
eyes slowly to look at one of the crew, and the
crewman he looks at, his head and limbs
resemble that of a praying mantis with over sized eyes.

Somewhere in deep space closer to our galaxy, a disruption followed by a spiraling of space matter suddenly appears. Next, the UFO begins to exit.
On board, everyone still stretched, and seen through the bridge window the end of the black hole appears. The second they exit the end of it, everyone snaps back to normal...the reaction is as if being punched.
James starts feeling his whole body and smiles while saying, "I'm alive! I'm alive!"
He turns to Deek who doesn't look surprised at all and asks, "How? How did we just manage that?"
Deek simply replies, "What is you call physics."
"That ship, where is it," asks James with concern. "Destroyed it is." James wears a look of relief and turns around towards the bridge window revealing light speed travel. He points towards the bridge window and says, "Onward mattes!"

   Back home on the dark desert road leading to the Taylor's Ranch, Davis leans back on his car with arms crossed waiting for Nelson and Barnes to arrive. Suddenly in the distance, headlights appear coming up fastly towards Davis. After a moment, the vehicle being the black SUV, pulls up behind Davis's car and stops. Nelson and Barnes exit and start walking towards Davis. Davis shoves off the car, faces them while placing his hands on his hips then says, "Well it's about damn time!"

   At the Taylor Ranch, Debbie now asleep in her SUV, and in her hands, she holds the picture of her and James.

   Just above Earth's atmosphere in space, Deek's

ship suddenly appears out of light speed, and flies towards Earth. On the bridge, the crew still at the controls, as Deek's blue containment beam shuts off and he walks away from his station towards the entrance ramp that leads to the lower portion of the ship. James looking at Earth through the bridge
windows says, "We made it! I'm home!"
He then takes out the coin that Burke gave him and stares at it while saying, "I won't forget you Professor." Deek returns from the lower section, and walks to his control console. James puts the coin away, and turns to Deek, "So how does this serum,
evaporation thing work anyhow?"
"Hurry we must!" Deek ignoring his question as his blue containment beam comes on and they suddenly fly in faster towards Earth. Looking out the bridge
window, Earth's hot ozone layer appears and disappears quickly, as James begins to grip his chair again.

   Outside the ship, a clear misty steam begins to exit the rear portion of the ship's very edge. The ship suddenly begins to pick up more and more speed, as it levels off at approximately three miles above Earth.

   Inside the cockpit of an Airliner, a pilot and copilot at the controls, when suddenly Deek's ship zips right by them. They look at each other. "Did you see something," asks the pilot.
"No. Must have been one of them experimental planes." They both nod their heads.

   Back aboard the UFO, James with a frightened

look briefly shouts, "WOO." as the ship travels thousands of miles per hour, dodging planes and mountains the whole time.

  On the ground at Max's gas and convenient store, Tommy closing the store, finishes locking the door, then turns and pulls out a pocket-radio and places the earphones on, then turns on the radio. He rocks out as he walks away from the station. Suddenly Deek's ship streaks across the sky. Tommy sees it and stops rocking out, as his eyes fix themselves on the sky, and his jaw slowly drops. Suddenly he sees it again, and pulls the earphones off and stares at them!

  On the dirt road to the Taylor's Ranch, Davis's car now out of the ditch, and Nelson and Barnes still there, as all three of them also watch the sky as Deek's ship makes a pass every other second. "What do ya suppose it is Chief," asks Nelson. Davis replies, "Maybe them damn Tre'token creatures."

  Aboard the UFO, James now laying low in his seat grips it as hard as he can while squinting, as the view through the bridge window is totally obscure of any structure what so ever.

  Six miles high above Earth looking down, the blue streak from Deek's ship is seen, and getting faster by the second, until it encircles the entire globe in a matter of just eight seconds, then beginning to slow down for four seconds until it's no longer visible.

On board, James still squinting and gripping his chair, opens one eye while saying, "Is it over yet?" Deek replies, "Over it is." James eases back up in his seat and opens his eyes, then release his chair and his hands remain in a grip. "Earth, is it safe now Deek?" Deek replies, "Hope so we do." Deek smiles.

  On the dirt road, Davis and his rookies watch in the near distance, as Deek's ship heads for the Taylor Ranch location. Davis shouts, "Come on," as he gets in his car, starts it up, and peels out shooting rocks and dust all over Nelson and Barnes, as they try to get in the black SUV.

  At the Taylor Ranch, Debbie still lays asleep in the driver's seat, when suddenly her SUV begins to shake, then rock back and forth. She wakes up frightened, while all of the lights start flashing, horn honking, and engine starting and stopping. She starts to scream as the wind also gets heavy. Suddenly it all stops, and out of nowhere about fifty yards in front of her, the UFO starts to land. All the animals begin to act spooked once again. Debbie's eyes widen, and her mouth opens as she stays in her SUV for the moment, just watching in amazement at the incredible sight of the UFO landing. After a moment, the UFO lands, and bright lights suddenly shine on the ground from it. Next, the access ramp begins to open until fully extended to the ground. The animals now begin to settle down. Debbie still with a frightened look remains ever so still. Suddenly she sees a pair of feet walking down the ramp, then legs, and finally the whole figure of a man. Debbie decides

to slowly get out of her vehicle, not removing her eyes for
even a second, as she completes her daring exit, and stands
next to her vehicle, now with a look of
hope, as the man's dark figure clears the light
pollution. Debbie takes a step forward, then stops.
She sees James' face smiling, and she runs towards
him...finally reaching him and almost tackles him
as they embrace.
"Oh James, I thought I'd never see you again."
Debbie with tears of joy as James hugs her tightly
and says, "You know me sweetness...I can't stand
to be without you for a second." They quickly
lock lips for a moment...and while kissing, Debbie
opens her eyes and sees the crew carrying off the
Taylors on their shoulders. She unlocks lips
quickly while still staring at them. James turns
around while still holding her, and she curiously
asks, "What are they doing James?"
James grins and replies, "They...would be the
Silustrians. And what they're doing...is a long
story." Debbie looks at James, then back to the UFO and
sees Deek walking down the ramp, as the rest of
the crew returns to the ramp, walking back
into the UFO. Deek stops at the end of the ramp
and awaits James' farewell. James looks at
Debbie and says, "I've gotta go say goodbye to
my friend." Debbie just nods, as James turns her
loose and walks over to Deek. James starts the
farewell. "Well...I guess this is it Deek."
Deek nods once, as James continues,
"It was quite a ride, I can tell ya that."
"I thank you, James." Deek smiles and James
says, "And we thank you Deek, for believing in
the importance of peace and life...and answering

the call in a time when desperately needed."
Deek nods once again, then extends his hand.
James extends his hand and they shake hands.
"Take care Deek."
"Take care I will."
They finish shaking and James takes a couple of
steps back slowly, then turns and walks back to
Debbie. Halfway to her, he stops and turns around
to see Deek halfway up the ramp, facing him…as
Deek holds up a peace sign and smiles. James
smiles and holds up a peace sign, then Deek turns
and walks up into the UFO, and the access ramp
begins to close. James returns to Debbie's side
and they hold each other, watching the UFO
take off…as the wind once again blows
everywhere. The UFO about a hundred or so
feet off the ground begins to move away quickly,
and the wind stops. Debbie and James kiss heavily
once more. In the barn on the ground, the Taylors begin to
regain consciousness.

On the road almost to the Taylor's, Davis driving
sees the UFO flying away. He floors the gas
even more.

James and Debbie finally stop kissing, then turn
and start to walk back to their vehicles.
Davis suddenly arrives speeding up and stops,
gets out of his car quickly, and runs up to James
and Debbie. "We thought you was a goner. What did they
do to ya? Or take ya for that matter?"
James replies, "Chief, right now at this
moment…I've only got one thing on my mind."
James looks at Debbie and smiles. Davis takes a

deep breath and says, "All right you two…I suppose you've been through enough already. Get on outta here." James and Debbie still smiling at each other, and James says, "There's some folks in the barn that might need some attention Chief." Davis runs in the direction of the barn as James and Debbie walk to their vehicles. They walk over to Debbie's and stop. Debbie suddenly turns to James with a look of concern.

"There's an alien Virus James!" James calmly replies, "Was a Virus. Hey, how'd you know about it?" Debbie sighs and replies,

"It's a long story." James briefly displays curiosity, then grins and says, "I'll drive."

"What about your Van?"

"It can wait." Debbie smiles and hands James the keys, then runs around to the passenger side, and they both get in. James starts it up, turns around, and pulls away. Nelson and Barnes finally arrive and speed past James and Debbie. James' voice asks,

"Honey…have we any fresh milk at home?"

"Why would you be thinking of milk at a time like this?"

"Oh nothing…just curious."

  In space just above Earth, the UFO approaches. On the UFO in the same quarters that James first met Deek, lays James' boss, Olsen , restrained and only in boxers. Deek enters and uses the cylindrical device to wake him up.

In space looking at Deek's ship, Olsen's voice is briefly heard screaming with fright, then Lila the cow Moos, as the UFO zips out of sight.

To Be Continued…

ALIENS
BELIEVE TOO! 2
THE DARK SWARM

Written by

Brian Hiller

Introduction:

To begin, think of the following with an open mind. Imagine such a scenario as to the possibility of peaceful extraterrestrials helping us humans here on earth, and possibly other life forms in the Universe thwarting off threatening forces such as extraterrestrials of an evil caliber? To "know" of such an existing scenario would redefine everything we understand of extraterrestrials completely!

In this book I have created such a scenario that I feel gives a good example of what we here on earth might expect in the event.

Brian Hiller

ALIENS

BELIEVE TOO! 2

THE DARK SWARM

Table of Contents

Chapter One: First Contact *8-13*

Chapter Two: The Savior *14-23*

Chapter Three: Knowing *24-30*

Chapter Four: Home Away *31-39*

Chapter Five: Forward *40-48*

Chapter Six: Eve of Departure *49-57*

Chapter Seven: Dawn of War *58-67*

Chapter Eight: Biding Time *68-74*

Chapter Nine: Into the Unknown *75-83*

Chapter Ten: Out of the Darkness *84-102*

Chapter One
First Contact

The time is around three thirty p.m. in an upscale suburb of a quiet town in Arizona, as James Lowery, Chief Editor of The Daily Chronicle drives down the street in a new sports car, playing loud rock music and revving the engine. He waves at mothers walking their children home from school.

Two of the mothers converse in undertone while staring at James' display of ego foolishness.
He pulls into his driveway of a two story Victorian style home. He revs the engine one final time and shuts it off. He steps out and shuts the door ever so gently, then clicks the alarm and locks on his keychain. He leans in over the roof of his car and exhales deeply, then rubs the roof with the sleeve of his suede sports jacket, polishing it.

He then turns toward the street to notice the two mothers staring at him with a strong look of disbelief. James waves and the mothers quickly turn and walk away while giggling. "Have a great day," shouts James as the mothers totally ignore him and now walk away even quicker.

Suddenly a young boy's voice, James' son Pete Lowery, age six, is heard shouting, "Hey dad!" James turns to see Pete riding his bike up into the driveway. James jogs over towards Pete and greets him arms open, while Pete displaying a huge smile rides his bike into James' arms, stopping safely of course.

James smiles and delivers a little noogie to the top of Pete's head.
"How we do on the test today Buckaroo," asks James. No sooner said than done, Pete reaches into his backpack and pulls out a math test, then proudly hands it to James. James briefly looks at the test paper and quickly pretends to be shocked.
"Wow! Once again you've done it. A plus! Great job Pete!"
"Thanks dad! So this means I get to go over to Sam's?"
"Well, yes!"
"Yeah!"
With no delay, Pete turns his bike around then pedals as fast as he can down the driveway and into the street.
"Pete! Be back home in time for dinner!"
"Ok dad," shouts Pete as he speeds down the street and out of site. James turns and walks toward the front of the house.

   He arrives at the front door and it suddenly swings open. There, his wife Debbie stands with her arms crossed and looking angry. She points her finger at James, "I told you not to let Pete go over to Sam's today! Remember? We need to take him for his new shoes!"
"Oh honey, don't worry. We'll take him tomorrow, ok?"

"No! Not ok! That's what you said yesterday, and the day before that!
"Ok, I'm sorry."
"And don't you honey me either! And he'd better be back in time for dinner, or no you know what!"
"Yes dear."
After the scolding, James slowly leans in and kisses Debbie on the cheek.

   On a quiet and vacant backstreet, Pete rides his bike past an ice cream truck that is parked at a curb. Inside the ice cream truck, a mysterious looking man dressed up in a clown's outfit wearing shades, holds in his hands a strange looking scanning device. The scanning device appearing to be tracking Pete's movement. It suddenly lights up with a flashing red indicator and the clown looks at Pete then immediately starts the engine.

   Pete turns down another street and the mysterious man follows him intently. Suddenly out of nowhere, an old black sedan also turns the corner, burning rubber. Pete looks behind him to notice the creepy clown gaining on him. Pete pedals as fast as he can, cutting through a city park. The old black sedan speeds up and suddenly hits the ice cream truck with a pit maneuver causing it to roll over and stop on its side.

The sedan locks up the breaks and does a one eighty, then stops thirty yards from the ice cream truck which now rests near the park entrance. Pete also stops and turns to look at the ice cream truck and black sedan.

The creepy clown crawls out of the ice cream truck, growling and reaching into his pocket. The sedan door opens and a strange looking man of average build and height, wearing a trench coat, wide brimmed hat and a ski mask exits and walks to the rear of the car.

The clown now standing, holds a small laser pistol in his hands while the man just stands still, as if a show down of the best. Pete still frightened but ever so curious, watches them face each other off. The creepy clown suddenly points and shoots a red laser beam at the man, and the man swiftly shrugs left avoiding the beam, as it takes out the sedan's rear window.
"Oh," says the man as he reaches down the front of his pants and pulls out a two and a half foot long laser gun, the barrel somewhat resembling a musket.

He aims and shoots at the creepy clown, and a red round beam of light quickly encircles the clown, the clown instantly shaking and screaming, as he is burnt to a pile of smoldering ash in seconds. Pete now more frightened quickly begins to pedal away.

The strange man looks at Pete, "Oh brother." The strange man gets back in his car and pursues Pete.

Chapter Two
The Savior

Many light years away in space, an enormous fleet of strange looking starships that resemble the shape of shurikens, the "Mulchre", orbit a large mysterious planet, Nebtus. A small sun exists in the distance.

Aboard one of the ships three mysterious looking Mulchre aliens with blood red eyes and heads a little larger than humans, wearing dark shimmering cloaks walk down a corridor. They converse, the one in the middle their leader Lord Krralmoom speaks,
"All resources are diminished. Move on now we shall."
"Yes my lord," says Krralmoom's advisor to his immediate right. With a bit deeper and authoritive tone, the Mulchre commander, Commander Dakknol, to the left of Krralmoom speaks,
"I will begin the necessary arrangements before departure my lord…and seek the truth of this new world, Earth."
"Very well Commander," says Krralmoom.

Dakknol stops walking, then Krralmoom and his advisor as well, facing each other.
"If you'll excuse me now my lord," says Dakknol. He bows then exits right towards what appears to be the ships commons quarters.

Inside the quarters many other Mulchre sit at tables drinking, eating and conversing.

Dakknol walks up to a table and sits. Across from him, sits new leader Lord Orrius of the Tre'toan. "You will tell me now of this Earth," demands Dakknol. Orrius grins and replies, "Have you met my demands Commander? Time grows short."
"No more games!"
"Relax Commander. You will receive the information you so desperately seek, as soon as I am on my way far from the sight of you." Orrius grins again.

Back on Earth inside James and Debbie's house, Four hours have passed as James sits on his plush couch in his living room, holding the television remote flipping through channels. Debbie paces behind him with great worry as of Pete's where abouts. "Six thirty James and no sign of Pete. Had a feeling this might happen." James shuts off the television while standing up, then walks around the couch and gently holds Debbie's shoulders.
"Ok, it is late. Don't worry baby. I'll go and get him. I'm sure he's alright." Suddenly the door bell rings. "That's probably Pete now," says James as he smiles and walks to the front door.

James enters the foyer and unlocks the front door. He immediately opens it, hoping Pete will be there, but to his surprise, instead the strange man from the shoot out with the creepy clown stands before him. The man's wide brimmed hat slightly tilted down.

"Pardon me, can I help you," asks James.
The strange man holds his right hand open, displaying a bright platinum looking coin and replies, "Would you possibly have change for this sir?" James now appearing very puzzled slowly takes the coin from his hand and observes it closely. James' eyes suddenly widen as the strange man lifts his head while smiling, revealing his true identity...professor Landin Burke, his friend whom he met six years ago in a battle against the Tre'toan. "Professor? What are you doing here?" Burke removes his hat and replies, "It's good to see you again James. Might I come in?" "Sure, sure." They briefly shake hands as James welcomes Burke inside. James hails Debbie, "Honey?" Debbie walks up quickly into the foyer also with sudden puzzlement as to the sight of Burke. "Honey, I'd like you to meet an old acquaintance, friend of mine, professor Landin Burke."

Burke smiles and holds out his hand to greet her. Debbie resists and says, "Wait...you're that guy with the aliens James told me about?" Burke briefly wears a look of guilt while looking at James. Debbie continues, "What is he doing here James? No offense Mr. Burke."
"None taken," says Burke.
"What are you doing here professor," asks James. Burke answers, "May we go have a seat and I'll explain?"

Everyone walks into the living room and sits down on the couch. Burke begins, "What a lovely house you have." James replies, "Thanks. So what brings you here, back to Earth?"
"Well…there's no easy way to put this. Your son is in grave danger." Debbie displaying fear of Burke's words asks, "Pete? Where's my son?"
"Relax ma'am. He is in safe hands for the moment."
"Safe hands? Where?" Burke looks at James then Debbie, "Aboard my ship."
"What," shouts Debbie. James asks,
"Professor, you're telling us that Pete is aboard a UFO as we speak?"
"I can explain everything, but first we must leave here immediately."

Somewhere in space just above Earth, Burke's UFO present. On the bridge aboard the UFO, several short bluish grey Silustrian aliens controlling it. By the bridge window, Silustrian alien Deek sits alongside Pete, looking forward out the window at Earth. "Wow. Amazing! None of my friends will believe me when I tell them."
"Funny it is. Your father thought as much the first time as well."
"You know my dad?" Deek nods and replies,
"Your father, brave he is." Pete looks at Deek with curiosity, then returns to the fascinating sight of Earth through the bridge window.

Suddenly an alarm sounds throughout the ship. Deek quickly stands and jogs over to a radarscope located on the center control console. The scope reveals a small red dot traveling towards Earth at great speed. Pete jogs up and stands next to Deek and asks,
"What is it?"
"Hurry we must!" In space just above Earth, a dark object is seen briefly entering the atmosphere.

Back on Earth in James and Debbie's house, Debbie and Burke all standing now. James and Debbie are now bickering as Burke shouts,
"We must go now!" James and Debbie shut up quickly, as a second later the doorbell suddenly rings.
"You folks expecting company," asks Burke. James and Debbie both look at Burke and reply, "No."
"Where's your back door?" asks Burke.
"This way," Says James as he grabs Debbie's hand and runs toward the back of their house, Burke on their heels.

The front door suddenly blasts open and two Tre'toan agents dressed in black, holding laser guns enter looking all around. At the back of James and Debbie's house, the back door swings open and James, Debbie and Burke head down the alley.
"Hurry! My car's just around the corner," shouts Burke. The agents run out of the backdoor just in time to see them turn the corner. They immediately follow.

Burke's old sedan visible, as Burke runs up and gets in…James and Debbie entering the front as well, Debbie in the middle, James riding shotgun. Burke turns the ignition key, but the engine hesitates to start. "C'mon you piece of junk," shouts Burke. The car still hesitating to start, so Debbie looks at Burke and says, "Maybe you should be nice to it?"

The agents now turn the corner and see them. "Okay. Nice car," says Burke as he tries to start it again, and this time it starts. He puts it in gear and peels away. The agents aim their guns but too late to get off a shot. They quickly run back to whatever source of transportation they possess.

In Burke's car, James and Debbie holding each other tightly as Burke floors the gas pedal. "Hold tight folks! Won't be too long till we're safe," shouts Burke.

In front of James and Debbie's house, a black sports car like never seen before is present. The doors suddenly open upward and the agents hop in. The doors close swiftly and it peels away with a supersonic sound like no other.

Back in Burke's car, he pulls out a small communicator and speaks into it, "Deek! We're on our way! Your e.t.a.?" Deek's voice replies, "Three minutes professor!"

Aboard Burke's UFO, Pete still standing next to Deek asks, "My mom and dad with him Deek?"
"Yes. Not to worry."

Back in Burke's car, he still continues to speed down the road as fast as possible in order to get away from the agents. He looks in the rearview mirror briefly and says, "Blasted!" James asks, "What?"
"They're right behind us." James and Debbie quickly look back. "Faster professor," shouts James. "Hold onto something tight. It's gonna be close," says Burke. Burke quickly turns a corner at fifty or so miles per hour, drifting the whole course, as Debbie screams in fear. Burke successfully makes the turn and floors the pedal to the metal, now travelling down the main street in town. The agents turn the corner super fast and super perfect.

Back in Burke's car he talks to Deek through the communicator again, "Deek?"
"Yes professor?"
"Do you have a fix on our location?"
"Yes professor." Burke looks in the rearview again. "Damn, they're gaining on us."

In the agents car, the driver grins and says, "We have them now."

Hidden around the side of a downtown building, Chief of Police Miles Davis, sits in his car looking through a home and gardening magazine of sorts. He talks to himself while reading it,
"Free plant hammocks to the first fifty responses?" Suddenly he sees Burke's car fly by him.
"Not in my town you don't!" He turns on his car and sirens then floors it into the intersection, and is suddenly hit by the agent's car. His car spins like a top briefly then stops. Not a scratch on the agent's car as they continue their pursuit of Burke and the Lowery's. Davis only remains shook up and holding the steering wheel, looks down at his magazine to notice his free hammocks entry ripped.
"Damn it! My free hammocks!"

Back aboard Burke's UFO a monitor shows his car speeding down the street. "Ready for extraction professor," says Deek.

In Burke's car, Debbie asks, "Extraction? What does he mean by extraction?" A laser beam suddenly hits the rear tail light on Burke's car. Laser beams continually flying by them. Debbie screams and ducks into James' lap. "James, hold the wheel," says Burke, as James does so and holds the steering wheel. Burke pulls out his long laser gun, leans out the window and returns fire, but missing.

Overhead, Burke's UFO finally arrives and positions right over his car. A blue beam suddenly shines down on his car, and Burke, James and Debbie begin to disappear. A laser beam hits the back of Burke's car and blows it up skyward.
The agent driver shouts, "Agrr!"

Inside a separate cavity on Burke's UFO, Burke, James and Debbie present. Burke quickly jogs away towards the bridge. "Hurry! Come along," he shouts. Debbie gasping with fright says, "So that's what extraction means." On the bridge, Burke quickly arrives next to Deek and Pete. "Get us out of here Deek, quick!" An exterior view of Burke's UFO, as it zips away at the speed of light, gone in a fraction of a second.

Back on Earth, the agents car suddenly transforms into a sleek UFO, then zips up and away into space.

Back on the bridge of Burke's UFO, James and Debbie arrive, and Pete instantly shouts,
"Mom! Dad!" He runs into their arms. Burke looks at Deek, "That was too close. Are we being followed Deek?"
"The scanners, pick up no evidence of pursuing craft."
"Good." Burke looks at the Lowry's, smiles then sighs.

Chapter Three
Knowing

Returning to the commons inside the Mulchre ship, where the Mulchre commander Dakknol last visited Tre'toan leader Orrius, he still sits at the table. Commander Dakknol walks up to him and stops. "Enough with the games Orrius! I've news for you. Lord Krralmoom has informed me to give you no further time with the delay of this Earth's coordinates. Provide us with them now!" Orrius remains calm and replies, "Very well Commander, they are aboard my ship. I shall go and send the coordinates to you."
"I shall accompany you."
"Our deal Commander?" Orrius stands up, and Dakknol quickly pulls his gun and points it at Orrius. "No more deals," says Dakknol loudly as he signals Orrius to start walking at gun point.
"You're making a terrible mistake Commander."
"You're the mistake! Move!" They walk out of the room and down the corridor to a large set of doors that open upwards as they arrive before them. They stop walking. "I warn you Commander, your are making a terrible mistake." Dakknol signals with his gun again, "Move!" Orrius walks through the entrance then quickly turns on Dakknol with his eyes glowing red. Dakknol tries to move but is frozen. Orrius grins and Dakknol begins to shake, then passes out and hits the floor. Orrius turns and continues to walk through the entrance of what appears to be the ship's landing bays.

Back aboard Burke's UFO, Debbie and Pete stand looking out the bridge window, while James, Burke and Deek stand by the control console.

"So professor…now you can tell us what this is all about," asks James. Debbie looks at James and Burke, then walks over with Pete to hear as well. Burke turns to Deek, "Deek, could you take young Pete here for a tour of the lower ship?" Burke winks at Deek briefly. "Yes professor." Debbie quickly responds, "You sure that's a good idea?"

"Not to worry ma'am. I assure you he's safe with Deek." Deek escorts Pete away and Debbie says aloud, "Be careful Pete!" "I will mom!"

With Pete and Deek now out of sight, Burke begins with his explanation as to why the Tre'toan seek them out. "Remember six years ago when we had our first run in with them?"

"Yes," replies James.

"Well…turns out they didn't get what they came for then."

"What were they actually looking for then professor," asks James.

"Your son." James and Debbie both reply, "Our son?"

"Yes. You see, your son is believed to be what many know as the Zensmittorith. The one being in the known Universe that is capable of unlocking many things that most of us can't begin to understand."

26

"How do you know this professor," asks James. "Well, don't be disappointed with what I'm about to tell you." Burke takes a long breath then continues, "I took on the liberty of what you would say, keeping a close eye on things if you will." Debbie crosses her arms and asks, "And just what was your close eye fixed on?" Burke takes another long breath, and exhales while looking at James, then Debbie. He continues, "All of you." "What," shouts Debbie. "Forgive me, but as you can see, it was the right thing to do." Debbie looks at Burke and then James with anger and says, "Did you know about this James?"
"No honey! Not at all!"

   Meanwhile in the lower quarters of the ship, Deek shows Pete around. Pete looks up at the ceiling to see a cluster of unique mechanical equipment hanging down…needles, drills, claws and other strange devices. "What's all that neat stuff Deek?" "Necessary equipment for study."
"Study? Study of what?"
"Professor's research."
"Oh." Pete walks over to the equipment's control panel. The panel fitted with a number pad and buttons. "What's this for Deek?" "Control of devices. Touch do not." Pete being ever so curious, avoids Deek's warning and presses a button, and the equipment begins to lunge downward from the ceiling.

"No," Deek shouts as Pete and him dive to the floor to avoid being harmed by the out of control equipment. An alarm begins to sound throughout the ship, as the equipment probes for Pete and Deek.

On the bridge, Burke looks at a monitor showing Pete and Deek cornered by the equipment. James and Debbie appearing panicked as Burke begins to run away towards the lower quarters. "Not to worry! I'll be back," shouts Burke.

Back in the lower quarters, Deek and Pete still cornered. Pete bravely stands up and presses several number buttons on the control panel, ten or so to be exact, and the equipment miraculously shuts down. The alarm stops as well. Deek stands up while looking at Pete with great curiosity. Burke arrives to see the equipment has stopped, and Pete and Deek unharmed. "Deek, how did you do it," asks Burke. Deek shakes his head and looks at Pete.
"It is true," says Burke.

James and Debbie quickly arrive and hug Pete.
"Are you okay," Debbie asks Pete.
"Yes mom." Pete looks at Burke, "Sorry professor. It won't happen again." Debbie looks at Burke, "Safe huh?" She takes Pete by the hand and leads him away. James looks at Burke,
"What happened here professor?"

"My theory proven, that's what."
"Theory?"
"Yes…knowing for sure."

   Returning to the exterior of Krralmoom's ship, a small Tre'toan fighter ship jets out of a landing bay quickly. Aboard the fighter craft is none other than Lord Orrius at the controls…escaping the clutches of the Mulchre. He flips a switch on a console. "Report," he says aloud. The agent driving the car from the earlier chase with Burke and the Lowry's voice replies, "Forgive me lord Orrius. The humans escaped."
"No! You fools! This changes everything! How did they escape?"
"With help my lord, the Silustrians."
"Curse them blue blooded terrasites! Return to base! I have to figure a new strategy."

   Back aboard the Mulchre leader Krralmoom's ship in his counsel chamber room, Commander Dakknol takes a knee in front of Krralmoom, who is seated on a dark marble like chair some six foot high. The room is dimly lit, and a small beam of light shines on Dakknol. "My lord, forgive me. The Tre'toan leader Orrius has escaped, and with him the coordinates to Earth." "Not to worry Commander. We've recently received enough intelligence to find it ourselves." Dakknol looks at Krralmoom curiously. "How my lord?"

"You forget of the seer's Commander."

"Thus is true my lord."

"You may return to the bridge and await my further orders."

"As you wish my lord." After Dakknol rises, Krralmoom concludes, "When finished with this Earth, Tre'toa shall be next." Dakknol grins, then turns and walks away.

# Chapter Four
Home Away

Returning to the bridge of Burke's UFO, the Lowery's, Burke, Deek and crewman all present. Burke and the Lowery's all sitting near the bridge window, Pete in between James and Debbie.
"I tell you James, it is true," says Burke. James replies, "It's just so hard to fathom professor." Burke stands and looks at James, then sways him with his finger, "Come. I've something to show you that will clear this all up." Burke walks over to the control console next to Deek, and James follows.

   Burke begins working a monitor, it revealing video footage of Pete and Deek's encounter with his personal lab equipment. James arrives at Burke's side and asks him, "So what is it you feel you need to show me?" Burke continues to work the monitor and asks James' "Ever wonder why your son gets straight A's?"
"He's a smart, hey! You've kept too close an eye on us huh?"
"Doing only what was necessary. Ok. Here, take a look for yourself." James looks at the monitor showing Pete and Deek's encounter. "So what am I looking for," asks James. Burke pauses the video then tells James, "Watch closely." Burke plays the video showing Pete pressing the buttons on the equipment control pad. James looking says, "So he pushed a few numbers and fortunately got lucky."

"Not on your life could he be so lucky. Only I know the correct sequence, and believe me, only I am capable of turning it on or off…with the exception of your Pete now."

"Ok, suppose you're right…and Pete's this Zen's whatever? What do you think the Tre'toans want with him?"

"Whatever the reason may be, I can assure you it's of bad intentions." James and Burke then look at Pete.

Light years away in space, a dark reddish planet in the near distance, Tre'toa. Orrius' ship streaks by towards it. On the planet surface, Steam spews upwards from the ground all around on the entire surface. A large reddish stone structure with one large landing bay entrance door opens. Orrius' ship arrives and enters through the large bay opening. Inside the landing bay of the structure, the two agents who gave chase to Burke and the Lowery's earlier, stand on a catwalk as Orrius' ship completes its landing cycle.

With his ship finished landing, a walk ramp extends out of his ship. Orrius exits the ship and walks toward the agents. The agents tighten up as Orrius walks up and stops in front of them. "I will not tolerate incompetence again," shouts Orrius. Both agents immediately reply, "Yes lord Orrius!" Orrius begins to walk away and the agents follow.

"I must now think of a new strategy. One that will prove vital against the Mulchre."

  Back aboard Burke's UFO, all the Lowery's sitting in front of the bridge window, as Burke walks up with a tray of silver cups. He hands everyone a cup and James asks, "What's this professor?" Burke sits next to Pete and replies, "Drink up. It's good." The Lowery's all smell a white milky substance in the cups. Burke chuckles and says, "Relax. It's good old fashioned one hundred percent milk."
"So…are we headed where I think we are professor," asks James.
"That we are, Silus. And the Queen will be delighted to see you again." James suddenly spits out milk and replies, "Thanks for the reminder, friend." Debbie looks at James with the utmost curiosity and says, "Oh? The Queen?" James now looks at Burke who is trying his hardest not to laugh and says, "Long story honey."
"Oh? I'm all ears, honey."

  A planet, Silus, in the near distance that resembles Earth, as Burke's UFO streaks by and descends towards it. Back inside the UFO, Pete stands leaning on the bridge window seeing Silus for the first time says, "Wow! It looks like our planet!" Burke walks up and stands next to him and replies, "Yes, it does. However a lot different in many many ways."
James adds, "You can say that again." Debbie gives James the eagle eye.

Only a quarter mile or so above the surface of Silus, the elegant Capital City in view as Burke's UFO fly's towards an enormous landing platform…it filled with dozens of other UFO's. All sorts of UFO's fly all around the city. Burke's UFO lands and the entrance ramp extends. A moment later, The Lowery's, Burke, Deek and crewman all exit the ship. "Wow! Amazing," Pete says with great excitement. Debbie also in awe to the first sight of it. "Welcome to Silus," says Burke with pride.

Returning to the interior of the Mulchre Lord Krralmoom's ship, in a strange dimly lit chamber sits two odd and old looking Mulchre women, Seer's, wearing dark hooded capes sitting in the middle of the room across from each other in black marble chairs. Their faces barely visible as a strange crystal looking sphere approximately a foot in diameter, rises up out of the floor between them and stops at their eyes height. Krralmoom enters the chamber and stands just a few feet away and then orders them, "Begin." The Seer's place their hands on the sphere and it begins to pulsate with a variety of colors. They begin chanting strange noises and a moment later a hologram appears above the sphere, displaying the planets in our solar system. They look up at the hologram and shockingly their eyes look as if burned out long ago. Krralmoom orders them again, "Further!"

The Seer's begin to chant again and the hologram reveals speeding by all Earth's outer planets until stopping at the sight of Earth. Krralmoom stares at the sight of Earth with great anticipation.

Returning to planet Tre'toa in the chambers once owned by the late Lord Zemious, Orrius' brother, Orrius sits on his throne, contemplating his new strategy. His personal servant enters and briefly bows. "My lord, I have news of the information you have so requested of the Earthlings."
"Do tell."
"The Earthlings, indeed they are on Silus."
"Grrr! Leave me! Now!"
"Yes my lord." The servant bows briefly and exits quickly, while Orrius continues his contemplating.

Back on Silus in the Capital City, Burke and Deek escort the Lowery's through the illustrious city square towards many interesting large domed structures. Many Silustrian aliens and humans as well, walk about the city. Burke looks at Debbie, "So, what are your thoughts about Silus?"
"It's nice, so far." After a moment more of walking, Burke walks ahead and says, "This way folks."
He and Deek lead the way towards a very different unique domed structure, his and Deek's home. Once everyone is inside, Burke closes the door, it resembling that of a house door on Earth.
"Make yourselves comfortable," says Burke.

"This is cool," says Pete, as he looks all around the dwelling at Burke's collections of paintings, statues etc. Everyone sits down in the living room on couches and James says, "Not a lot's changed since my last visit." Pete yawns then lays his head in Debbie's lap and falls asleep. Burke stands behind his bar and pours drinks. "Drink anyone," he asks. "Thanks, but I'll pass," replies James. "I'll take one," says Debbie. "So what now professor," asks James. "We relax and get some well deserved rest, and worry about it tomorrow." James nods, "Ok. Sounds like a good plan to me." Burke hands Debbie her drink, then Deek. She watches Deek down his entire drink in seconds, then burps loudly. Deek smiles and Debbie looks at him strangely.

Back aboard lord Krralmoom's ship, him and commander Dakknol walk down a corridor. "We've plotted the coordinates for Earth my lord, and will be ready for departure soon."
"I look forward to see this Earth for myself. Long has it been since we've encountered a planet with such great resources."
"Yes my lord, long it has been."

Back on Tre'toa in Orrius' base, he and his commander, Commander Trenn, and several other officers walk together down a corridor that leads to the landing bays. "Am I to understand my lord, we are to engage in battle with the Mulchre," asks Trenn.

"Yes…but maybe not alone?"
"Not alone? We have an ally?"
"Not for certain Commander."
"Who is this uncertain ally you speak of?"
"An arch enemy at the moment."
"The Silustrians? You can't be serious?"
Krralmoom stops walking and looks at Trenn with his eyes glowing red, "Yes Commander! It will do you wise not to question my judgment any further!"
"Yes my Lord. As you wish."

From a short distance away of Orrius' base on the surface, enormous Tre'toan freighter ships accompanied by smaller fighter craft, exit the base and ascend upwards into the dark night sky.

Back in Burke's house on Silus, it's morning as we see only James' face, him in a deep sleep. Something causes him to snarl and wave his hand in front of his face. Suddenly out of nowhere, a strange old man's face all wrinkled and bald moves in very close to James'. The old man smiles and stares at James. James suddenly opens his eyes and screams while jumping up and landing on the floor. Debbie and Pete sleeping on a couch across from James also wake up from the noise and stare at the old man. Burke runs into the living room, "It's ok! It's ok! This is my dear friend Januu Yasuun. He's ancient descendant of the Akkinuu."

James stands up and says, "Your friend here needs to learn some manners."
"My apologies James. He's here for a reason of great importance."
"Oh? What would that be,' asks James.
Januu takes a step forward towards James and says, "A great darkness is coming. Darkness that shall consume all that is vital in our Universe."

Chapter Five
Forward

James sits down and listens to Januu continue. "Long ago, a dark race of beings, the Mulchre, lived upon a world of abundant life and resource, but a new tyrannical ruler, Lord Krralmoom became ever so discontent and full of greed. Soon him and his faithful followers destroyed their world, and many more soon after to follow. His dark veil of evil now draws nearer."
"Just how near are you saying," asks James.
"Your world lay in their path of terror."
"Earth?" Januu nods. "How do you know this," asks James. "For I have seen it to be so." James now with a look of puzzlement looks at Burke, "Your friend here professor…how can we be sure what he's saying is true?" Burke looks at Januu and says, "Show him." James looks at Januu as Januu moves in close to James. Debbie and Pete just stare with great curiosity. James resists a little, but then suddenly closes his eyes. Januu closes his eyes and lays his hands on James' head.

James begins to have visions of the Mulchre slaughtering civilizations of many races, and destroying worlds. He then sees our solar system, followed by the Mulchre ships above Earth. Januu removes his hands from James' head and James awakens with fear and panic, gasping for air. He looks at Debbie, Pete and Burke then says, "What just happened?"

"A true vision of what's to come soon," replies Burke. "How do we stop it," asks James.
"The way is not an easy one. The Mulchre strong in numbers, and defenses strong as well," says Januu. Burke sits down next to James and says, "Januu is here to help us in any way he can. In light of a certain new fact, he's told me of a way to possibly stop the Mulchre…but it's a dangerous one."
"A dangerous one? Like what?
" Januu and I will explain it later. But first we have a luncheon engagement with the Queen."
James immediately says, "Uh, go ahead without me. I'm not hungry now." Debbie looks at James and says, "Oh no you don't. You're going James Lowery." Debbie grins at James. "Guess I'm hungry after all."

On the now desolate and burnt planet Nebtus, many Mulchre ships begin to ascend through the smokey remnants of what was once a great planet teaming with life and resources. Their prerogative complete…total planetary annihilation.

Aboard the bridge on Krralmoom's ship, Dakknol stands before many crewmen at their stations, as Krralmoom enters and stands beside him. Both looking at the bridge window. Dakknol turns to Krralmoom and says, "We are ready for departure on your command my lord."
"Proceed Commander."

The crewmen begin to navigate, as the stars begin to move forward looking at the bridge window. Dozens of Mulchre starships follow in formation.

   Returning light years away to the bridge of Orrius' ship, he sits in the command chair clenching his fist, knowing he draws near to Silus. Commander Trenn stands beside him. "When we near Silus Commander, send a friendly transmission on all frequencies."
"I will do so my lord."

   Back on Silus, Burke, Deek and the Lowery's all walk into a large entrance that leads to Queen Mirla's Dinner Hall. James looking a little on edge of course, from the last time being in the company of Queen Mirla. Once inside, we see the beautiful Queen Mirla, half Silustrian, half human,
sitting at the opposite end of a thirty foot long table. She sees James and instantly smiles with great joy. She quickly stands up and runs to his arms. "James," she shouts as he tries to avoid her hugging. Debbie looking furious at the sight of it. "So good to see you again James." "Like wise," replies James. Mirla stops trying to hug James and looks at Debbie, "You must be the lucky Lady?" "As a matter of fact I am." Mirla then looks at Pete, him smiling. "Hello. And who might you be," she asks Pete. "Pete."
"Handsome like your father. Welcome to Silus Pete."

Burke addresses Mirla, "My lady."
"Come, sit," says Mirla as her and everyone sits at the table, James sitting furthest away from Mirla, behind Debbie. "It's good to see you all back safely," says Mirla. "Yes, safe we are my lady, for the meantime," says Burke. Mirla turns sideways and claps her hands, hailing for the feast to be served. "Wonder what kind of food is coming," Debbie whispers to James. "If it's anything like last time, it's ok." A brief moment later, a large food service cart is rolled in by an older human gentleman dressed in servant's attire and wearing an apron. He pushes the cart next to Mirla and stops, then begins to serve her food. James looks more closely at the man and his eyes widen. Low and behold it's his old boss Dan Olsen from the Daily Chronicle. James frozen with shock seeing Olsen. "Here you are my lady," says Olsen as he serves Mirla. Olsen kisses Mirla's hand then looks up to notice James staring at him
 and now looks shocked himself. "Lowery? Is that you?" Burke and Deek both look at each other with guilt from abducting Olsen six years ago.
"Oh my god! It is you! How? You've been declared missing and dead for six years!" Burke clears his throat as everyone watches Olsen walk up to James. "Missing? Dead?" Olsen briefly laughs and continues, "You mean more like kidnapped and forced here against my will?" Olsen looks at Burke and Deek, then back to James who now stands up, "So…still work at the Chronicle?"

"Well, yes."
"Good good good. Still working the field?"
"Not exactly."
" Oh? What are you doing now?"
"I've been…the new Chief Editor ever since your disappearance." Olsen very angered says, "Well I'll be! You've got my job now? Beginning to make sense!"
"Was your job! And no! I had nothing to do with your kidnapping!"
"Really now?"
"Yes, really! And maybe if you weren't such a hard ass, and believed in aliens, none of this would've happened to you in the first place!" Olsen balls up his fists, then James. "Gentlemen," shouts Burke, breaking up the argument before the bell rings. Olsen angrily turns and walks away, and says to Mirla on his way out of the hall, "Excuse me your Highness." He takes off his apron and throws it to the ground, then turns the corner out of sight.

   James looks at Deek then Burke and says, He's still a hard nose."
"I heard that Lowery," Olsen's voice shouts from afar. James says to Burke, "I was gonna ask you why and how about Olsen, but since the reminder, no need." "Mm," mumbles Mirla stuffing her face. Everyone looks at her and giggles.

Returning to the bridge of Krralmoom's ship, he sits in the command chair, as Commander Dakknol enters the bridge via an elevator entrance, and stands next to Krralmoom. "My lord, I've question of this Earth's possible defenses. We know nothing of this new world, and would be un wise to assume not to expect opposition upon our arrival."

"You needn't worry Commander. I assure you, our weaponry and defenses are far superior than that of Earth's."

"How do you know this to be my lord?"

"This Earth…its position in this sector of the Universe reveals it is indeed a young planet yet. And we Mulchre millions of years old."

"Wise you are my lord."

The Mulchre ships continue to press onward at great speed towards their new initiative of darkness, Earth.

Back on Silus in Queen Mirla's Dinner Hall, everyone remain seated, eating and drinking. James asks Burke, "So what's this danger you were talking about earlier professor? Stopping these Mulchre beings?"

"Well, Januu believes there is one possible way that may stop their treachery, even put an end to them for good. But it does however involve a dangerous method, that may possibly reveal the solution we seek."

"What is this method professor," asks James. "It involves your son." Debbie immediately responds, "No James!" She then wraps her arms tightly around Pete. Pete looks at Debbie, "Mom, maybe we should listen to him?" Suddenly Januu enters, everyone watching him walk up to the table. Burke stands to greet him, "Ahh, there you are my friend. Thought you might have forgotten about us." Burke shakes Januu's hand then speaks to him in undertone, "I'm just getting around to it. Bare with me." Januu nods and takes a seat across from James, Debbie and Pete. Burke sits next to Januu. Burke continues his conversation with the Lowery's, "As I was saying, Januu here can possibly reveal what it is we can do to stop the Mulchre. You've witnessed his capabilities."

"I'll say," says James." Burke continues, "If Januu could perform a successful mind transference with Pete, we may find the vital answer we so desperately need…of course with both you and Pete's permission only." Debbie looks at Pete, James, then Burke, "I don't know. It sounds too dangerous to me." James asks Burke and Januu, "What is this transference thing you're talking about?"

"A joining of minds. Two as one, unlocking the prime mortal secrets one may possess hidden away," replies Januu. "And how is this done," asks James. "Telepathy," replies Burke. "Still sounds too dangerous," says Debbie. "Yes, it can be, but not for your Pete. It is I that risk uncertainty," says Januu.

James asks Januu, "What uncertainty?"
"Eminent danger." "A very brave and noble species you are Januu," says Mirla. "I understand the risk your Highness, and if need be, sacrifice all in order to save worlds." Burke looks at Januu, "I would certainly hope something of that nature would never be-fall you my friend." Pete looks at Debbie and says, "Mom, I think we should try. I'll be ok." Debbie and everyone else shocked at Pete's statement. James looks at Burke, then Januu and asks, "If we allow you to do this…you're absolutely one hundred percent sure no harm will come to my son?"
"Yes. Safe your son will be."James then turns to Debbie and Pete with reason in his eyes. Debbie hugs Pete and asks him, "Are you sure Pete?" He nods, then Debbie looks at Januu and nods.
"To my sanctuary we must go," says Januu.

Behind the side entrance where Olsen exited earlier, he stands quietly, eavesdropping the entire time.

Chapter Six
Eve of Departure

Mean while, returning to the bridge of Orrius' ship, light speed is visible through the bridge window for a brief moment then stops. Planet Silus in the distance. Commander Trenn enters and walks up to an officer seated at a console. "Open all communications channels," he commands. A holographic monitor suddenly appears in the center of the bridge.

Back on Silus, Burke, Deek, Januu and the Lowery's walk into an old ancient looking temple, located on the outskirts of the city. Sirens blaring from the city are suddenly heard. Everyone turns and looks towards the city. Burke looks at Deek, "Deek, stay here while I see what's happening. I'll return as soon as possible." Deek nods, then Burke runs away towards the city. The sirens suddenly stop, and Januu looks at everyone, "Come, tis safe now." Everyone enters the temple.

Burke arrives in the city square, as hundreds of fellow Silustrians stand and stare up at a large monitor on the front of a tall building. Orrius' face on the monitor. "Citizens of Silus do not be alarmed. I seek council with your leaders, with good intentions." Burke remarks, "Good intentions, hu! That'll be the day." Orrius' face fades out and Burke walks away quickly towards Mirla's palace.

Returning to our friends Deek, Januu and the Lowery's inside the ancient temple, Januu leads everyone down a corridor to an open entrance located at its end. Everyone enters a large chamber, dimly lit by way of torches on its walls. Several ancient alien statues, tapestries and symbols adorn its walls. Januu walks to the center of the room, then sits on the bare floor legs crossed. "What is this place," James asks Januu. "Sacred temple of Akkinuu," replies Januu.

Januu looks at Pete, "Come, sit," he asks. Pete sits down directly across from Januu, then Deek, Debbie and James sit as well, forming a circle. Januu smiles at Pete and asks, "Are you still not frightened?"
"No. I'm ok."
"Tis good. We shall begin now. Close your eyes and think of your favorite thing."
"Ok." Pete nods then closes his eyes. Januu closes his eyes as well. Januu carefully places his hands on Pete's temples. Debbie and James watch intently. Januu suddenly jerks his head, remotely viewing unlocked revelations and secrets within Pete's mind. In Januu's mind, he sees stars, planets, wormholes, and the Mulchre approaching Earth. His head jerks again, and he then sees an ancient Mayan temple, and briefly a mysterious looking crystal prism. Januu suddenly begins to breath heavy and tremble. He suddenly collapses to the floor, incoherent. Pete opens his eyes, appearing fine.

James and Deek quickly rush to Januu's aid. . James rests Januu in his arms, "Hey! Januu? Are you ok," asks James as Januu slowly opens his eyes but half way. "Hurry you must. Soon too late," says Januu weakly. "Where? What," replies James. "Your son, he knows what must be done." James looks at Pete and Debbie, then back at Januu, who now appears to have slipped away. Januu no longer breathing. James quickly listens for any sign of breathing from Januu, but sadly hears none. He looks at Deek and asks, "Is there anything you can do Deek?" Deek shakes his head no and lowers his head in sadness. A complete silence now fills the chamber upon Januu's passing.

  Back at Mirla's palace in the command center, Burke, Mirla and several Silustrian officers, among them Silustrian alien Jim, present and looking up at a monitor displaying Orrius' face again. "I am Chancellor Burke. With whom do I speak, and state your business?"
"Orrius, leader of the Tre'toan. I seek to render a solution with a common enemy of ours, the Mulchre."
"Oh? And we're to believe you after all the multiple attacks and interference with us and Earth? And most recently with your agents!"
"We both know chancellor, the Mulchre must be stopped. I give you my word."
"Huh! Your word? Tell me Orrius, what is your interest with the Zensmittorith?"

Orrius plays off Burke's question, "I've no idea what you are implying. My only wish is to stop the Mulchre. They head for Earth as we speak!"
"And tell me, do we have your word, that your medaling with us, Earth, and any other worlds will cease?" Orrius hesitates a little then answers, "Yes. No further medaling will occur."
"Just a moment," says Burke as he leans in next to Mirla. "My lady, I realize your hatred for them as well, but under the circumstances, we could use their help. The Mulchre are strong and outnumber us by far." Mirla nods, and Burke returns to Orrius.
"We will make an acception this one time, and on our terms. And no tricks, or there will be hell to pay! Agree?"
"Agreed chancellor."
"We'll contact you soon with the tactical data."
Orrius nods and his face fades out. Burke looks at Mirla, "I sure hope we don't regret this later?"

Returning to lord Krralmoom's chambers upon his ship, he sits at a table eating what appears to be some sort of slimy skin and bones. Commander Dakknol enters and stands before him. "My lord, we shall be entering the Earth system in seven cycles."
"Very well. Inform me when we have arrived within one cycle."
"Yes my lord." Dakknol bows briefly then exits.

Back on Silus in Burke's home, everyone present except Januu, sitting down with a look of morning about their faces. Burke looking upset the most upon his dear friend Januu's passing.
"Shall never forget him. The bravest of all he was."
"Our sincere condolences professor, says James. A brief moment later James adds, "I know it's not the best time to ask…but what was with the alarms from earlier?"
"You wouldn't believe me if I told you."
"We're all ears professor."
"Believe it or not, we've made a new ally. The Tre'toan of all beings wish to help us stop the Mulchre. I believe it's only to save their own necks as well."
"Are you for real professor," James asks with disbelief. "I'm afraid so James." He then looks at Pete while asking James, "So, Pete knows now what we must do?"
"Yes." Burke still looking at Pete, "You may be our only hope son." Burke smiles, and Pete smiles as well. "We must leave now, before it is too late," says Pete. Burke replies, "Yes, we must be going now." Burke stands, then Deek. "Deek, prepare the fleet for departure. I'll notify the Queen and be with you shortly."
"Yes professor." Deek exits the house.

Back in space by Silus, on the bridge of Orrius' ship, Orrius now sits in the command chair, and commander Trenn stands next to him. Trenn looking a little unsure asks Orrius, "My lord, when we encounter the Mulchre…what if their shields are too impenetrable?"

"We'll have to worry about that when the time arises Commander." Trenn still in doubt asks Orrius, "And what if the Silustrians," Orrius angered with Trenn's questions stops him and says aloud, "Enough Commander! You dare question my judgment?"

"No my lord. Forgive me."

"I'll hear no more of this Commander."

"Yes my lord." Suddenly Orrius' communications monitor appears, and a crewmen looks at Orrius, "My lord, chancellor Burke of Silus."

"On screen," Orrius commands, and Burke appears, his presence aboard his UFO. "Lord Orrius?"

"Yes chancellor?"

"We will begin our departure in twenty minutes, Earth time. I'll send you all the necessary tactical data shortly."

"Very well chancellor. I look forward to this venture."

"I'll bet." Burke fades out.

Aboard Burkes UFO, him, Deek, the Lowery's and all crewmen present, as Burke stands at the main control console with Deek. The Lowery's all sitting down. "Deek, ready us for takeoff."

"Yes professor," replies Deek as he begins working the controls.

Meanwhile outside of Burke's UFO, Olsen who is still dressed in servant's attire looks all around then sneaks aboard just before the entrance ramp begins to close.

Back aboard on the bridge, Deek and crewmen still working the controls, while Burke stands in front of the Lowery's. "Ok folks. Hold on tight. This ride could get a little bumpy," says Burke as he walks away over to Deek. "Hail lord Orrius Deek." Deek nods and touches the coms link screen. The holographic monitor appears with Orrius' face present. "Yes chancellor?"
"We are now departing for our rendezvous with you and your fleet. From there, you shall accompany us portside till we've made contact with the Mulchre. Understood?"
"Yes chancellor, understood."
"Very well. Sending the coordinates now. Seems awkward to say this…but, good luck."
"Like wise chancellor." The monitor disappears then Burke and Deek both exchange glances of questionable reason.

Over looking Burke's UFO docked on the landing platform, his and dozens of more UFO's begin to ascend into the starlit night skies of Silus.

56

Queen Mirla and the majority of Capital City residents all look up and cheer for our departing brave galactic keepers of the peace.

   On the bridge of Orrius' ship, he gives the order to Trenn, "Move the fleet forward to the rendezvous coordinates commander."
"Yes my lord." Trenn turns to the flight officer, "Move the fleet to the rendezvous with the Silustrians."

Viewing the Tre'toan fleet, all ships thrusters ignite and they quickly move forward and out of sight.

Chapter Seven
Dawn of War

Returning aboard lord Krralmoom's ship in his chambers, he lays asleep on his bed when a strange door chime suddenly rings. He awakens and sits up, "Yes," he asks aloud. Commander Dakknol's voice replies, "It is I Dakknol my lord!"
"Enter!" The door swiftly opens and Dakknol enters and stands before Krralmoom. "My lord, we will be within one cycle of Earth soon."
"Very welcomed news commander." Krralmoom stands up and leaves his chambers, Dakknol following.

   On the bridge of Krralmoom's ship, he and Dakknol enter and walk towards the bridge window. Through the bridge window, Earth's solar system is seen in the distance. Krralmoom staring at it in awe, as Dakknol points at it, "There…that is the location of Earth according to the seer's."
"Yes, a magnificent sight."
"Indeed it is my lord. Indeed."

   Back near Silus on the bridge aboard Burke's UFO, him and Deek stand at the main controls, while the Lowery's remain seated for the moment. Burke addresses Deek, "Patch me through to Jim." Deek touches the coms link and the holographic monitor appears with alien Jim's face present. "Jim, the moment is upon us when we must part ways. You are in control of the fleet for now. Good luck be with you all."

"Good luck be with you all too professor."
The monitor disappears and Burke looks at the Lowery's, "Ok folks, hang on tight! It's gonna get a little bumpy now." Debbie looks at James with great concern. Burke gives Deek the order, "Full speed ahead Deek!" Deek nods and places his hand on the screen of the main console, then spreads his fingers and the ship begins to travel at light speed immediately, gone out of sight in a fraction of a second.

   Somewhere in deep space, the Tre'toan fleet present in a holding pattern at the rendezvous, as the Silustrian fleet arrives quickly and stops.

   Inside Jim's UFO, he and his full crew present, as he brings up his holographic monitor. Orrius' face appears, "Who are you? Where is Chancellor Burke?"
" Jim I am, commander of the Silustrian fleet. Chancellor Burke tending to a matter of great importance he is. Lead us into battle with the Mulchre I will. Coordinates locked and ready."
"A matter of great importance you say? Hmm…very well. Let us proceed." Jim nods and his holographic monitor disappears.

   The Silustrian fleet suddenly forms a tight formation alongside the Tre'toan, then all ships quickly jump to light speed.

Back aboard Burke's UFO, Deek, Burke, and the crewmen operating the ship, as the Lowery's remain seated. "Are we approaching the Constance Horizon soon Deek," asks Burke. "Yes professor. Two minutes till entry it is." James overhearing Burke and Deek turns to Burke and asks, "Are you gonna do what I think you're gonna do?"
"Yes. It's the only way to get there in a feasible amount of time. And time is something we're running out of." James turns back at Debbie and Pete, "Honey, Pete, trust me on this. Whatever you do, close your eyes and keep them shut till it's over, ok?" Debbie now looking very scared nods and closes her eyes. Pete appearing ok nods and places his hands over his eyes.

Through the bridge window, the appearance of a wormhole begins to become visible…swirls of light and dark matter mixing together as if orchestrated. "Thirty seconds till entry," says Deek, as the ship begins to shake a little from the massive force of the wormhole. James puts his arms around Debbie and Pete, comforting them through the scary experience. "Here we go! Hang on," shouts Burke, as they enter the amazing mysterious wormhole. The ship now shaking ever so more, as Pete's curiosity gets the best of him and he peeks through his fingers.

Below in the lower quarters, Olsen hangs on to a strap located on one of the crates he hides behind.

Above Olsen's head on a shelf, one of Burke's research tools becomes dislodged from the shaking and falls on his head. "Oww," he shouts, rubbing his head, then looking around the crates to see if he's been heard.

Back on the bridge, Burke looks at Deek, "Did you hear that?" Deek shakes his head no. Suddenly, everyone and everything on the UFO sort of begins to stretch forward due to the incredible forces of the wormhole's effects.

Deep inside the wormhole looking at the UFO, It amazingly appears stretched, that as of the shape of a cigar.

Back on the bridge, Pete not at all afraid still peeks through his fingers and smiles while he looks at his nose appearing to be six inches long. "Cool," he says.

In a remote area of our galaxy revealing only distant stars, Burke's UFO suddenly appears, jetting out of the opposite end of the wormhole, instantly returning to its original state.

Back on the bridge, everyone and everything also back to normal, as Burke now holds a laser pistol looking at Deek, "I'll be right back." He runs away towards the lower quarters.

James, Debbie and Pete watching Burke and James asks, "What is it professor?" Burke ignores James and continues his trek to the lower quarters.

In the lower quarters, Olsen remains hidden behind the crates, as Burke enters and stops, then looks all around with his laser pistol drawn. "Anyone in here," he shouts. Olsen now aware of Burke's presence, remains completely still and silent.
Burke begins walking slowly to the area of the crates. Olsen begins to feel a cramp in his leg, and tries his hardest not to make a sound, but can't help it and groans as low as possible. Burke hears him and points his pistol toward the crates. "I'm warning you! If I must, I'll vaporize your ass! Now come out!" Olsen slowly walks out from behind the crates with his hands up and stops. "You," says Burke aloud. "Yeah, me!"

James enters and is shocked at the sight of Olsen. "What are you looking at," Olsen shouts at James. Olsen continues, "If it weren't for you, I wouldn't be in this damn mess!" James points his finger at Olsen, "I'll have you know, that if you weren't such an ass, you probably wouldn't be in this damn mess, now would ya?" Burke breaks it up again, "Alright! That's enough! You sound like two hens fighting over a rooster." James and Olsen both look at Burke with raised brows.

Burke addresses Olsen, "You, are going to remain right here for the time being till we sort things out." "Yeah, right here." Olsen smirks at Burke, then Burke and James walk away.

Returning to the Silustrian and Tre'toan fleets, they still travel at light speed on course for a war engagement with the Mulchre. On the bridge aboard Jim's UFO, he signals to his coms officer to notify the Tre'toan of their approach out of light speed.

In our galaxy in the kuiper belt, the Mulchre ships now traveling very slow, launching explosive projectiles, and laser canon fire at the many large asteroids present there…clearing a safe path for travel. The Silustrian and Tre'toan fleets suddenly appear out of light speed just a few meters behind the Mulchre.

Aboard Jim's UFO, he addresses Orrius on his monitor, "Assume attack formation above them we will."
"We shall flank them from below."

On the bridge of Krralmoom's ship, he sits in the command chair while accompanied by Dakknol and his advisor at his side. Warning lights and an alarm suddenly go off throughout the bridge, due to the approaching Silustrian and Tre'toan fleets.

A large spherical holographic monitor appears in the center of the bridge, displaying the Silustrian and Tre'toan ships closing in. The communications officer turns to Krralmoom and Dakknol, "Tre'toan craft and another of unknown origin engaging us!" "Filthy Tre'toan! Hu! They stand no chance! Deploy the dark fighters," orders Dakknol.

Viewing the Mulchre starships, dozens of fighter craft that resemble somewhat miniatures of the Mulchre starships quickly exit and engage the Silustrian and Tre'toan ships. Laser fire exchange begins instantly and heavily. A now massive dog fight on the edge of our galaxy. Several ships from all sides being destroyed, and the Mulchre dark fighters keep exiting and engaging…out numbering the Silustrian and Tre'toan by far.

The Mulchre starships continue blasting their way through the kuiper belt, oblivious of the ongoing war all around them.

In space with Earth in the near distance, Burke's UFO fly's by and towards it.

Aboard on the bridge, Burke, Deek and the crewmen at the controls, as the Lowery's remain seated. Burke looks at James and Debbie, "Might I borrow your son for a spell now?" James and Debbie ok with a nod.

James then looks at Pete, "Go ahead Pete. Gonna stay here with mom." James winks at Pete. Pete gets up and walks over next to Burke and Deek who are both standing at the main control console. Burke and Deek looking at an atlas of Earth on the console screen. "Take a look here Pete," asks Burke. Pete leans over the console to look at the atlas. "Pete, do you know on here where it is we are to go?" Pete nods, then points at the location on the atlas, it being South America. "Interesting. South America it is."

Just above Earth, Burke's UFO streaks by and enters the atmosphere, out of sight in seconds.

Returning to the war on the edge of the kuiper belt with the Mulchre, ships from all sides continue their engagement in battle, while the Mulchre starships continue to press forward through the kuiper belt…firing dozens of explosive projectiles and every laser cannon at the mass of asteroids. Several ships from all sides being destroyed in the process.

On the bridge aboard Krralmoom's ship, he gives the order, 'Increase speed!" Dakknol turns to Krralmoom, "My lord, it is still dangerous to proceed with greater speed than that of which we travel now."
"I will say when it is dangerous Commander!"
"Yes my lord." Krralmoom looks at the helmsmen, "Increase speed!"

The Mulchre starships increase speed now hitting asteroids as they go, but attaining no damage, as some Silustrian, Tre'toan ships and Mulchre fighters are pulverized and destroyed from the asteroid debris created from the Mulchre starships.

Chapter Eight
Biding Time

Somewhere in the deep jungles of South America, two South American men wearing straw hats and leading pack mules walk down a lush green path on the edge of the dense jungle. They suddenly stop, looking and listening all around them. The strange humming sound form Burke's UFO becomes present, as the two men look up and see Burke's UFO passing above them. They and the pack mules quickly run away extremely frightened.

   Aboard on the bridge of Burke's UFO, Burke, Deek and all the Lowery's stand around the control console, as Pete points at the areas of travel on the atlas. "Right there," Pete says with excitement. "Set us down about here Deek," says Burke while pointing at the atlas. Deek nods and works the controls.

   In a small clearing surrounded by the dense jungle, Burke's UFO approaches and begins to land. All the local animals now begin to flee the area, with fright in their voices…monkeys, panthers, birds, even some insects. Once fully landed and the UFO's engines off, complete silence fills the entire area. The entrance ramp now lowers downward.

   Back inside by the entrance, Burke casually gestures the Lowery's to exit, "Shall we?" The lowery's exit while Burke turns to Deek, "Stay here and keep a close eye on Olsen." Deek nods then Burke exits.

Outside the UFO with everyone exited and now several feet away, James looks at Pete, "Son, are you sure this is the right place we're supposed to be?" "Yes dad, I'm sure."

On the edge of the tree and vine riddled clearing, is an ancient looking stone statue, resembling that of the ancient Mayans. Everyone walks up to it and stops with great curiosity in their eyes. "Wow, wonder what this old thing is," says Debbie. Burke moves in closer for a further examination of it. He studies it for a moment, and begins to translate an ancient inscription upon it, "Those who dare pass of this point…prepare for certain…death." James and Debbie now looking worried, and Debbie turns to Burke, "Um…maybe we should heed this warning?" "Ah, native superstition to keep the curious onlookers away is all," says Burke. Pete looks at Debbie, "Mom, we have to go that way," Pete points past the statue at what appears to be a vine overgrown path. "See? Pete says that way," says Burke. Burke pulls out his laser pistol and begins to lead the way down the path, and Debbie asks him, "Oh? What do you need that for then?"
"Just in case a wild beast happens to lunge out at us." Burke looks at Pete, smiles then winks. Pete smiles and winks back.

Back inside the UFO, Deek looks all around for Olsen, seeing him nowhere around where he's supposed to be.

Just outside the UFO, Olsen runs toward the statue next to the path Burke and the Lowery's entered.

Returning to the battle in space within the kuiper belt with the Mulchre, the fighting still in full swing, as the Mulchre starships begin to successfully exit its dense asteroid belt, entering our inner solar system. All Mulchre ships pick up momentum, as well do the Silustrian and Tre'toan, keeping the fight going.

While exiting the kuiper belt as well, Alien Jim's UFO is hit by a repelled remnant of an asteroid, smashing his UFO sideways.

On the bridge of Jim's UFO, an alarm sounds as sparks emit out of the control consoles. Jim and crew doing their absolute best to remain in control of the ship. The alarm and sparks stop as the holographic monitor appears with Orrius' face present, "We can no longer continue! Only three of my ships including my own remain!" The monitor disappears, as Jim and crew now wear a weary look about their faces.

Orrius and what remain of his fleet, turn and flee the battle.

Back on the bridge of Jim's UFO, a crewmen looks at him, "Life support systems, severely damaged they are." Jim looks down at his control console and pounds his fist.

Back on Earth somewhere in the deep jungles of South America, Burke and the Lowery's continue their trek through the dense trees and vines on a path that leads to only where Pete knows of its final destination. "How much further Pete," asks Burke. "Just a little more," replies Pete. The terrain now begins to slope downward, as they continue to press on through the dense jungle, arriving to whatever destination awaits them.

Behind a tree just some twenty or so yards behind Burke and the Lowery's, hides Olsen, tailing them for whatever reason.

Burke's communicator on his belt beeps and he grabs it then answers it, "Yes Deek?"
"Professor, Olsen aboard the ship no longer."
"Blasted! Alright Deek, just remain aboard the ship and wait till you hear from me again."
"Yes professor." Suddenly an old rope and board bridge appears at the end of the path that leads over a tremendously deep canyon, some thousand feet deep. Everyone stops and looks at it. Burke places a hand on one of the top ropes and gives it a little tug. Dust and an old walk plank fall away. "Best we take our time crossing here."
"I'll say", adds Debbie. Burke begins to cross the ancient rickety bridge first.

Back in space near the ice blue planet of Neptune, the Mulchre ships now traveling thousands of miles per hour, as the Silustrians alone continue their fight with the Mulchre dark fighters, in what now has become only a hope of biding time for whatever miraculous task Burke and the Lowery's can pull off. Sadly, only half the Silustrian fleet now remains in their endeavor to stop the Mulchre.

On the bridge aboard Jim's UFO, the faint sound of an alarm sounds as Jim looks at the crew, and they stop what they're doing and look at him. "Short the time is. Die soon we will." His crewmen realizing thus being the truth, now wear a sadness about their faces. Jim continues, "A last fight we have." The crewmen suddenly appear calm and confident, then nod their heads. Jim raises his fist, "For the Queen and Silus!" All crewmen raise their hands as well and respond, "For the Queen and Silus!"

Suddenly we see Jim's UFO speed up through the barrage of Silustrian and Mulchre dark fighter craft, and head towards one of the lead Mulchre starships. Jim's UFO quickly positions directly in front of the Mulchre starship, then suicide dives at super speed towards the ships bridge window, entering successfully and exploding on impact. The effect causing multiple explosions throughout the ship, it too then exploding into a massive fireball of burning debris.

On the bridge aboard Krralmoom's ship, Krralmoom remain seated with his advisor standing to his left, and commander Dakknol leaning over the coms console. Dakknol looks at Krralmoom, "We've lost our secondary command ship!" Krralmoom looks at Dakknol with anger, "Because of your incompetence and knowing of the Tre'toans treachery is the reason!" Complete silence fills the bridge, as all crew personnel look at Krralmoom and Dakknol.

Chapter Nine
Into the Unknown

Back on Earth in the deep dense jungle of South America, where are friends professor Landin Burke and the Lowery family trek towards whatever unknown destination their son Pete leads them to, they all carefully and successfully manage to cross the ancient rickety bridge. They continue their trek through the dense jungle. As soon as Burke and the Lowery's are out of sight, Olsen appears on the opposite side.

  He looks down into the seemingly bottomless ravine, then also just as Burke did, places a hand on the top rope and tugs on it. "Oh hell. Why why why am I doing this," he asks himself as he begins to cross the bridge. He cautiously watches his footing, until the fifth step in a walk plank suddenly breaks and he quickly grabs the top ropes, "Ohhh," he shouts with fear of falling. Safely able to hang on, he watches the pieces of walk plank fall away till out of sight.

  On the path ahead where Burke and the Lowery's travel, Burke signals everyone to stop and be quiet, "Shhh." He listens for a moment and James whispers, "What is it?"
"Oh, I guess it's nothing. Let's continue." Everyone continues walking down the tree and vine infested path.

Olsen now back on his feet and walking ever so carefully across the bridge mutters, "Damn you Lowery."

Much deeper in the jungle on the mysterious path, Burke and the Lowery's now sweating and appearing a little exhausted, come upon what looks to be a clearing some thirty or so yards ahead. "There's a clearing up ahead," says Burke, and everyone picks up the pace. After a few moments of dodging the trees and vines, they reach the clearing, and are amazed to see an ancient Mayan temple, towering some one hundred feet high to the top of the dense jungle canopy, one of which that may have never been seen or discovered before since its inhabitants left it. "Amazing," says Burke. Burke then looks at Pete, "What now Pete?"
Pete points at the temple, "There! Come on," he shouts as he then runs towards the temple. "Pete! Wait," shouts Debbie and James, as she runs after Pete first, then James and Burke.

Pete reaches the temple and begins to climb its vine and fern ridden stone steps. "Pete no," Debbie shouts as she runs up to him just in the nick of time when his foot slips on a vine and he falls backwards, into Debbie's arms. She cradles him, "Peter James Lowery, you almost seriously hurt yourself!" "Sorry mom." She sets him down as James and Burke arrive.

James places his hands on Pete's shoulders, "You alright son?" Pete nods, "Yeah, sorry dad."
"It's ok Pete. Just try and be careful, ok sport?" Pete nods again and Debbie looks at James, "Oh, why do we have to do this? It's crazy!" James places his hands on Debbie's shoulders and looks her in the eyes, "Because we have to. To save lives, Earth." James hugs Debbie and Pete says, "We have to hurry!"

Returning to the battle in space between the now narrowed down to half Silustrian fleet and the Mulchre, all ships resume traveling thousands of miles per hour towards Earth. The Silustrian ships fighting in close and away of the massive Mulchre starships, trying their best to inflict damage and possibly slow them down. But the dark fighters keep coming despite their efforts.

On the bridge of Krralmoom's ship, commander Dakknol turns to Krralmoom, "Their fleet is dwindling! These beings are no match for the Mulchre!"
"Indeed they are not Commander."

The dogfight between the Silustrian and Mulchre continues, as the Mulchre continue to press onward towards earth with predatory persistence.

Back on Earth in the dense South American jungle, Olsen now stands just two steps away from making it across the ancient rickety bridge. He takes two steps and on the last step the plank breaks, him falling through but grabbing both the upper ropes. "Ahh," he shouts as the braiding of the ropes begin to unravel and snap. "Oh no no no no," he says while carefully working his hands on the ropes, inching his way closer to the safety of the ledge.

The ropes suddenly break completely and Olsen throws his arms toward the ledge, luckily able to grab it, as the entire bridge falls out of sight. "Whew. That was close." Olsen climbs up to safety, then continues his trek following Burke and the Lowery's.

Back at the Mayan temple, Burke looks at Pete and asks, "So Pete, we must go up?" Pete nods and Burke adds, "Wish there was a safer way." Burke looks up towards the top of the temple, and everyone else does the same. "Last one to the top gets to live and tell about it," says James, as they all begin their assent on the temple…James and Debbie holding Pete's hands.

On the path near the temple, Olsen lurks behind a tree, watching Burke and the Lowery's climb up the vine and fern infested stone steps of the temple.

He mutters, "Great. This isn't a town. What the hell are they doing? A Mayan temple?"

At the top of the temple, Burke and the Lowery's all arrive safely. They all now look at what appears to be an enclosed entrance, with a large stone door that looks as if never been opened since it was closed by those who constructed it. Ancient hieroglyphics adorn the large stone door. Burke examines them closely and says, "This isn't Mayan. In fact I've never seen anything like it before. Hm?"

James looks at Pete, "What do we do now son?" Pete points at the door and replies, "We gotta go in there.'
"I had a feeling you were gonna say that. How do we open it?" Pete walks up next to the door and sticks his four fingers in four small holes located behind the cover of a fern on the wall, and a triggering mechanism is heard as the door begins to open upwards with a stone grinding rumble, followed by a bellow of dust exiting. Pete stands back into Debbie's arms, and a brief moment later the door finally ends its upward track, with a loud thud.

Suddenly the sounds of bats are heard, as they fly out of the entrance at great speed. Debbie quickly covers her and Pete's heads and screams aloud, "Ahhh! Bats!" With the bats all gone now, Debbie calms down as Burke pulls out his communicator.

He speaks into it. "Deek, we're at some sort of ancient temple. We're Going inside of it now. If you don't hear from me by night fall, lock onto my signal and bring the craft."
"Yes professor," replies Deek as Burke walks up to the entrance and turns to everyone, "I'll lead the way." He turns and begins to enter into the unknown darkness that awaits him, and the Lowery's. The Lowery's follow Burke inside.

Olsen still lurking behind the tree at the mouth of the path, comes out and begins walking towards the temple. "Can't fathom for the life of me I'm doing this."

Returning to the ongoing battle in space between our friends the Silustrians and the ever fearful Mulchre, Saturn now visible in the distance as the battle with the Mulchre gets more and more seemingly hopeless for the Silustrians…dozens and dozens of dark fighters keeping the Silustrian craft at bay. Only five percent of the Mulchre dark fighters have been destroyed, while seventy percent of the Silustrian fleet is now gone.

The Silustrian craft now move in much closer to the city sized Mulchre starships, to hopefully be more effective with their lasers, and provide more cover for themselves as well.

Intense laser fire now exits the Mulchre starships upon the Silustrians near approach to them. The Silustrian craft firing everything they've got at the starships, but doing no severe damage or slowing them down whatsoever.

    Back on Earth inside the mysterious ancient temple, Burke holds up a small but intense light device somewhat the shape and size of a pencil. He leads the way down a cobweb infested corridor, the Lowery's still right behind him. "I've got a bad feeling about this," says Debbie.
"Don't worry mom. It'll be ok," says Pete with complete confidence.

    They finally arrive at the end of the long dark and cobweb infested corridor, that now splits into two more…one left and one right. Burke looks at Pete, "Ok Pete, so far so good. Which way now?" Pete uses his thumb and gestures to the right. Everyone enters the right corridor.

    Little does Burke and the Lowery's know, that Olsen trails just behind them, lurking in the shadows.

    After a few moments of Burke and the Lowery's walking down the right corridor, they reach its end, a dead end at that. More unrecognizable ancient hieroglyphics adorn the end wall, carved into it.

"Well, what now," says Debbie shrugging her shoulders. Burke holds his light closer to the end wall, to get a better look at the hieroglyphics. "Fascinating," says Burke, as Pete walks up to the wall and begins pushing on it. Nothing happens, then Pete looks at everyone, "Come on, help me." Everyone then joins in to help Pete push on the wall, and it moves just two inches and stops, followed by a ratcheting sound within the wall. Everyone backs up a few steps and suddenly the floor opens downwards from behind them, a twenty foot long slide trap floor. Everyone instantly slides and screams on the way down into the unknown except Pete, him enjoying the ride wearing a huge smile.

Chapter Ten
Out of the Darkness

Olsen runs up to the now gaping hole in the floor and looks down. He remains quiet and out of sight for the moment, while seeing Burke tap his light back on.

Down in the mysterious unknown area, everyone appears to be alright as they all stand up. Burke shines his light all around in what appears to be an enormous hallway with more unknown ancient hieroglyphics all about its walls and ceiling. "Wow, wonder what this place was used for," says James. "One thing's for sure, you can bet they didn't have invited guests in mind when they built it," replies Burke. Burke shines his light up at the slide trap floor to see it is still some six and a half foot high, able to grab, but way too steep to climb up.

Olsen still above them and out of their sight, suddenly has the urge to sneeze. He holds it at bay for a brief moment then lets it out, "Achoo!"
Burke and everyone else looks up. "Who goes there? Olsen, is that you," asks Burke. Olsen shows his face in the rays of Burke's light, "Of course it is! Who'd ya expect, Bigfoot? Oh, but maybe he exists too?"
"Why are you shall I say stalking us?"
"Stalking? Huh! My curiosity's got the best of me."
"Curiosity killed the cat."
"Curiosity, cats, whatever! From the look of things, I'd say I'm the one holding all the cards now, eh?"
"What is it you're getting at exactly?"

"You, Mr. steal my job there and his family are gonna want a way out of that pit your stuck in, and I want a new deal, capiche?" James glares at Olsen. Burke continues, "What sort of deal, might you be referring to?"

"Well for starters, my damn life back, here on Earth!"

"What makes you so sure we won't manage a way out of here?"

Olsen chuckles then replies, "Without my help, you're all gonna be here for a long long time."

"Oh? We'll just see about that." Burke takes out his communicator and speaks, "Deek?" A brief moment goes by with no reply from Deek. "Deek, can you hear me?" Still no reply from Deek, Burke looks up at Olsen, "What have you done?"

"Me? I've done nothing. Looks like destiny's calling the shots now. So we have a deal?" Burke stares at Olsen for a moment then answers, Oh…alright. We have a deal."

"Good good."

"But we're not finished with what we came here for yet. So maybe you'll be so kind as to find us something useful to help us out of here, while we finish with our business?"

"Sure. I'll be right back. And don't hang around too long down there. Might become a permanent part of the scenery." Olsen turns and walks away while laughing. "If I knew of another way out, he'd surely be the only permanent part of this place," says Burke.

Burke turns to Pete, "Ok Pete, what now son?" Pete points toward the opposite end of the long dark hall and replies, "Down there." Everyone begins to walk down the long mysterious dark hall.

Returning to space at the sight of the ongoing battle between our Silustrian friends and the ever so fearful Mulchre, the cat and mouse dog fighting persists…still traveling at thousands of miles per hour.

Aboard on the bridge of Krralmoom's ship, the communications officer turns to Dakknol who now stands next to Krralmoom, "Commander, no signs of eminent danger on the coordinates we travel." Krralmoom looks at Dakknol, "See Commander? Nothing to fear. And soon the feeble attempts of these incapable and lacking beings will be of no importance as well." Dakknol confidently replies, "Yes my lord. Soon they shall be no more, and this Earth ours for the taking." Both Krralmoom and Dakknol wear an evil grin.

Back on Earth in the ancient undiscovered temple, Burke and the Lowery's walk down the dark and mysterious hall. They finally come to its end, and to the right is a large entrance opening. Everyone stands looking through the entrance at a very large chamber with more ancient hieroglyphics all about the walls, ceiling, and strangely the floor as well.

Everyone slowly walks into the chamber, Burke shining his light all around. The chamber cold and silent as if the dead were deader. Pete walks quicker than everyone towards the center of the chamber, compelled by some mysterious force to do so. Debbie also walks quickly behind Pete, him now standing still in the very center of the chamber, staring down at the floor. James and Burke now walk up to Debbie and Pete.

  Pete then gets on his knees and stares at some carved hieroglyphic stones, four to be precise. "What do you make of that professor," asks Debbie. "Yes, quite interesting," replies Burke. Burke kneels down to get a closer look, and Pete places his hand onto one of the carved stones that looks like a hand, then pressing down on it, and the four stones begin to agitate as if a jack hammer were hammering upon them.

  Pete stands up and everyone backs away several feet, as the carved stones suddenly rise up out of the floor and stop just inches high, then quickly spread out diagonally and stopping. Next they witness the incredible sight of a mysterious four inch high, clear Mayan temple shaped prism slowly rising up out of the floor, resting upon a stone pedestal. The pedestal rises to a height of approximately three and a half feet then stops. Everyone stares in awe as Pete walks up to it then carefully picks it up and places it in his hands.

Debbie now with a look of concern calls out Pete's name, "Pete!" He turns around and faces everyone with a smile. The prism suddenly begins to glow with a static type of electricity, and flamboyant light emitting from within, causing no harm whatsoever to Pete. "We need to go now," says Pete as the prism now stops glowing. He begins walking towards the entrance and everyone else as well.

Behind them, the pedestal begins to shake. Everyone stops and looks at it, as it then falls to the floor and shatters. Next a stone door above the entrance begins to close downward. Everyone turns to see it. "Hurry! Run," shouts Burke, as everyone quickly begins running towards the entrance. James picks up Pete on the way out. Burke makes it through the entrance first, then Debbie, followed by James and Pete…James having to roll under the door with Pete just in time as the door falls shut with a thunderous pounding. James and Pete stand up and James sighs, "That was way too close."

Returning to space somewhere between Mars and Jupiter's orbit, the ever so brave and willful remaining Silustrian fleet, continue their now seemingly impossible effort to thwart off the Mulchre from reaching Earth. The Mulchre's defenses too impenetrable for the Silustrians weaponry, or possibly any other.

On the bridge aboard Krralmoom's ship, the navigational officer turns to Krralmoom and Dakknol, "We are now within one quarter cycle of Earth."
"Slow to one quarter power upon one eighth cycle from Earth," Dakknol orders. The communications officer now turns to Krralmoom and Dakknol with urgency, "My lord, Commander, the enemy has broken off the attack!"

The now dwindled down and tired Silustrian fleet, realizing they alone cannot defeat or slow the progress of the Mulchre, quickly evade the battle, flying away in all directions.

Back on the bridge of Krralmoom's ship, Dakknol stands next to Krralmoom who still remains seated in the command chair. Dakknol turns to the communications officer, "Where has the enemy gone? Have you tracked their last trajectory?"
"Sorry to inform you Commander, they have evaded us. Their last trajectory unknown." Dakknol then looks at Krralmoom, "My lord, these beings must be in league with not only the Tre'toan, but perhaps the beings of this Earth as well. You are sure we stand to face no eminent danger from these Earth beings?" Krralmoom looks at Dakknol with angered eyes, "Again you question my intellect commander! Do not disgrace me again!"

Dakknol bows and answers, "Yes my lord. Forgive me. My thoughts betray me."
"Now recall the fighters. We must replenish our forces before we reach Earth…in the event if there is any eminent danger that may occur."

Returning to Earth inside the mysterious ancient temple, Burke and the lowery's all arrive back at the trap floor location where they last left Olsen, him leaving to find them a way up from the lower hall. Pete still holds the mysterious prism with firm hands, guarding it. Everyone looks up for any sign of Olsen, but him nowhere in sight. "Olsen," shouts Burke but no reply. He shouts his name again while looking up, and Olsen appears at the edge of the trap floor. "Shout my name any louder and this place is liable to crumble to the ground."
"And I thought you'd be drowning in quicksand by now, or perhaps eaten by piranhas."
"Ha ha, very funny."
"Well, did you get something to help us out of here?" Olsen turns and walks out of sight, then a large vine suddenly falls down to them. Olsen returns to the edge. "That's gonna have to do," says Olsen as he holds the vine in his hands tight.

James turns to Pete, "Pete, you go first, ok?"
Pete nods then lifts up his shirt and tucks the prism in between his shirt and pants. "You want me to hold that for you instead Pete," asks James.

Pete shakes his head no and replies, "Only I can hold it dad." Pete begins to climb up the vine. After a moment he makes it all the way up with Olsen's help. Debbie now climbs the vine. She gets almost to the top and her hands begin to give out. She begins to slip and Olsen grabs her hands and pulls her all the way up. She then thanks Olsen. James and Burke remain below talking. "After you professor?"
"No, after you James. I insist."

James climbs the vine while Olsen, Debbie and Pete all hold the vine firmly. James makes his way up the vine to the top with ease. "Ok! Here I come," shouts Burke. "He mutters, "I'm getting to old for this stuff." He begins climbing the vine, everyone above holding onto it with a firm grip. He gets halfway and begins to lose his strength, struggling to pull himself up any higher. "Come on professor! You can do it! Just a little bit more and I'll help you up," shouts James.

Suddenly the trap floor begins to slowly close upwards to its original position.
"We've got a bigger problem than I now," shouts Burke. "Hurry professor," shouts James, as Burke looks at the trap floor approaching him. He begins with all his might to swing on the vine. After a few swings, he jumps off onto the trap floor, a successful landing, but begins to slide backwards towards the opening.

"Hang on," shouts James as he himself jumps to the trap floor with the vine in hand, landing successfully next to Burke. With the trap floor only a couple of feet left before closing on Burke's legs, James grabs Burke and pulls him with all of his might to safety. The trap floor shuts with a loud pounding.
"I am too old for this stuff. Thank you," says Burke to James, as James then helps Burke to his feet.

Back at the small clearing where Burke's UFO remains landed, Deek stands outside looking in the direction of the path to the temple. Suddenly from above him, the remaining Silustrian fleet arrives and remains stationary above him. Deek looks up at them and waves briefly, then enters back into the UFO.

Returning to space with Earth's moon in the near distance, the Mulchre still travel on a direct heading for Earth.

On the bridge of Krralmoom's ship, Earth is visible in the distance through the bridge window. Dakknol still standing next to Krralmoom who still remains seated in the command chair addresses the helmsmen, "Slow engines to five percent." The helmsmen nods and slows the engines. The communications officer turns to Dakknol, "Detecting small signs of life on the Earth moon, but no eminent danger Commander."

Krralmoom stands up and walks to the bridge window, staring at Earth's magnificence. Dakknol also staring at Earth walks up to Krralmoom's side. They both now stand at the edge of the window, and Krralmoom says, "The sight before us is self explanatory, why this Earth has allies. It looks to contain a great abundance of resources."
"Yes my lord, it does. And very soon it will be ours for the taking."
"Yes Commander, ours."

   Back on Earth in the mysterious ancient temple, Burke, Olsen and the Lowery's all walk down the final corridor leading out of the temple. Burke leading the way suddenly stops and turns to everyone, "Stop!" Everyone stops and James asks him, "What is it professor?"
"It would seem to me, that every time we or possibly being the prism get near an entrance, the entrance closes." Burke now looks at James and Debbie with reply. "You've got a good point," replies James.

   Burke continues, "I suggest we make a run for it from this point on, yes?" Everyone nods, and James picks up Pete and places him on his shoulders. Burke begins a count down, "Five, four, three, two, one!" Everyone quickly begins running down the corridor towards the light at the entrance. Surely enough as soon as they get within thirty or so feet of the entrance door, Burke's theory now a fact.

The entrance door begins to close downward and Burke shouts, "Hurry! It's closing up!" Everyone now runs their fastest to make it out in time. The stone door now half way down, as everyone begins to exit...Burke first, followed by Debbie, Olsen, then James and Pete. As soon as James and Pete exit, the door falls shut with a tremendous sound resembling thunder echoing throughout the entire temple. "Just in the nick of time again," says Burke while wiping away the sweat from his forehead. Olsen leaned over gasping for air replies, "This is crazy. You're all crazy."

James takes Pete off his shoulders and sets him down. Suddenly the sound of a laser is heard, and the falling of tree limbs. Everyone looks up and sees a thin blue laser beam cutting a huge hole out of the high jungle canopy above. After an entire hole is visible, Burke's UFO descends down through it and lands twenty yards away from the steps of the temple. Above the hole in the canopy, the rest of the Silustrian fleet present and remaining stationary.

Burke waves at Deek visible through the bridge window, while everyone but Olsen appears delighted to see Deek arrive. Pete takes out the mysterious prism and holds it with both hands, staring at it intently. It suddenly begins to glow again with its flamboyant static electricity, but this time with a strange humming sound that of a synthesizer.

The prism now begins to pulsate steadily. Pete's eyes close and the prism now begins to levitate slowly out of his hands. It catches Burke's attention and he places his hand on James' shoulder nudging him, "James look." James looks then Debbie and Olsen. "What the," says Olsen. Everyone remains silent and still except for Debbie, as she calls his name, "Pete," then putting her arms on his shoulders and being zapped a little by his involvement with the prism. The prism begins to rotate in a clock wise order, then levitate higher and higher.

   Returning to space on the bridge of Krralmoom's ship, Dakknol still stands next to Krralmoom who is seated once again in the command chair. He addresses the helmsmen, "Full engine stop!" "Order the fleet to move into forward position of us commander, and ready for battle if need be," orders Krralmoom. "Yes," replies Dakknol. He turns to the communications officer, "Order the fleet to our forward position ready for battle!"

   The entire Mulchre fleet moves into position in front of Krralmoom's ship, in a tight holding pattern.

   Back on Earth at the mysterious ancient temple, everyone except Pete, just stares in awe watching the mysterious prism rise higher and higher.

Pete still remains standing with his eyes closed in a trance. With intense speed, the prism shoots straight up as if being shot out of a gun, piercing through tree limbs like they were butter, as it leaves everyone's sight. Pete collapses towards the ground but James and Debbie catch him in time.

Returning to space on the bridge of Krralmoom's ship, Dakknol turns to Krralmoom, "All ships ready and awaiting your command my lord." The communications officer looking at his screen with great curiosity shouts, "Commander, an unknown energy source is closing in on our position!" Krralmoom and Dakknol both look at the communications officer. "From what point of origin," asks Dakknol. "Earth!"
"Inform the fleet at once!" An alarm now sounds throughout the bridge.

In space just above Earth's atmosphere, the mysterious prism now glows bright blue as it streaks by at supersonic speed on its heading towards the Mulchre.

Back on Earth at the ancient temple, Burke and Olsen watch Pete and Debbie holding Pete in their arms, trying to revive him. "Pete! Come on baby! Wake up," shouts Debbie.

    Burke gets on his communicator, "Deek, can you hear me?"
"Yes professor." Deek's voice replies.
"Bring the medical kit and fast."
"Yes professor."

    Back on the bridge of Krralmoom's ship, the alarm continues to sound as Dakknol now leans over the communications console next to the officer, viewing the prism closing in on the scanner screen.
"On my mark, all ships fire," he says aloud. After a moment watching the prism get nearer, Dakknol gives the order, "Fire!"

    All ships fire their lasers repetitively in the direction of the prism.

    The prism is bombarded with the repetitive laser fire, but incredibly the laser beams just deflect off the prism.

    Back on the bridge of Krralmoom's ship, Dakknol still leans over the communications console watching with disbelief, as the prism continues its approach. "How can this be," he shouts. He then looks at Krralmoom with uncertainty. "You told of this world being weak and less intelligent!"
"Hold your tongue Commander! The information obtained of this world was accurate! This may be just trickery, or perhaps a probe of some sort."

Just a thousand or so yards from the forward position of the Mulchre fleet, the prism suddenly stops, while lasers still bombard it. It now begins to glow a bright red with reddish static electricity.

Back on the bridge of Krralmoom's ship, Dakknol still looks at Krralmoom with anger now. The communications officer next to Dakknol says aloud, "The object has stopped!" Dakknol looks at the screen, "What is it doing? All ships cease fire," orders Dakknol.

The laser fire stops bombarding the prism, as it now strangely begins to change its structure, breaking apart into miniatures of itself, a dozen to be precise. They suddenly spread out in a horizontal line spanning a miles distance equally, then stopping. They now glow bright red as if miniature stars, and humming loudly.

Back aboard Krralmoom's ship in the seer's chamber, the two seer women sit across from each other, with their hands on the levitating crystal ball. Above them the holographic image of the miniature prisms. They lower their hands, look at each other, then hold hands and smile with a look of relief.

In space just in front of the Mulchre ships, the miniature prisms suddenly explode, each with the capacity of a nuclear bomb.

Amazingly they explode only in the direction of the Mulchre.

On the bridge of Krralmoom's ship, he stands and shouts, "NO!" Everyone on the bridge now stands and watches the great wall of intense fire destroy every Mulchre ship in its path, as it approaches them. Just a few seconds before the flaming wall of fire reaches them, Dakknol calmly says, "We are dead." Krralmoom's eyes widen and he screams as the wall of fire devours his ship.

The dark swarm, Mulchre have been defeated, thanks to some unknown ancient technology that lay in wait for this very moment.

Back on Earth at the ancient temple, James and Debbie still hold Pete in their arms, as burke finishes waving a capsule of smelling salt under Pete's nose. Pete begins to awake, slowly opening his eyes and looking at Debbie and James. Tears of joy roll down Debbie's cheeks as she hugs him. "Oh Pete, thank goodness you're ok," says Debbie. Debbie pulls away from hugging Pete, and he looks at James and Debbie, "It's safe now. Their gone."
"Who's gone Pete," asks James. "The bad people." Everyone looks at each other briefly, then back to Pete. Deek standing behind Burke addresses him, "Professor, the fleet ready to return home they are."
"Yes Deek. We can go home now, all of us."

Pete now stands up, then everyone begins to walk down the temple steps. Olsen adds, "And that does include me too, here on Earth. A deal's a deal!" Everyone shakes their heads at Olsen's remarks, as he continues to ramble on.

It's twelve o'clock in the afternoon a week later, as James sits in his office chair, leaning back with his eyes closed and feet on his desk. A sudden knocking on the door, "Yes," James asks aloud. The door opens and low and behold it's Olsen, holding a box of pizza. "Here's your lunch, sir," Olsen says sarcastically. James opens his eyes and says, "Just put it on the desk and leave thank you." Olsen tosses the box of pizza on James' desk and replies, "Not a problem, sir." Olsen smirks at James then turns and walks out the door. He slams the door real hard and walks away with a grin. James' voice yells, "Olsen!"

Later that same day, Pete rides his bike home from school, and is being followed by a couple of bullies from school also on bikes. They yell at him, "Peter Peter pumpkin eater!" Pete ignores them and then one of them shouts, "What's a matter Lowery, chicken?" Pete stops pedaling his bike and plants his feet firmly on the ground. His eyes suddenly glow white as a light, and the bullies' bike's freeze with them stuck on them as well. Suddenly two trash cans fly in and knock the bullies off their bikes. They scream and run away in the opposite direction.

Pete smiles and his eyes return to normal, as he rides away.

To Be Continued...

ALIENS
BELIEVE TOO! 3
RETURN OF THE AKKINUU

Written by
Brian Hiller

Introduction:

  This book like the two before it, deals on the basis of the possibilities of the existence of Alien life forms existing throughout the known Universe… yet in the fictional realm. In this book, I reveal a mysterious power force, one that is to be reckoned with, and teaches us a valuable lesson…not to take anything in life, including life itself, for granted. It is my sincere wish that all readers will enjoy this book.

Brian Hiller

ALIENS

BELIEVE TOO! 3

RETURN OF THE AKKINUU

Table of Contents:

Chapter One - Confrontations
Chapter Two - The Unexpected
Chapter Three - Hour of Discovery
Chapter Four - Bridging the Gap
Chapter Five - Assault on Terathis
Chapter Six - Search and Rescue
Chapter Seven - Narrow Escape
Chapter Eight - Arrival of Hope
Chapter Nine - Tomb Of Kattarus
Chapter Ten – Final Judgment

Chapter One
Confrontations

It's mid afternoon somewhere in a small town in Arizona in front of a high school, as students return to their classes from lunch period. A young man, sixteen year old Pete Lowery walks up the front steps and is greeted half way up by a young girl, sixteen year old Lynn Sanders. They both smile and Pete opens conversation, "Hey, how's Mr. Thompson's art class going?"

"Well…if you wanna call coloring by numbers with mustard and ketchup art, then I guess ok." They both now laugh, as an older man, Mr. Thompson, half bald and wearing glasses, Lynn's art teacher himself walks up and addresses Lynn, "Don't be late for class again Ms. Sanders. You have two tardies accounted for already." Lynn looks at Pete, "Gotta get to class. Call me later, ok?"

"Sure," replies Pete as Lynn quickly turns and jogs away. Mr. Thompson briefly smiles at Pete, then turns and walks away as well.

   Three hours later in front of the high school, the bell rings and all the students begin exiting the school from every possible exit.

   In the school parking lot, Pete is present and walks up to a high performance motorcycle. He grabs his gloss black helmet off the handle bars and puts it on, then zips up his black leather riding jacket.

He then gets on the motorcycle and starts it up, revving the engine just a little bit. His friend from earlier, Lynn Sanders walks up and greets him, "Hey Pete, where ya headed?"
"Gotta go straight home today. My mom's birthday."
"Oh wow! Tell her happy birthday for me."
"Ok, I will." Pete closes the black tinted visor on his helmet, then puts the motorcycle in gear and starts to pull away. "Bye," he shouts to Lynn.
"Don't forget to call me," she shouts to Pete, as he gives her a thumbs up then races away.

   In the middle of town at a four way traffic light, it turns red as Pete pulls up to the light and stops. The sudden sounds of more motorcycles present as four more male bikers pull up next to him, two on each side. They rev their engines a little as one of them flips open his visor and looks at Pete, him being Chinese American, "You think your bike so fast huh," he says loudly to Pete. Pete just ignores him. "Hey! I'm talking to you def American boy!" Pete flips up his visor and casually looks at him and says, "And I'm not listening to you." The other biker instantly wears a look of anger.

Pete shuts his visor and notices the light turn green. He then races away performing a wheel stand, leaving the other bikers far behind. The disgruntled biker shouts, "Get him," as they race away giving chase after Pete through traffic.

   In front of the police station also located in the middle of town, Chief of Police Miles Davis exits the front doors and walks down the front steps towards his cruiser. He carries in his hand a Styrofoam cup with coffee in it, sipping. Suddenly Pete races by at eighty miles per hour and Davis immediately drops the coffee and runs to his cruiser, hops in and starts it up. The other bikers also race by, as Davis lights up the tires backing out, turning on his lights and sirens, then lights up the tires again giving chase. "You boys picked the wrong day to be messing around on my turf," Davis says aloud.

   On the far end of town, Pete quickly takes a right turn towards the train yards, and in the distance a railroad crossing guard begins to descend downward at the tracks. The other bikers turn right as well still perusing Pete, as Pete continues full throttle down the street.

Davis then turns right, drifting around the corner and speeding up in hot pursuit. He gets on his radio, "This is Davis!" I'm in pursuit of several street bike racers headed toward the train yards! Anyone in the vicinity?" A moment goes by with no reply.
"Damn! On my own!"

The other bikers look back to see Davis now behind them, then quickly split up down alleys. Pete still races toward the tracks with the crossing guard all the way down now. The sound of an approaching train in the near distance is now present.
Davis still in pursuit of Pete, "Got you now sucka! Ain't nowhere for you to go."

As Pete approaches the tracks, he looks back at Davis, then ahead and amazingly performs a bunny hop with his bike, jumping over the crossing guards, through an open box car from the train and successfully makes it through. He continues to race away. Davis in complete amazement locks up the breaks, just stopping one inch from the crossing guards. "No way, that's impossible," he says in disbelief as he just stares forward, as the train continues rolling along down the tracks.

Suddenly a voice from one of his fellow officers on his radio, "Sir, we're in route now. What's your location?" "My location? A little late to be asking me about my location, bozos!" The officer on the radio clears his throat and responds, "Sorry sir."
"That you are."

   In a quiet upscale suburb, Pete quickly pulls into the beautiful two story Victorian Lowery home. He parks his bike between the house and garage. He takes off his helmet, rests it on the handle bars, then dismounts and walks up to the side door.

   Inside the house in the kitchen, the side door opens and Pete walks in. A note lay on the counter. Pete shouts, "Mom? Dad? I'm home!" With no reply, Pete then sees the note and picks it up. It reads: *Pete, me and your father had to leave to our dinner engagement early. Sorry about that son. We love you, and will be home soon. There's some fresh tuna salad I prepared in the fridge. Love, mom and dad.*
"Great," Pete says disappointed as he unzips his jacket, then opens the fridge and takes out the tuna salad.

Pete walks up stairs and opens his room door while taking a bite of his tuna salad sandwich, and low and behold, Professor Landin Burke dressed in a trench coat and hat sits on Pete's bed with a girly magazine in hand. Pete doesn't act surprised at the sight of Burke. "Hmm? Things have really changed since I've been away," says Burke as he flips through the pages. Pete quickly walks up to Burke and rips the magazine out of his hands, "Is there ever gonna be a time that you might be a little considerate and knock, or something like that," asks Pete as he sets his sandwich on his dresser. Burke calmly looks at Pete and replies, "Is that tuna salad?"
"Or, even bother me somewhere else a little less private?"
"Like maybe at the corner Diner downtown? You could tell everyone I'm your grandfather."
"Well, yeah. Something like that at least. So what is it this time that brings your presence into my room?"
"For starters, it still seems I haven't stressed to you enough how important it is for you to be more inconspicuous."
"Inconspicuous?"
"Yes."
"Like what?"

"Like using your power in plain view of the authorities?" Pete chuckles a little and says, "Oh, that was nothing." Burke stands and says, "You should be so fortunate you haven't been identified as of yet."

"Anything else you have a problem with professor?"

"Something else much more important to discuss."

"Like what," asks Pete with curiosity.

Burke removes his hat and explains, "Long ago, a great race of beings with great knowledge and wisdom were nearly wiped out. Only a handful managed to survive and exile to safe haven upon the planet of Cathelle."

"What race of beings professor?"

"My dear deceased friend Januu Yasuun's people, the Akkinuu. News has it that their location has been discovered by an old arch enemy, the Korrinion, a race of powerful, and ruthless beings as well. And now an effort by the Silustrians and myself to secretly make way for Cathelle and warn them of this news is under way. And if possible, assist them."

"So, what does this have to do with me," Pete asks while now wearing a look of greater curiosity.

Burke briefly sighs and replies, "I need your help Pete."
"Whoa, wait a minute."

Just outside the front of Pete's house, Chief Davis slowly drives by, looking around at all the houses. He spots Pete's bike parked near the garage and suddenly stops, staring at it with wonder. He looks around for a brief second, then opens his door and gets out, quietly shutting the door then walking towards the house.

Back in Pete's room, Burke and Pete continue debating Burke asking for Pete's assistance in aiding him on a trip to Cathelle, to warn the Akkinuu of the present danger. "I can promise you everything will be ok," says Burke.
"If that were the case, then you wouldn't be asking me this, right?"
"Well, yes and no."
"Just because I'm endowed with a gift, doesn't mean I have to go off to some strange world light years away and do whatever!"
"This isn't just a whatever I'm asking."

Back outside in front of the Lowery's house, Davis enters the front porch and knocks on the door. A moment goes by and no answer.

Back in Pete's room he asks, "Did you hear something?" Burke shrugs and replies, "No. Back to the important issue now."

Back outside, Davis now tries the door handle, but it's locked. He then makes his way around to the side door via the garage. He arrives then tries the door knob, and it turns. Davis takes out his gun and enters cautiously. "Hello! Anyone home? Lowery, you here," Davis says aloud. Pete opens his bedroom door and looks around and continues, "I could've sworn I heard something or someone." Burke replies, "I know for a fact I wasn't followed. Probably just the wind. Now, are you going to come with me to Cathelle? It is of dire circumstances Pete." Pete finishes looking around then closes the door, locking it and replies sarcastically, "Dire? Just what would I tell my mom and dad…hey mom, hey dad, going for a little trip with the professor. I'll be back in oh say, a hundred years."

Down stairs at the bottom of the staircase, Davis still armed looks up the stairs and begins to walk up. Burke continues, "Your parents, no one will even know you were gone. In fact…I'll have you back in time for supper. It'll be as if you never left!" Burke smiles as Pete replies, "And how is that possible?" "Simple, I've a time displacement convertor aboard my vessel. Only wish I had it years ago. But that's beside the point. So, are you coming or not? It'll be exciting!"

Just outside Pete's bedroom door, Davis still armed cautiously walks up to it and leans in to eavesdrop on Pete and Burke's conversation. In the room Pete and Burke continue, Pete asks Burke, "You're serious, aren't you?" Burke wears a serious look and replies, "Of course I am. Time is of the essence, and I truly need your assistance Pete."
"I see. I haven't been gone far from home since the last time we left with you. Hard to believe in the last ten years, I haven't been anywhere." Pete chuckles a little then continues, "Ok, let's say I go with you, and something goes wrong?"
"I assure you, everything will be just fine. You have to trust me on this."

"Trust you? I don't know." Burke looks at his watch and says, "We've only a few minutes now."
"Only a few minutes for what," Pete asks curiously.
"Before we, I must be going. So what shall it be?"
Pete scratches his head then replies, "Oh, ok. On one condition."
"What might that be?"
"No matter what, you get me back home safely, and in time for dinner, like you promised. Agreed?"
Burke smiles, "Yes, agreed." Burke shakes Pete's hand then lifts his coat sleeve to reveal a communication wrist band. Burke taps on the screen twice, then looks at Pete, "Get ready, here we go."
"Wait! I'm not ready yet!" Suddenly a blue beam of brilliant light appears on them. The whole room glows blue. Just on the other side of Pete's bedroom door, Davis still armed shouts, "This is the police! Open the door now!" After a brief moment of nothing happening, Davis tries the door knob but it's locked. He then takes a step back and kicks the door in, just as the blue beam of light, Burke and Pete disappear without Davis seeing it happen. Davis with gun aimed says, "All right! Come on out! I know you're in here!"

He looks all around the room cautiously, only to find no one present. "Damn, where did they go?" He puts his gun away then walks up to Pete's dresser and leans in looking at the tuna salad sandwich Pete made earlier. He sniffs it, then picks it up and begins to eat it as he walks away.

Outside the house approximately fifty yards above it, Burke's UFO hovers momentarily, then suddenly streaks away into the vast blue sky as Davis exits the front door. He hears it and looks up curiously, but doesn't see it. He shakes his head then walks away toward his cruiser.

Chapter Two
The Unexpected

Burke and Pete now walk onto the UFO's main bridge, as a few other Silustrian crewman sit at various controls operating it. They see Pete and smile at the sight of him. Pete nods and smiles back, as a familiar voice nearby says, "Greetings Young Lowery. Grown you have." Pete turns to his left and see's Deek at the main flight controls, just as he remembered him from ten years ago. "Hello. You're Deek, if my memory serves me correct?"
"Yes, Deek I am. Good to have you with us again." Pete and Burke walk up next to Deek and stop, while Pete says, "Yeah, let's hope it's good."

Burke begins pushing several buttons on the main control console while addressing Deek,
"Have you laid in the course for the Lexium system?"
"Yes. On our way there now we are."
"Where's this Lexium system we're going to? How far," asks Pete. Burke and Deek continue working the controls and Burke replies, "Oh, about twenty or so light years away…give or take a few." Pete's eyes widen, then he asks, "Twenty or so light years? Holy crap!" Deek looks at Pete and says, "Holy? Crap? Understand I do not."

Pete Continues, "Just how long are we gonna be gone for? I do know a little about physics." Burke replies, "That's good to know. You should, being who you are and all." Pete sighs, "Yeah yeah yeah I know, the Zensmittorith. So how long?" "In our time, could be only hours, days. But in Earth time, years." Pete cuts in, "I know…give or take a few." Burke smiles and finishes with the controls, then looks at Deek, "Ok Deek, full speed ahead." "Yes professor." Deek engages the light drive and light speed instantly displays through the bridge window. Pete looking at the bridge window takes a deep breath and exhales, "I can't believe I'm doing this."

   Back on Earth in Pete's town at a local high end restaurant, his father James lowery, and mother Debbie Lowery dressed for the occasion, sit at a table drinking red wine and conversing. "I really wish Pete could be here with us," says Debbie. "Me too honey. But this was the only opening they had." "Hard to believe at this hour in this small town." James chuckles and replies, "Yeah, you can say that again."

James then wears a smile as he reaches into his jacket pocket and pulls out a little wrapped gift for Debbie. He hands it to her as she smiles as well.

"Happy birthday honey," says James as Debbie unwraps the gift revealing a small jewelry case. She opens it and smiles from ear to ear. "Oh wow James. It's beautiful!" Debbie pulls out a platinum necklace and holds it up…other people stop and stare. "Thank you honey, says Debbie as she then leans a across the table and lays a huge kiss on James. "Hmm hmm," your dinner is here Mr. And Mrs. Lowery," says a waiter with a large platter of food resting on his arm. James and Debbie refrain from kissing and sit up straight, "Great. Thanks," says James as the waiter sets their dinner on the table. The waiter finishes then asks, "More wine sir, madam?" James grabs Debbie's hand lovingly and replies "Pour on my good man. Pour on."

Just outside the restaurant, Chief Davis drives by and notices James' sports car parked there. He whips in and parks. He quickly exits his car and uses his shoulder radio, "I found Mr. Lowery. All units continue your sweep." He then walks into the restaurant.

Back inside the restaurant, James and Debbie raise their glasses for a toast. "Happy birthday to the most beautiful, loving, intelligent and sexy woman in the world," Says James. They both toast then begin to drink as they are interrupted by yours truly Chief Davis, "Lowery?" James and Debbie both look at Davis and James replies, "Well hello Chief. What brings you around this neck of the woods?"
"I'm afraid it's about your son." James and Debbie both instantly look worried, and James asks, "About our son? What is it Chief?"
"About an hour ago, I was at your residence, and witnessed your son and some other person vanish into thin air, inside your house!" James and Debbie both looking shocked. "Inside our house? Why were you in our house? Where is our son," asks Debbie.
"Earlier today, I pursued some kids on motorcycles street racing, and they got away. I spotted a motorcycle matching one of their descriptions at your residence, so I knocked on your door and received no answer. I then proceeded inside and upstairs. What happened next was impossible. After hearing and knowing your son and another individual, an older man's presence in the room discussing plans of leaving, I entered the room.

Once inside, they were already gone, into the thin air! I searched your entire house and property, but no sign of your son or the stranger." Debbie looks at James with fear, "Oh my god James…Pete." James holds Debbie's hands and calmly says, "Don't worry honey. I'm sure there's a logical explanation." James then looks at Davis and adds, "Right Chief?" Davis replies, "Let us hope so. I have everyone searching everywhere for your son. Hopefully we'll find him, or at least something that will lead us to his whereabouts." James and Debbie both now wearing a look of worry and despair, as James says, "Thank you for all you're doing Chief."

"Don't mention it. It's the least I can do. Do any of you know what may have occurred, the stranger…your son's disappearance?" James and Debbie both shake their heads no. Davis continues, "If you hear anything or think of anything that will help, give me a shout." Davis turns and begins to walk away while James and Debbie stand up. Davis stops walking and turns to them, "Say, you wouldn't suppose it might be those," Davis whispers, "Tre'token creatures again would ya? I remember, even have nightmares still about them things." James replies, "I don't think so chief."

"Alright, I'll be in touch." Davis turns and walks away, and James looks at the waiter from afar and loudly says, Check please!"

Back in deep space light years away traveling at light speed aboard Burke's UFO, Burke and Pete now sit in front of the bridge window…stars and constellations streaking by ever so quickly.
"So how long before we reach this Cathelle," asks Pete. "Oh, about a half an hour." Pete looks at the bridge window and asks, "What if the Korrinion are already there, and we're too late to warn them? Have you given that any thought?"
"That I have my lad, which is why several Silustrian scout vessels have already been dispatched to the Lexium system, and will rendezvous with us upon our approach to Cathelle." Pete tightens hip lips then looks at Burke and says, "Hmm, clever thinking." Burke smiles then replies, "Yes, always good to be a step ahead of the game, especially out here." Pete chuckles and adds, "I hope you're right professor, for all our sakes."
"Yes, I hope so as well. Not to be worried too much Pete. I'm sure everything will be just fine."

Back on Earth at the Lowery's house, James' car is parked in the driveway. Inside the house in the foyer, the front door opens and James and Debbie enter quickly, James closing the door immediately as well. They both stand still and look all around for a moment and James says, "I think it's safe honey. C'mon." James and Debbie hold hands as they begin walking toward the staircase. Upstairs, they arrive at Pete's room, seeing the doorjamb broken from Davis' handy work. They both continue to enter Pete's room. Once inside, they both browse all around, looking for any clue as to what may have befallen Pete. After a moment, James and Debbie realize there is no trace of anything that could possibly lead them to the truth of Pete's disappearance. Debbie starts to shed tears and looks at James as he sits on the edge of Pete's bed. He holds out his hand to her and she holds it, as she also sits next to him. He gives her a hug and says with assurance, "Don't worry honey. Something tells me that Pete is gonna be ok. I just know it."
"I know…I need to be strong, and hope for the best, right?" She looks at James and he replies, "That's right honey. We need to be strong and think positive." Debbie nods and lay in James' arms.

Back in space aboard Burke's UFO some fifteen or more light years away by now, him and Pete still sit by the bridge window. Burke leans back in his seat, crosses his arms relaxed while looking forward out the bridge window, as light speed travel resumes.
"I can remember when I was a young lad such as yourself. Those were the days, not a care in the world…just hanging out with friends, partying as it's called today, and girls." Burke smiles at Pete then looks back at the bridge window continuing,
"Yes, girls. Made plenty of time for many breakups." Burke laughs a little as Pete stays amused by Burke's conversation. "Then I met her."
"Her? Who is, or was her," asks Pete.
"Rose, the one women who didn't say no to me. The one I wanted to spend eternity with." Burke looks at Pete and adds, "Ahh, forgive me for boring you with my melancholy stories."
"I'm not bored at all professor. In fact…find it sort of interesting, to a certain degree."
"Yes, a certain degree, or two." Burke and Pete have a brief laugh, then Pete asks, "So, what happened professor…with Rose?"
"That my boy is a story within a story itself. Someday I'll tell you all about."

Deek addresses Burke, "Approaching the Lexium system soon professor!" Burke pats Pete on the knee, "Well, here we go. You're in for a treat!" Burke then stands up and walks over to the controls, assisting Deek with the arrival out of light speed.

   In a remote area of Lexium space, Burke's UFO appears out of light speed, and continues moving forward at idle speed towards what appears to be several small planets of various shades and colors in the distance, surrounding a small but bright sun. Among the planets, one stands out more so due to its vast colors of blue, brown, green…almost such the colors of Earth. Its atmosphere gleams with iridescence. Back aboard Burke's UFO, Burke and Pete both stand near the bridge window. Burke holds out his hand in presentation, "I give you the beautiful Lexium system!" Pete stares in awe at the mysterious but breathtaking view. Pete leans on the ledge of the bridge window,
"Wow…I could swear that that planet right there," Pete points at the planet momentarily, "looks almost identical to Earth!"
"Yes, I have to agree with you. Its resources are abundant as well, yet its culture is far different then

that of Earth's."

"How so professor?"

"Oh, you will soon see for yourself how much."

"So that's Cathelle?"

"Indeed it is." Deek addresses Burke again, "The fleet, received our signal they have, and orders they await." Burke turns to Deek, "Tell them to rendezvous with us, and inform the Cathellion council of our arrival." Deek nods, "Yes professor." Pete remains still, staring at the mysterious and magnificent view of Cathelle for the first time, as they draw closer to it. "Whatever happens Pete, we must keep it secret why we are here, ok," asks Burke.

"Ok professor. Not a problem."

Chapter Three
Hour Of Discovery

Back on Earth at the Lowery's home, James and Debbie are present in their living room…Debbie sitting on the couch, and James pacing back and fourth, thinking hard about what could've happened to Pete." "What are we gonna do James," asks Debbie. "I don't know." Suddenly the doorbell rings, and Debbie and James both walk quickly to the door. James opens it to the sight of Davis standing there. "Hello Chief. Any good news," asks James. Davis takes a breath and exhales, then replies, "Nothing yet. Sorry. But my men and I are working on it. I've put out an A.P.B, and hopefully something will turn up. Could I come in for a minute?"
"Sure. I was gonna ask you to anyway." Davis looks at James curiously and enters, and James closes the door. Everyone walks in to the living room and sits down, Debbie right at James' side clutching his arm. James asks Davis, "Chief, you said it was the voice of an older man you heard?"
"Yes. And oddly, he sounded as of having an accent.?"
"An accent," asks James.
"Yes, like British, English or something like that."

James' eyes widen, then he asks, "Did it sound something like this, James impersonates Burke, "Hello my good man! Care for a sip of tea?"
Davis now looking at James astonished answers, "Yes! Say…how did you do that? Sound just like the guy?" Davis now looking ever more curious.
James replies, "You're not gonna believe me when I tell you this."
"Oh? Try me."

  Back in space some twenty or so light years away near the planet Cathelle in the Lexium system, Burke and the Silustrian fleet's UFO's approach the beautiful mysterious planet. Just above the capital city of Cathelle, Terathis, Burke and the fleet descend through clouds towards a large landing platform located atop a tall skyscraper. The city appearing super advanced then that of Earth…antigravity vehicles and ships of all different shapes and sizes flying all around, and holographic images line the walls of the tall buildings everywhere. And strangely enough, the beings in the holograms appear to be human looking in nature. The sky, also appearing similar as the skies over Earth on a partly cloudy day.

Aboard Burke's UFO, Pete looking at every possible area of the city says to Burke, "I see what you mean by different, very different in fact."

"Wait till you see the rest of it. It's truly a remarkable world." Pete looks at Burke, "The rest? I'd love to, but I gotta be back home upon the time we agreed on."

"Yes. Yes of course. As soon as we're finished with our business here, I will return you safely home. And not a minute later." Pete nods and returns to the amazing view of Terathis and says, "From the look of things here, I wouldn't say it's dire. So what's the real reason to have me along professor?" Burke places his hand on his chin and strokes his beard while replying, "Well…just in case something does go wrong before we can warn them of the impending threat, I feel your presence could possibly be most valuable." Pete turns and looks at Burke with a curious grin and says, "What about all that, I should be more discrete with my abilities mumbo jumbo you preached earlier?"

"Well…that was then, and for good reason. And now, now could be for good intended purposes only, and only such."

"Ok." Pete chuckles and adds, "Whatever you say."

"Good. Glad we have that out of the way."
Burke takes a deep breath and sighs with relief.
"Come, we have an important engagement." Burke walks away, Pete and Deek follow.

On the landing platform, all the Silustrian UFO's land and exit ramps descend, as two very tall men in classy uniforms that appear to be royal sentries walk towards Burke's UFO. Burke, Pete, Deek and all the remaining Silustrian crewman exit their UFO's. The two sentries arrive in front of Burke, Pete and Deek then stop. They bow and one of them speaks, but in a language unknown to Pete,
"Greetings." Burke bows and replies in their language, "Thank you. Greetings to you."
"The council is aware of your presence, and request your company." The two sentries turn and walk away towards a large octagon shaped elevator in the near distance. Burke turns to the Silustrian crew, "Remain here! We shant be long!" They all nod and remain by their UFO's. Burke, Pete and Deek follow the sentries. "This is kinda cool. Getting the royal treatment," says Pete. Burke adds, "See? Not so bad a decision you've made."

"So where are these Akkinuu people we're here for," asks Pete. Burke quickly speaks in undertone, "Shhh. We must remain quiet about it for now. They are not right here. I must find a certain individual here who knows." Pete nods with a very curious look, as the sentries stop at the sides of the elevator and gesture them to enter. Everyone enters the elevator, the door closes swiftly but quietly, then descends out of sight.

   Returning back home to Earth inside the Lowery's home, James, Debbie, and Chief Davis still sit in the living room, while James finishes explaining to Davis what he thinks happened to Pete. "And that's what I think happened. Professor Burke took him on a joy ride. Where to, we don't know. And hopefully not too far away either. It's the only logical explanation."
 "And you're absolutely, one hundred percent sure of this," asks Davis. "Yes. I feel very sure about it. I just hope the professor doesn't do anything crazy with my son." Debbie looks at James angered upon his words. Davis adds, "Like fighting those Tre'token creatures?" James replies,
"The Tre'toan are no longer a threat.

It's what we don't know with Pete's whereabouts that worries me."

"And me," Debbie adds.

"Alright. I guess that's that," says Davis as he stands up. He continues, "Don't know what cockamamie story I'm gonna tell everyone down at the station, but I'll think of something. And in the meantime, if you folks have any way of contacting this Burke character, I suggest you do it. Although he may be far out in space somewhere." Davis turns and walks toward the front door chuckling," Man! Crazy!" Debbie shouts at Davis as he walks out the front door, "Don't let the door hit ya, where the good lord split ya!" The front door closes and Debbie turns to James and hugs him, tears begin rolling down her cheeks. "Oh James, what can we do? That damn friend of yours has our Pete! Why?" Debbie grits her teeth and adds, "What I'd like to do to that Burke right now if he was here." James pats Debbie's shoulder and says, "Now don't you worry honey. Our Pete's gonna be back home soon, ok?" Debbie wipes the tears away and nods, as James continues comforting her. "James, is there any way we can contact Burke?" James shrugs his shoulders and replies, "Not that I know of at the moment honey."

Returning twenty or so light years away to the mysterious capital city Terathis on Cathelle, Burke, Pete and Deek now walk down a huge long corridor by escort of the two sentries. The walls and ceilings laden with gold and platinum looking panels in various shapes and sizes. The flooring looks as if one shimmering sheet of painted white glass were carefully laid. Other sentries stand guard at all the entrances along the corridor, and all armed as well with what appears to be some sort of shiny chrome laser pistols holstered on their hips. Pete looks at Burke and asks, "When was your last visit here professor?"

"Oh, about a decade ago."

"Let me guess…Rose, right?" Burke looks at Pete and jokingly replies, "Have you been reading my mind?" Burke chuckles and continues, "No, I was merely here reassuring relations between Silus and Cathelle. For many centuries, relations with them have remained very good. And I hope it to stay just as such."

The sentries arrive at a large open entrance at the end of the hallway and gesture everyone to enter. Burke, Pete and Deek enter, and the sentries follow.

Through the entrance is a very large council hall, the ceiling some fifteen feet high. At the opposite end sits three elderly council members dressed in formal outfits, one woman and two men.
The woman sits in the middle, quite attractive, with brunette hair pulled back into a bun. She wears a unique pendent in the shape of a star around her neck, blue in color. The two men appear standard clean cut and shaved with grey hair.

As everyone follows the sentries to greet the council members, Burke stares at the woman council member and whispers, "No…it can't be." Pete replies, "What professor? Can't be what?" Burke ignores Pete's reply, and Pete notices Burke staring at the woman. The woman begins to smile condescendingly at Burke for whatever reason unknown. Everyone stops just several feet away from the council members, as one of the sentries introduces Burke and party, "Chancellor Burke of Silus!" Burke briefly smiles, then attempts to speak and is quickly interrupted by the woman, "Chancellor…your unexpected visit to Cathelle is of great interest to us.

Why are you here today, along with a large percentage of your Silustrian fleet?"

Burke replies, "I, we are here on a simple sight seeing visit. This is Pete Lowery from Earth," Burke introduces Pete, and Pete waves. The council members smile and nod. Burke then introduces Deek, "And my dear friend Deek from Silus." Deek smiles and waves his hand. The council members smile and nod to Deek as well. Burke continues, "As for the extra Silustrian company…when traveling great distances such as this, it's much safer to journey in numbers, in the event anything should befall one." The two male council members nod in agreement with Burke, while the woman continues to stare at Burke condescendingly. She stands up and addresses Burke, "Chancellor…may I have a word with you privately?" Burke nods and says, "You may." He then looks at Pete and Deek with widened eyes, then walks towards the woman. They walk to the side of the hall, and through a doorway out of site. Pete asks Deek, "What's going on Deek?" Deek looks at Pete and shrugs his shoulders.

In another corridor just outside the council hall, Burke and the woman stand closely facing each other.

"You have some nerve showing up here, and unannounced as well," says the woman very angrily. Burke stares her in the eyes and replies, "Me? I seem to recall you having the nerve to run away from me, and your only child!" The woman suddenly slaps Burke's face hard. His lip instantly bleeding and he replies, "The truth hurts, doesn't it?" He pulls out a handkerchief from his pocket and holds it on his lip, while she remains silent but still angered. Burke cradles her star pendant in his hand and says, "It's even a wonder you still keep this much wear it. I remember when I gave it to you." She calms down as Burke releases the pendant. He continues, "What happened?" Rose remains silent. "I am sorry about your father's passing. Honorable for you to take his place as head of the council." She looks down at the ground briefly, then back at Burke still speechless. Suddenly from around the corner, Pete enters and leans on the doorway. Burke says, "Pete, meet Rose. You may have to pardon her at the moment…she seems to be at a loss for words presently." Pete looking at them with arms now crossed and leaning on the doorway, walks over to her and extends his hand, "Pleasure meeting you ma'am." She smiles and grabs his hand in return.

Pete suddenly squints his eyes and briefly has a vision of a new born child crying alone in a crib. He snaps out of it just as Rose replies, "Pleasure meeting you too Pete." They finishing shaking, and Pete looking immobilized for the moment. Burke and Rose look at Pete very curiously now upon his reaction to meeting her. Deek and the other council members enter through the doorway and stop, just looking at everyone. Burke places the handkerchief back in his pocket and says to Rose, "In light of this enchanted meeting…may my friends and I now be on our way?" Everyone now looking at Burke as Rose replies, "Be on your way." She then turns and walks away in the opposite direction down the corridor. One of the two male council members looks at Burke, "Excuse us. Enjoy your stay here," then him and the other man turn and walk away down the corridor in Rose's direction. Burke says, "She always was short on goodbyes. Come, we have important work to do."
Burke turns and walks away, Pete and Deek follow, while Pete now looks at Burke with great curiosity.

  Rose tucks around a doorway and begins crying, holding her face with both hands.

Chapter Four
Bridging The Gap

Back on Earth at the Lowery's residence, several hours have passed since Pete's disappearance with Burke. The sun just now begins to pierce its way through the dark blue skyline in their back yard. Inside the house in the kitchen, James in his pajamas pours a cup of coffee while reading his newspaper. He finishes adding some creamer and sugar, then takes a seat at the table, newspaper still in hand. Debbie then enters wearing only a gown, and sits at the table directly across from him, still appearing very upset about Pete's disappearance.

"I can't stand this, not being able to do anything about it," says Debbie. James looks over his newspaper at her and replies, "Me either honey. It's not right at all of Burke doing this. And when they return, Burke had better have a damn good explanation!"

"Damn right he'd better! What gives him the right," Debbie says aloud. "Exactly my thoughts," James adds. He continues, "Whatever the reason, it's gotta be a logical one. I mean…the professor is a very logical person, and I don't think this event would be of an illogical nature. I don't see that. We just have to wait honey. Like it or not, it's all we can do for now.

Debbie stands up and walks away, while James watches her exit the kitchen. James shouts, "I love you honey!" She doesn't reply. James stares down at the table with hope and wonder.

Back on planet Cathelle, Burke, Pete and Deek exit an elevator located on the ground floor just feet from the city sidewalks. Many people, and Aliens of different species walking along the sidewalks, and a variety of small crafts landing and ascending all over the city. "Wow," says Pete, as he marvels at the incredible new world of Cathelle. Burke turns to Pete, "Are you feeling a little hungry yet? I'm starved!" Pete nods and Burke continues, "I know a great place not too far from here. Come." Burke turns and begins walking away, Pete and Deek follow.

A few moments later, Burke, Pete and Deek arrive in front of a fancy looking restaurant called Ma Belle's. Everyone enters through an open entrance. Once inside, they sit at a table off to the side, and out of nowhere a voice shouts, "Landin!"

Burke, Pete and Deek look and see a large Alien woman, skin color purple, wearing what looks like a blonde wig and yellow waitress outfit approaching them. She carries a platter of ice waters. Burke quickly stands up to greet her. She stops in front of Burke excited and instantly hugs him. "Good to see you Belle," says Burke. They finish hugging and she says, "Where you been stranger? Off on another one of your adventures?"

"Well, you know me Belle." She chuckles strangely then says, "Yeah, I've always known you, but not good enough." She winks at Burke then turns to Pete. "Who's this handsome young man?" Pete smiles briefly, then Burke introduces Pete to Belle, "Pete, this is Belle, the owner of this fine establishment, and dear friend of mine." Pete extends his hand to Belle and they briefly shake hands. "Pleasure," says Pete. Belle winks at Pete then looks at Deek, "Hi Deek. You keeping this hunk of handsomeness out of trouble?" Belle looks at Burke, then back at Deek. Deek smiles and nods. Burke sits back down and Belle places the ice waters on the table for them. "So how have you been Belle," asks Burke. "Same old same old. Business as usual." "How's the family?"

"Oh you know…family is family." She chuckles strangely again then asks, "So what can I get you?" "Some nice big Jarron steaks with a side of potatoes…and a little information possibly," replies Burke. Belle looks at Burke, "What kind of information?" Just as Burke begins to speak, Rose shows up out of the blue and walks up to Burke. Burke says to Belle, "Hold that thought." Belle gives Rose a dirty look, winks at Burke then walks away. Burke still seated and shocked at the sight of Rose says, "Well I'll be. What are you doing here? Did you have us followed?"

"No, I followed you myself. Look…I'm not big on words these days. I know I have a lot of explaining to do, and I just need you to know…I was confused back then, and I'm very very sorry. I'm a different woman now." Tears begin to roll down her cheeks. Burke's eyebrows raise with amazement as she continues, "I'm truly sorry for what I did, to you, and our son." She holds her face again and cries heavily, and Burke stands up and holds her in his arms. "There there. It's ok. All is forgiven." After a moment, She looks at Burke, and him her, then they kiss passionately for a moment.

When they pull away from kissing, all the other guests in the restaurant clap their hands. Pete now looking at the two, smiling and shaking his head. Rose looks at Burke with serious question and quietly asks, "Our son, where?" Burke replies quietly, "He's just fine. Now is a bad time to discuss this. I will tell you soon. I promise you." She nods in agreement and hugs him. Burke then gestures her to join them, "Join us."

"Oh I'd love to, but I have some work to finish up with back at the council."

"Come on, join us! You can finish your work later. I insist." Rose smiles and says, "Well, since you put it that way, ok." Rose then sits next to Burke. Pete then looks at Burke, hinting to him about getting information from Belle. Burke paying Pete no mind, caught up in the moment with Rose. Pete then clears his throat loudly enough to get Burke's attention, then jerks his head in Belle's last known direction. Burke finally realizes Pete's motions and says to Rose, "Please excuse me for just a moment? I'll be right back." Burke stands up, then grabs Rose's hand gently and kisses it. She and him smile, then he walks away. Pete and Deek look at Rose and smile briefly, and she returns a brief smile.

Back on Earth inside the Lowery's home, James sits comfortably on the couch in the living room, still in his pajamas watching television. On the television, a UFO documentary showing UFO's entering Earth's atmosphere. Debbie walks in and stops in front of James, dressed up in a navy blue suit holding a shiny navy blue purse. James looks at her, "You're going in to work?"

"Yes. There's no one available to cover for me today. Unlike you, who can take the day off when he wants to. Besides…I need to keep my mind occupied on something, other than wanting to strangle your dear friend Burke!" She walks away quickly with authority in her stride, and James shouts, "Drive safely honey! I love you!" The front door is heard slamming shut, and James resumes watching television.

At a four way stop, Debbie arrives in her small compact car and stops. She begins to pull away and is suddenly cut off by a man driving an old pickup truck. She slams on the brakes stopping, and the man continues driving away while looking at her out his window and shouts, "Where'd you learn to drive lady, online?"

Debbie looking at the man now very angered, slams her hands on the steering wheel, and proceeds to drive away.

  Inside a local television news station, Debbie walks down a long corridor now appearing calm cool and collective. Many other employees mull up and down the long corridor, exiting and entering rooms.
A middle aged half bald man holding papers walks up to Debbie and says, "You're on in one minute. Here's your stuff." He hands Debbie the papers and walks away. Debbie stops walking and takes a deep breath, then continues to walk into the live television news set. All television crew on cameras and grips ready to roll on cue, as Debbie walks behind the news desk and takes her seat. She appears a little unfocused at the moment, as the man that gave her papers, now wears a headset and says quietly while counting down with his finger, "Five, four, three, two, one." Debbie quickly straitens up and smiles. "Good morning. Welcome to the morning news. We're gonna take a short commercial break, and be right back." The news director gives the signal to go to commercial, then walks up to Debbie, her now looking relieved, yet unfocused.

"Are you ok? What's wrong," he asks. Debbie breathes in and exhales, "I just need a moment. Nothing's wrong. I'll be ok." The man nods then walks away, as Debbie tries to regain her composure.

  Back at Ma Belle's restaurant on Cathelle, Burke exits the kitchen area and waves to Belle as he walks back to Rose, Pete and Deek. Pete and Deek finish up stuffing their faces, while Rose smiles at the sight of Burke's return. He takes a seat next to Rose again and she asks, "So what's with your friend there?" "Belle, She's just a good friend. I've known her for quite some time."
"Oh. I see. Well, I think I should be getting back now. They might call out the council guard if I'm gone for too long." She chuckles and Burke replies, "Heavens, we wouldn't want that now would we?" Burke stands up and lets Rose out from the table. They face each other and Burke says, "I'm so very glad to see you again…and to have mended the bridge that, well you know what I mean." She smiles and says, "Yes." They both then kiss passionately again, then pull away ever so slowly.

Burke reaches into his pants pocket and pulls out a small silver communications device. He grabs Rose's hand and gives it to her. She looks at it, then him. Burke says, "I'll be in touch. Call on me whenever you want or need to. Ok?" She nods and replies, "Ok, I will." They both smile again and Rose walks away. Burke turns to Pete and Deek, "Glad to see you boys have had your fill." They look at Burke and both shrug their shoulders. Burke continues, "I have the location now. We must get there as soon as possible." Deek and Pete now exit the table, and Pete play slugs Burke on the shoulder and says, "You old slugger. Way to go!" Burke smiles and replies, "To be honest, I didn't see it coming." Burke chuckles then looks at Deek, "Deek, I need you to return to the fleet and remain there till further notice, ok?" Deek nods and replies, "Yes professor. Understand I do." Deek turns to Pete while walking away and nods with a smile. "Take care Deek," Pete shouts. Burke and Pete also turn and walk away and Pete asks him, "So, who and where is yours and Rose's son?"

"That's a long story…one that you're sure not to believe me when I tell you."

"Really? Lay it on me."

"Later. First we need to see to it, that our Akkinuu friends are safe and secure…far away from here." Pete nods, "Ok, I'm all ears after that." Burke nods as they continue walking away.

Meanwhile back on Earth in the parking lot at Debbie's work, she walks towards her car and drops her keys. She stops and picks them up, then looks up and sees James standing before her with one arm behind his back. James smiles and pulls his arm out revealing a dozen roses. He extends his arm with the flowers and she smiles, as tears run down her cheeks. They both hug each other immediately. "Oh James," She says happily. "I love you honey, more than you'll ever know," says James. "I know. And I love you just the same," she replies.

Chapter Five
Assault On Terathis

In space viewing planet Cathelle in the distance, a strange looking fleet of starships in various shapes and sizes, metallic looking in nature slowly travel towards it. They are the Korrinion, a human like race of beings that are highly intelligent, intellectual, advanced and driven by a common cause...seek out those who have opposed them in the past with complete vengeance. The Korrinion once a very powerful race, dared to impose their own laws upon many worlds. A time soon came when the galactic council ruled to put an end to the Korrinion's ways, by means of a great war upon their home world of Korrin. Many willing recruits from many other worlds, obliged the galactic council in an effort to put an end to the Korrinion's one way plans of dominance upon innocent unsuspecting worlds throughout the Universe. Among them, the Akkinuu, the Korrinion's greatest arch enemy. One leader now remain among the Korrinion, himself actually being a descendant of the Akkinuu...driven by jealous rage of his denial by the Akkinuu, to be granted a seat on the high council, due to his devious ways, and unclear of his true intentions.

Aboard on the bridge of the Korrinion command ship, their leader Lord Rhim Baynyu, mid thirty's, dressed in a shiny black leather type outfit, stands with arms crossed looking out the bridge window at Cathelle. There are several crewmen on the bridge at various controls. "All engines stop," Baynyu commands aloud. His and all other ships pause. An officer Commander Hunn, dressed in military style attire then enters the bridge via elevator, and walks up to Baynyu's side and stops. "My lord, we await the vital information you seek from our contact on the planet."

"How much longer Commander? Time grows weary, as well does my patience."

"Not much longer my lord Baynyu. Expect a communication within the hour." Baynyu turns to Hunn, "One hour, then we begin our assault Commander."

"Yes my lord." Hunn briefly bows as Baynyu walks away. An officer seated at a radar tracking console views a small ship entering their sector. He says aloud, "Commander, a Cathellion scout ship entering our sector!" Baynyu stops and turns in his direction, and Hunn quickly walks over to look at the radar screen.

"Send them our regards Commander," says Baynyu. He turns and continues walking away. "Fire on that vessel," Hunn says aloud. Another officer at a gunnery console pushes a red button.

Far from the Korrinion fleet, a small Cathellion vessel flying in towards them is suddenly hit with a mysterious translucent type missile, that spreads upon the entire hull, devouring it quickly till nothing remain…with a very brief, but loud scream of agony echoing away into the darkness of space.

Back on Cathelle in the capital city Terathis, it is now night fall and lightly raining, as a shuttle cab lands at an alley. Steam spews upwards from sewage drains as the passenger door slides open. Burke and Pete then exit the cab, Pete looking all around with caution and curiosity. Burke turns to the cabby and flips him a gold coin. "Keep the change," Burke says aloud, as the passenger door closes and the cab fly's away swiftly. Burke turns and looks down the dark and deserted looking alley, "Well, this is the place Belle told me of. Reminds me of back home a little…Earth that is, dark and cold."
Burke begins to walk down the alley, Pete follows.

As Burke and Pete make their way down the dark and rain drenched alley, they pass several bums sleeping in the shadows…mumbling in their sleep and persevering the cold night rain. After a moment, they finally arrive at a large door with a small light high above it. Burke looks at Pete for an instant, then back at the door and knocks four times. A brief moment goes by and no answer. Burke knocks four times again and suddenly a little peep window slides open. The face of an old woman present behind the door. "Go away! And tell your slimy boss we'll have his filthy money tomorrow," the old woman shouts then slams the peep window shut. Burke looks at Pete with a raised brow, then looks at the door and says aloud, "We are not here for money! We are here seeking our friends!" The peep window quickly opens again and the old woman asks, "Oh? Just who are you?" Burke replies, "Chancellor Landin Burke of Silus. And this is my dear friend Pete Lowery of Earth. We mean you know harm. We wish only to find our friends." The old woman's face disappears from the peep door and the door itself suddenly opens all the way, revealing a middle aged looking man dressed in pajamas wearing a thick coat, smiling at the sight of Burke.

"Landin Burke! Great to see you!"

"It's great to see you again as well Azzar."

Azzar extends his hand and Burke and him briefly shake hands. Azzar continues, "Do forgive me. Come inside." Burke and Pete enter and the old woman leans her head out the doorway, looks up and down the alley, then closes the door behind them. Once inside the dwelling, oil lamps rest on tables dimly lighting the interior filled with old paintings, worn furniture, beaded drapery and a fireplace with a few logs burning. An old tea kettle lightly steaming hangs over the fire.

Azzar walks over to a table and pulls out a couple of chairs for Burke and Pete. "Come, sit. I'll get you both something to dry off with. Be right back," Azzar says as he scurries away to another part of the dwelling. Pete looks at the old woman just staring at them, then looks at Burke briefly as he takes a seat at the table with him. The old woman wearing an old worn out dress and worn sandals, quits her staring and walks over to the fireplace and begins pouring what resembles tea from the kettle. Pete leans in towards Burke and quietly says, "So it seems you've known these people, Akkinuu, a long time."

"Yes I have as a matter of fact. For quite a while."

The old woman walks up to the table and sets down two cups of hot tea for Burke and Pete. She smiles as Burke takes his cup and gestures, "Thank you." Burke looks at Pete with suggestive courtesy, and Pete picks up his cup, "Thanks."

Azzar returns with two dry towels in hand, and behind him, a beautiful middle aged pregnant woman in a nightgown wearing a gold shawl.

"Here you are," says Azzar as he hands Burke and Pete the towels. "Thank you," both Pete and Burke reply. Burke stands up and takes the woman's hand, "Pleasure to see you again lady Lorrian." Burke kisses her hand then releases it as she smiles and replies, "You as well chancellor."

"My, soon to be expecting a wonderful new addition I see." She smiles and rubs her stomach and replies, "Yes, our second edition actually." She looks at Azzar and they both smile at each other.

"Oh, do forgive me," says Burke as he turns to look at Pete still sitting down at the table finishing with his towel. Burke gestures Pete to stand and he does so. Burke continues, "This is a good friend of mine, Pete Lowery of Earth. And you'll soon find that he's not your average ordinary Earthling." Everyone looks at Pete. Pete looks Burke straight in the eye.

Burke continues, "He is the one...the Zensmittorith." Azzar, his wife lady Lorrian and the old woman all suddenly get on their knees and bow to Pete. Pete shakes his head and says, "No no no. No need for that, really." Pete chuckles briefly then they all rise back to their feet. They all then rush to Pete's side with great honor for his presence among them. Pete looks at Burke, and Burke grins then winks. Pete rolls his eyes.

Back at the Cathellion council building, Rose now sits in front of a mirror in her penthouse, accompanied by her house maid Eseret. Eseret stands behind Rose brushing her hair.
"I'm so thrilled to have him back in my life," says Rose in regards of Burke. She continues, "Long have I waited for this day to come, and explain to him my deep regret and love for him."
"So happy for you councilor." Rose smiles and looks at Eseret in the mirror, "Eseret, we're friends. You can call me Rose." Rose grabs Eseret's hand and smiles again. Eseret smiles in return, "Ok, Rose." Suddenly from behind them, one of the councilmen from earlier walks up and stops with his hands behind his back. Rose turns and looks at him.

"How dare you enter my place without proper notification councilor Norro," Rose shouts. Norro then smiles and pulls his hands from behind his back, revealing a laser pistol in his right hand. He points it at them and replies, "As you can see councilor, I'm definitely not here properly, and don't care so either. But, I am here to know something that you, and you alone know of, and are going to tell me." Rose and Eseret both in shock at the moment. "Why? How is this possible," asks Rose. "No concern of yours! Now tell me…where are the Akkinuu hiding?" Rose stands up and rests her hands on her hips, "Are you serious? You actually think I know that? You're delusional! Who's behind this?"

"None of your concern! Chancellor Burke! He knows! You met with him earlier! Yes, I've been watching you, and you will now disclose the Akkinuu's location, or else? " Without Norro's knowing, Eseret secretly grasps the chair behind her, remaining calm and unsuspected. Norro takes a few steps forward and stops just a few feet from them, then aims his pistol at Rose's head.

"Now councilor! Tell me now, or I will be forced to kill you, and your lackey chamber maid."

Eseret then suddenly picks up the chair with all her might. She swings it at Norro, hitting him on his right shoulder and knocking him to the floor. His pistol fires a shot missing them and hits the ceiling. Eseret looks at Rose and shouts, "Run!" Norro now begins to make his way up off the floor as Rose looks at Eseret hesitant of running away.
Eseret shoves Rose and shouts, "Go now! Get help!" Rose runs around Norro as Eseret begins to take another swing at him. Rose stops very briefly and looks at Eseret, then runs out of the door. Norro quickly points his gun at Eseret as she swings the chair at him, and shoots her in the chest, killing her instantly.
"You stupid girl," Norro shouts. He then spits on her, turns and gives chase after Rose.

  In the corridor that leads to Rose's penthouse, she runs as fast as she can, and notices several centuries lay dead on the floor. She continues running and suddenly laser fire from Norro's pistol blasts all around her feet. She reaches an elevator and presses the down symbol, and the door swiftly opens. She runs in and the door closes. Norro Shouts with anger, "Ahhh!"

He arrives at the elevator and shoots the controls, sparks and fire everywhere.

   In the elevator shaft, it quickly stops. Inside the elevator, Rose now on her knees looks up with worry. She gets to her feet and tries the controls, but nothing works. She then begins pounding them, and still nothing.

   Back at the elevator entrance where Norro blasted the controls, he tries to open the doors but can't. He then reaches into his pocket and pulls out a digital timer revealing all zeros. "Damn," he shouts, then runs to a door just feet away with the word staircase above it. He opens it and runs in.

   Returning to the bridge aboard Rhim Baynyu's ship, Baynyu enters via elevator and walks to his command chair and sits. Commander Hunn and crew all present, Baynyu addresses Hunn, "Time is up Commander. No word from your source. We must now for go an all out assault on the capital…the council building especially. All ships prepped and ready Commander?"
"Yes my lord, on your command."

"Proceed." Hunn turns to the communications officer, "All ships advance toward the capital!"
All the Korrinion ships engines fire and quickly move forward towards Cathelle.

Back on Cathelle in the elevator where Rose is now stranded, she suddenly remembers the communication device Burke gave her just a while ago. She reaches in her pocket and pulls it out. She quickly flips it open and taps on the screen.

Inside the secret dwelling where the Akkinuu, Burke and Pete are, they all now sit at the table drinking tea. Burke speaks, "It is the utmost importance, that you pack and leave here as soon as possible. You know the Korrinion will seek you out and destroy you. Their hatred for the Akkinuu runs deepest of their enemies."
"Where shall we go? How much longer must this continue," lady Lorrian asks. She then looks at Pete and asks him, "You, the Zensmittorith, keeper of secrets, force to be reckoned with…what would you have us do?" Pete quickly responds, "I'd be getting my butt up out of here as quick as possible lady. That's what I would do, like yesterday?"

"Then we shall leave for the temple of Kattarus," says lady Lorrian. A beeping noise is suddenly heard coming from Burke's jacket sleeve. He pulls up the sleeve of his jacket and taps the screen of his communicator watch. He answers, "Hello?" Rose's voice answers, "Oh thank goodness! I need your help! Councilor Norro killed everyone and now he wants to kill me! Something to do with the Akkinuu!"

"Rose, where are You?"

"The council building! Stuck in elevator," their communications are cut short. "Rose," Burke shouts but gets no reply. Burke quickly taps the screen of his communicator twice, "Deek?" Deek's voice replies, "Professor, Korrinion attack ships inbound!" Suddenly loud air raid sirens are heard throughout the city.

  All over the city, people and aliens scream and scurry all about looking for safety in dwellings. High above the streets of Terathis, all air traffic diverts away from the city in every direction safely possible. Dozens of Cathellion fighter craft fly out of multiple hangers, and ascend towards the incoming threat of the Korrinion.

Back at the council building landing port, Deek stands at the foot of his UFO entrance ramp, still on a communicator with Burke. Burke's voice, "Deek, get the fleet up and have them assist the Cathellion military in defending the city!"

"Yes professor! What of you and young Pete?"

"I'm giving him my communicator! Lock on to his signal and pick up him and our new guests!"

"Yes professor!" Deek turns and runs up the entrance ramp into the UFO. A brief moment later, Deek and the Silustrian fleet quickly ascend away from the council building, Deek in the opposite direction.

Chapter Six
Search And Rescue

Back inside the Akkinuu dwelling, Pete now stands and paces with worry. He stops and looks at Burke, "This is just great! No danger huh? What are we gonna do?"

"It's what I need you to do Pete. Lead our friends here to safety and wait for Deek." Pete looks at Burke ever so curiously and asks, "Me? What about you? What are you thinking about doing professor?" Suddenly from out of the darkness in the dwelling, a young boy approximately age six, frightened, runs to lady Lorrian's side, clutching her waist, "Mommy what's happening?" She gently caresses his head and replies, "Don't worry my child. It's going to be alright." And still out of the shadows, yet another two dozen Akkinuu enter, just men and woman. Pete and Burke look at them, and Pete says, "Wow, this is gonna be fun." Burke addresses them, "Grab only what you need! We must leave immediately!" They all return to the shadows to retrieve whatever little necessities they need for the journey.

Burke walks quickly to the door and opens it. Pete grabs his arm briefly and asks, "Where are you going?"

"To get Rose. Here, put this on." Burke hands Pete his communicator watch. Pete puts it on.

"Are you serious? You could die," says Pete.
"I must try!"
"Why are you so eager to risk your life for that woman professor, after what she did to you?"
"She's your grandmother."
"What?" Pete instantly looking bewildered, as Burke quickly runs out the doorway and down the cold, dark alley. Sirens still blare all throughout the city. Pete remains in shock of Burke's revelation momentarily, as Azzar approaches him. "We are ready to go. I know of a safe passage under the city that will lead us far from the danger," says Azzar. Pete shakes it off then looks at Azzar, "Ok, lead the way." Azzar, lady Lorrian, her son, then Pete and the remaining Akkinuu quickly exit the dwelling and jog down the opposite end of the alley.

Back on top of the council building on the landing platform, Norro is present looking up at the air battle between the Cathellion and Korrinion in full swing, with the assistance of the Silustrian fleet. Norro takes out a small communicator and speaks into it, "You must hurry! The Akkinuu will escape!" Commander Hunn's voice replies, "Give me their location!"

"Forgive me Commander, but I was unable to achieve their location!"
"And we are unable to spare you!" Norro now wearing a look of fear, quickly turns and cowardly runs away toward the council entrance elevator. After a few seconds, a Korrinion fighter dives down on his position and fires its lasers, hitting Norro and killing him instantly.

In front of the council building entrance, Burke arrives on what appears to be a jet cycle. He almost flips over the handle bars parking it. He hops off and runs into the building. In the elevator where Rose still remains stranded due to Norro's handy work, she sits on the floor with her head and back against the wall, eyes closed. Inside the main lobby of the council building, it is desolate as Burke jogs to the main elevators. He reaches them and presses the up button on the first one of two, and nothing happens. He then tries to pry the doors open but no luck. He pulls out a small laser pistol and aims at the corners of the doors, blasting them. He then tries to pry them open again, and this time successfully able to pry them open. He carefully leans in and looks up, seeing Rose's elevator high above him.

"Rose," he shouts aloud, his voice echoing throughout the shaft. Inside Rose's elevator, she hears Burke's faint yell and immediately stands up and begins pounding on the doors and yelling, "In here! I'm in here!" Burke hears her pounding and yelling. He shouts again, "I'm here! I'm coming up to get you!" Burke looks straight across the elevator shaft and sees a small recessed ladder on the wall that leads all the way up. He stares at it, takes a few steps back, spits in his hands and rubs them together, then jumps across the shaft, "Uh," he shouts. He successfully makes it across, grasping the ladder and hanging on only with his hands momentarily, till getting a firm footing as well. He looks down, then up and begins climbing.

Back atop the council building, two Korrinion fighters and Rhim Baynyu's ship descend towards the landing port, as the battle in the skies between the Korrinion and Cathellion persists. Aboard on the bridge of Baynyu's ship, he stands up from his chair and addresses Hunn, "You have the bridge Commander." Hunn nods, "Yes my lord." Baynyu then turns and walks away, entering the bridge elevator.

Back in the elevator shaft, Burke continues climbing, halfway to Rose and short of breath. He suddenly slips and losses his footing momentarily, clinging on to the ladder. He then looks down, "Whew, that was a close one." He looks up and continues climbing.

Back atop the landing platform, the two Korrinion fighters land, while Baynyu's ship stops just feet from landing, due to its enormous size. Steam spews downward from ports underside the ship, as a ramp lowers to the platform. A dozen Korrinion soldiers armed with laser rifles jog down the ramp and form a line, pointing their weapons towards the council entrance. Baynyu now walks down the ramp and reaches the platform and stops. He looks all around for a moment, then continues walking toward the council building entrance. The armed soldiers lead the way.

In a deep, dark underground sewer system, Pete and the Akkinuu carefully make their way through inches of filthy rat infested sewer water. Azzar leads the way with a lantern. "How much longer till the end," Pete asks Azzar.

"Not much longer. We're almost there." Lady Lorrian suddenly holds her stomach and gasps for air in pain. Everyone stops and looks at her, while Azzar rushes to her aid and holds her. "What is it," asks Azzar. "Nothing…we need to continue. I'll be ok," she replies while shrugging off the pain. "No…we'll take a short breather, then continue," says Azzar. Azzar, lady Lorrian and their son lean against the wall together, as do the rest of the group, except for Pete. He senses something in the distance down the long dark of the sewer, listening ever so attentively for whatever it may be drawing near. A couple of Akkinuu begin talking and Pete holds up his hand, "Shh!" They stop talking and everyone looks at Pete, then forward into the darkness. Azzar quietly walks up next to Pete and whispers, "What do you hear?" Pete replies with whisper, "Some sort of crackling sound…like whips." Azzar now looking very worried whispers, "A gramphis. They were supposed to have been destroyed long ago."
"What is a gramphis," Pete asks. "You don't want to know. Most that see one, do not live to tell of them. We must turn back." Pete looks at Azzar,
"Hate to rain on your parade, but we're not turning back."

"We must."

"Come on…how bad can a gramphis be?" Suddenly a load roar with the sound of whips slashing is heard just feet from in front of Pete and Azzar. Pete remains staring forward as Azzar slowly holds up his lantern, revealing a hideous dark creature with a set of huge claws and whip tentacles. "Oh, that bad," says Pete. The gramphis opens its large mouth revealing long razor sharp teeth, then roars loudly again, spitting slime all over Pete. Azzar and all the Akkinuu begin backing away slowly, as Pete remains standing. Pete clears away the slime from his face and says, "Now why'd ya have to do that?" Pete's eyes suddenly glow white, then he holds out his hands and uses his power, picking up the gramphis and body slamming it several times, then hurling it several yards away. The gramphis now making a whining noise, turns tail and scurries away quickly. Pete's eyes return to normal as he wipes his hands together and says, "That'll teach ya." Pete turns around and sees all the Akkinuu bowed down, worshiping him. "You folks won't take no for an answer," says Pete. Azzar looks up at Pete smiling, "All hail the Zensmittorith!" All the Akkinuu respond, "Hail the Zensmittorith!"

Pete shakes his head, "Oh brother." Azzar and lady Lorrian's son staring at Pete says, "Wow! Can you teach me that?" Pete smiles at him and replies, "Don't know kid. Sorta gotta have it in ya." Pete looks at everyone and says "Let's go!" He turns and begins walking toward the dark of the sewer tunnel, Azzar rushing to his side with the lantern. Everyone follows.

  Back in the council building elevator shaft, Burke now just feet from the bottom of the elevator where Rose remains trapped inside. "Rose," Burke shouts. Rose replies, "Yes?"
"Stand back against the wall!"
"Ok!" Inside the elevator, Rose stands as close to the wall as possible. Under the elevator, Burke takes out his small laser pistol and aims at the center portion of flooring on the elevator. He shoots several times, till a circle of the flooring falls away. He then begins to climb his way up into the elevator, Rose assisting him.

  In the main corridor of the council hall, Rhim Baynyu and his armed soldiers now present and walking, searching every entrance as they go.

They soon arrive at the main council entrance and enter.

  Back in the elevator where Rose and now Burke stand, they finishing holding and kissing each other. Burke guides Rose away from the doors of the elevator, then takes out his laser pistol and blasts the corner of the control panel one time. He then approaches the panel and pries the cover off. "Be careful," says Rose. "Not to worry. This should be a breeze for me," he says as he begins pulling wires loose and rejoining them. After a moment of Burke's repair work, the control buttons light up. Rose smiles with relief and gives Burke another quick hug and kiss. "Ok, hold on. Here go's nothing," he says as he presses the button for the ground floor. The elevator begins to move quickly, but upwards instead. "Oh no," Rose says aloud with fright. Burke tries to pull the wires loose again, but is shocked and falls to the floor, still conscious though. Rose kneels down and asks, "Are you ok?"
"Yes…just a little toasty on the edges." The elevator suddenly comes to a stop and the doors open. Rose quickly helps Burke back to his feet, and they both cautiously peak their heads out and look.

They both then slowly begin to walk out of the elevator in the direction of the council hall entrance, which is located just thirty or so feet away. Suddenly Baynyu and his soldiers exit the hall entrance, and Burke and Rose quickly return to the elevator, unseen. Baynyu looks down the corridor towards the elevator for a moment, then turns and walks away in the opposite direction. "Who is that man, and soldiers," Rose asks quietly. "I don't know the man, but I do recognize the soldiers, Korrinion to be exact," replies Burke. "Why do they seek the Akkinuu, badly enough to engage in war with us," asks Rose. "Their hatred for the Akkinuu runs very deep. The great war two decades ago…the Akkinuu were mostly responsible for setting it in motion, putting a stop to the Korrinion's master plans of domination of many defenseless worlds. Sadly, only a handful of Akkinuu remain, due to a plague that nearly wiped out their entire race."

"Oh, I see. Where are the Akkinuu now? Surely you must know."

"Yes, they are in route to get as far away from here as possible." Burke peaks his head out of the elevator in Baynyu's last direction and notices him and his soldiers are now gone.

He looks at Rose, "The coast is clear. Let's go." Burke and Rose quickly exit the elevator and jog down the corridor hand in hand.

  Back in the cold, dark, rat infested sewer system under Terathis, Pete and the Akkinuu continue to make their way to safety far away from the city. "How much farther now," Pete asks Azzar.
"Just up ahead. There should be a ventilation shaft that will safely lead us out." Pete looks at Azzar with question, "Should be a ventilation shaft, or there is one?"
"Yes, it should be there."
"I thought you knew this way, from what you said earlier."
"Yes, I know this way. A dear friend told me of it." Pete grins at Azzar and adds, "Nice, a dear friend huh? Well I hope your dear friend was telling the truth?"
"Jaspy would never lie."
"Jaspy, hmm?" They reach the tunnel's end and Azzar holds up the lantern, looking around for the ventilation shaft that will lead them out. "There it is, over there," Azzar shouts and points at a ventilation shaft in the ceiling, equipped with a ladder.

"Good thing your friend, Jaspy was right," says Pete as everyone gathers around to get out of the cold, wet, rat and gramphis infested sewer. "Allow me," says Azzar as he begins climbing the ladder. Azzar reaches the hatch that leads to the ventilation shaft and tries to budge it open, but it won't budge. "It's locked from the outside! It won't open," says Azzar. He climbs down and looks at Pete, then everyone else looks at Pete as well. "Not to worry folks. I got this," says Pete. Pete walks over and stands under the hatch, looks up at it as his eyes light up white, then raises his right arm and motions with his hand as if unscrewing the hatch. The hatch suddenly begins to shake furiously, then bursts upwards and away from its casing. Pete turns and looks at everyone with his eyes still glowing white, "See? Not a problem." Everyone but Azzar and lady Lorrian's son turn their heads and look away in fear from the sight of Pete's eyes. Pete realizes his eye's still glowing and returns them back to normal. "Oh, sorry about that," says Pete. Everyone now looks at Pete. He then gestures everyone to the ladder, and they all begin to climb up and out.

Returning to the council building, Burke and Rose now present in the emergency stairwell, making their way down to the ground floor. Both hurrying as fast as they can, and both about out of breath. Rose stops and leans on the railing. Burke stops and also leans on the railing. "I need a rest," Rose says while gasping for air, Burke gasping for air as well.
"Or…a vacation?"
"Yes…a vacation. That sounds like an excellent idea."
"Come, we need to keep moving," says Burke as he straightens up. Rose nods then straightens up as well. They both begin their way down again when a door four flights below them suddenly opens. They both stop and peak downward over the railing, seeing two armed Korrinion soldiers exit and begin walking upwards. Burke looks up towards the nearest landing, with a door present. He grabs Roses arm, "Come on," he whispers to Rose. Burke and Rose quickly, and quietly make it to the door and Burke opens it and pulls Rose in, then closing the door. Once through the door, Burke and Rose see they are in a room with no other exits. Burke looks at Rose and gives her the signal to remain silent, as they hear the soldiers footsteps draw near.

Burke takes out his laser pistol, ready for any conflict with the soldiers. After a moment, he opens the door very slowly and peaks out and up at the soldiers walking up the stairs, now just two flights above him and Rose. He then looks at Rose and nods, and they quietly yet quickly exit the room and proceed down the stairs. Rose suddenly by accident almost trips and says aloud, "Ah!" The soldiers hear her and quickly stop and look down at Burke and Rose, who are now stopped themselves and looking up at the soldiers. The soldiers instantly start running down the stairs after Burke and Rose. Burke and Rose start running their fastest down the stairs as well.
"We have two council members in our sights! We're chasing them down a stairwell now, "says one of the soldiers aloud on his headset. Burke turns and shoots at them in the process of his and Rose's escape. He hits one in the shoulder, stopping him. The remaining soldier returns fire several times, but misses them. The laser fire exchange persists for quite some time, until Burke gets lucky and hits the soldier directly in the chest, stopping him instantly.

  In front of the council building, Burke and Rose run out through the entrance hand in hand.

Burke runs up to the jet bike and hops on. Rose hesitates and Burke looks at her, "Come on! Get on!." She then hops on the jet bike and puts her arms around him. Burke then starts it up and speeds away. Little does he or Rose notice, in the sky just behind them is Rhim Baynyu's ship, now engaged in the chase.

Aboard on the bridge of Baynyu's ship, him and his crew present, as he sits in his command chair with determination to capture Burke and Rose. Commander Hunn walks up next to Baynyu and stops. "My lord, most of our fleet have been eliminated, and we've sustained severe damage to our hull. Might it be a wise decision to break off our attack?" Baynyu just stares forward at a monitor displaying Burke and Rose in the distance speeding away through the city streets of Terathis. Baynyu suddenly pushes his hand sideways towards Hunn, and Hunn goes flying through the air, hitting the wall of the ship head first, so hard that his neck breaks. All the crew looks at Baynyu with fear, and Baynyu says, "Anyone else believe we should retreat?" The entire crew shake their heads and reply, "No my lord," then quickly look away.

Chapter Seven
Narrow Escape

Baynyu's ship engines suddenly begin to smoke and malfunction, losing acceleration quickly. On his command bridge, the navigator turns to him, "My lord, all main thrusters are malfunctioning!" Baynyu's face grows angry and he shouts, "No! Get them back online, now!" The navigator replies humbly, "Yes my lord. I shall do my best." The navigator turns to his control console and works his fingers furiously. Suddenly the sound of the engines and all power shutting down are eminent. Baynyu shouts again, "No!" He slams his fist down on the arm rest of his chair and breaks it completely off.

In the near distance overlooking the streets of Terathis, Burke and Rose still speed away out of sight to safety.

On the far edge of Terathis, Burke and Rose continue speeding away on the jet cycle towards barren looking desert land. "Rose," shouts Burke as she hangs on for dear life. "Yes?"
"Do you still have the communicator I gave you?"
"Yes! But it doesn't work!"
"Hang on!" Rose holds him tighter, as he throttles up and jets away twice as fast.

Back to where Pete and the Akkinuu are present in the ventilation shaft, they come to its end. A single grate with rusty hinges on the opening is all that blocks their way from safely escaping the city. Pete walks up to it and pushes on it, and it easily opens sideways, squeaking. Pete turns to look at everyone with a smile, "Well that was easy." Everyone and Pete now exit to the outside of what appears to also be barren desert. In the distance, the sun begins to rise, yet from a west to east direction, opposite that of Earth. Many tall mountains with snow caps are also seen in the far distance. Pete takes a moment to observe the landscape of this strange new world. He looks at Azzar who is now just exiting the ventilation shaft with his wife lady Lorrian and his son, she now holding her stomach again. Pete rolls up his sleeve to use the communication watch Burke gave him earlier. He taps on it once and waits for a reply from Deek. A moment goes by and nothing happens. He then taps on it again, twice, then three and four times, but still nothing happens. "Great! Just what we need at a time like this!" Everyone now stares at Pete with question as he asks Azzar, "Where to now? We can't stay here. We're sitting ducks out here."

Azzar walks up to Pete, then points over Pete's shoulder towards the mountains and replies, "There, just over that first mountain is where we can find safety." Pete turns and looks in the direction where Azzar points and says, "You gotta be kidding!" Lady Lorrian and her son walk up to Pete and Azzar. She also looks in the same direction and adds, "Yes, the temple of Kattarus...our only chance. We shall be safe there." Pete takes a deep breath, crosses his arms, then exhales and says, "Hoping any minute now I'm gonna wake up." He then turns to everyone and gestures them to follow. "Come on...let's get moving." Pete turns and starts walking toward the mountains, and everyone fallows his lead.

Back on Earth in the Lowery's residence, it is late night as Debbie lay wrapped in James' arms on the couch in the living room, watching television. On the television is an old alien sci-fi flick. Debbie looks at James and says, "It's been days. I've got a real bad feeling about Pete. This just doesn't seem right." James cuddles her, then kisses the top of her head and replies, "I know honey. I'm feeling the same way, helpless and worried in the same breath.

We can only hope that for whatever reason Burke decided to take Pete wherever, that it's nothing serious, and Burke does bring him back home soon, safely." Debbie's face now saddened, as she sheds a few tears and stares down at the floor with silence. James continues to cuddle her, and looks at the floor as well.

  Back on Cathelle somewhere far away from the capital city Terathis, Burke and Rose now stopped, off of the jet cycle and sitting on a small rock formation. The sun is now high and very hot as Burke and Rose both use handkerchiefs, wiping away their sweat. Burke pulls out the communicator he gave Rose earlier and taps twice on the screen. "Deek, come in Deek! Can you hear me?" After waiting for a brief moment, Deek's voice responds, "Yes professor?" Burke smiles with relief and says, "Where is your location? And have you picked up Pete and our friends?"
"Located above the planet we are. Picked up Young Pete and friends we have not."
"Why not?"
"Locate them we cannot. Signal is weak."
"What of the attack, the Korrinion?"

"Defeat them we have. Korrinion vessels, a few only remain."
"Ok…lock on to my signal and pick us up. And inform the rest of the fleet to continue assisting the Cathellion forces till further notice."
"Yes professor. Your way we are headed now."
Burke then taps on the screen of the communicator one time, then speaks into it, "Pete? Pete?" After a moment he puts the communicator away and looks at Rose. "It's no use. They must be free from the city and on their way to the temple by now."
"The temple? Temple of Kattarus?"
"Yes. Why so surprised? You do know of it, right?"
"Yes, but long since has it been forbidden for anyone to enter. The council established the ruling long ago, since your Akkinuu friends left the council." Burke stands up and adds, "And to my understanding, it was for good intentions as I recall." Rose now silent as Burke walks up to the jet cycle, opens a compartment on the center console and pulls out a round silver flask. He opens it then smells it. He then walks back to Rose and hands her the flask. "Here," he says as she takes it and opens it, then smells it herself. She looks at Burke strangely and asks, "What is this?"

"Doomga brandy. It's good, try it." Rose takes another whiff and hands it back to him.

"Thanks, but no thanks." Burke smiles and says, "Ok, suite yourself." He drinks the entire flask, then burps. "Pardon me."

"Some things never change," says Rose.

"Yes…some things," replies Burke. They both then share a little laugh together.

Returning to the skies over Terathis, Baynyu's ship now hovers motionless and alone, as just a few Korrinion fighters remain in combat with Cathellion and Silustrian forces in the distance. A bay door underside of Baynyu's ship begins to open. Inside the ship's bay, Baynyu himself sits in a fighter craft cockpit, ready for takeoff. The look on his face is of fierce determination. The bay door now fully opened, Baynyu takes off quickly out of the bay. Once outside, a Cathellion fighter crosses his flight path, and he fires upon it, destroying it immediately. He continues onward at great speed in Burke and Rose's last known trajectory.

At the base of the snow capped mountains where Pete and the Akkinuu journey to, they reach a narrow valley that appears to cut through. Strange looking trees that resemble pine trees, and rocks of different shapes and sizes are scattered throughout the landscape. Pete notices something very faint shining in the distance and stops walking. Everyone else also stops walking and Pete asks, "What is that?" "Our destination, the great temple of Kattarus," replies Azzar. Azzar holds up his hands and cheers, "Kattarus!" All the Akkinuu cheer as well, except for lady Lorrian who now holds her stomach in great pain. Azzar notices and quickly comes to her aid again. "We must hurry. It is almost time," she says to Azzar while short of breath. Lady Lorrian looks down at the ground and moans in pain briefly, as her water breaks. She looks at Azzar with fear, he then looks at Pete. "We must get her to the temple." Their son asks, "What's wrong mama?" She looks at him and replies, "It's ok. You're gonna have a new brother or sister soon." They both smile as Pete looks towards the temple, then back at Azzar and lady Lorrian. "I can get her there quick. No, I haven't delivered a baby before."

"I can help you with that," says lady Lorrian. With no time to waste, Pete walks up to lady Lorrian and gently picks her up in his arms, ready to go.

Azzar and her hug and kiss briefly. "Do not worry my love. All will be just fine," she tells Azzar. He smiles with tears as Pete turns towards the direction of the temple. Pete looks at her and says, "Hold on tight." She wraps her arms firmly around him, and he quickly takes off through the narrow valley, super fast, dodging rocks and trees with a breeze. Within seconds, Pete and lady Lorrian are far out of sight. Azzar picks up his son and puts him on his shoulders, then looks at everyone, "Come, we must hurry!" He then turns and jogs away, and everyone follows his lead.

  At the other end of the valley, there a very large ancient stone temple, temple Kattarus stands towering alone at the base of two very high mountains on each side. Four high turrets with a strange unidentifiable light source, accompany a large domed roof. The entire temple appears that of a fine polished stone or marble. The entrance located at the base of the structure, is centered and of average opening height, comprised of stone as well. A faint breeze blows through the surrounding perimeter, as if beckoning for the company of its long lost hosts.

In the near distance, Pete and lady Lorrian are visible, him still carrying her and running at incredible speed. Within seconds, they arrive at the entrance of the temple, Pete carefully slowing down and stopping just feet from it, and amazingly not short of breath. He looks at lady Lorrian and asks, "Is it ya know, safe?"
"Yes. There should be no one here. Long it has been since inhabited."
"Ok." With that said, Pete slowly enters into the mysterious uninhabited temple of Kattarus, lady Lorrian holding her stomach in pain.

Returning to Burke and Rose's location, they both sit beside each other on a large rock. Out of the sky, Deek appears with the UFO and lands just yards away. Burke smiles and stands up, then lends a hand to Rose. "See? Knew Deek would be here soon." Rose turns her head and notices in the distance, Baynyu's fighter closing in on them. "That can't be good." Burke looks at Baynyu's fighter and grabs Rose's hand, "Come! We must get on board!" They both run towards the UFO, the entrance ramp just now descending. After just a brief moment, they make it to the entrance ramp and run up into the

UFO. The entrance ramp closes quickly, then the UFO takes to the sky at supersonic speed, gone out of sight in a second.

 Inside the cockpit of Baynyu's fighter, he tracks Burke's UFO on a radar scope, and seeing Burke's UFO quickly disappearing off the scope. Baynyu growls a little, then turns his fighter towards their last known trajectory.

Chapter Eight
Arrival Of Hope

In the ancient temple of Kattarus, Pete still carry's lady Lorrian while walking down a large corridor lined with ancient looking statues of warrior and goddess type figures. The walls and ceilings also appear that of a fine polished marble and stone, illuminating the entire interior. The only sounds present are those of Pete's footsteps, and the very faint sound of wind bellowing through the open corridor. After a moment, they arrive at the corridor's end, and the beginning of an enormous domed hall. Pete stops and stares. "Wow," he says as he marvels at a kaleidoscope of paintings all over the ceiling, and light piercing its way through crescent shaped windows, illuminating a clear watered pool in the center of the floor. "There, the pool," says lady Lorrian. Pete nods and walks over to the pool and gently sets her down next to it. "What now," asks Pete. She then slowly gets into the pool only waist deep. "What are you doing," asks Pete. "This is the safest way, for both of us."
"Really?"
"Yes. You must join me." Pete scratches the back of his neck then replies, "Ok." Pete then slowly enters the pool as well. "Wow! It's cold!"
"My apologies."

"Oh no, I'll be fine." She then leans her head back on the edge of the pool, grabs the edge firmly, then begins to breath heavy and push, helping her baby enter the new world. Pete stands motionless, staring at lady Lorrian through the routine she and so many other expecting mothers have performed for so many centuries. She then raises her legs, her feet next to Pete's side. His eyes grow wide and he asks, "Um, what now?" While she breathes heavy and pushes, she instructs Pete to grab her feet, and he does so. "This is it…here it comes," she says as she growls one last long time. Pete almost looking traumatized at the moment, reaches down with both hands, feeling for the newborn. He gets a hold of it and quickly holds it up out of the water, it being a beautiful baby girl. The baby cries as he hands her to lady Lorrian, she now smiling and eyes filled with tears of joy. Pete now smiling as well, as lady Lorrian cradles her in her arms, and the baby stops crying. She looks at Pete with gratefulness, "Thank you so much Pete."

"Oh, it was nothing, really. Just glad to see you two are ok now." Pete exits the pool, and begins trying to ring out his clothes. "Yes, it was something, something very honorable. And I shall honor you."

She looks at her beautiful newborn baby and says, "I shall call her, Hope Petra." Pete smiles and adds, "I could live with that name. Thanks."

  Returning aboard the bridge of Burke's UFO, Deek and crew at the controls, as Burke and Rose sit near the bridge window talking. "You sure you know of the temple's location," he asks Rose. "Well, I remember it being somewhere near a mountain region. That's about all I remember."
"Great. That only helps a little, considering there are several mountain regions all over Cathelle." Burke thinks to himself for a minute, then adds, "I suppose we better start with the closet ones to the city first. Maybe we'll get lucky." Burke turns to Deek, "Deek, set a course for the mountain regions nearest the city!" Deek nods and replies, "Yes professor!" Burke turns to Rose and says, "All these years, and never once you nor I ever ventured there."
"Yes…hard to believe."

  Returning to the valley that leads to the temple Kattarus, Azzar still carries his son on his shoulders and walks quickly, as the rest of the Akkinuu follow close behind. He briefly looks back at them and shouts, "We are almost there! Steady your pace!"

Back in the temple, lady Lorrian now lay on the floor next to the pool, cradling her newborn baby girl Hope, while Pete walks around the huge domed hall. He walks up to the walls, examining them, touching them, and notices a small entrance behind an ancient statue of a man wielding a crescent shaped weapon in his hand. Pete turns to lady Lorrian and asks, "Where does this lead to?"
"The final resting place of the great Kattarus himself."
"Himself," asks Pete.
"Yes. He was the last Zensmittorith, beholder of all wisdom, and keeper of peace two thousand years ago. His last journey was in fact your world, Earth."
Pete turns and looks at the statue of Kattarus and says, "Is that so?"
"You the new Zensmittorith…your destiny lay before you now." Pete turns to her again and replies, "My destiny? Before me? What do you mean?"
"There, beyond the entrance to the great Kattarus, in his very tomb. Only you posses the power to gain entrance, and fulfill what you are destined to be."
Pete turns and stares at the eerie dark entrance.

Returning aboard the bridge of Burke's UFO, he now assists Deek at the main controls, viewing a monitor showing mountain terrain. Rose sits alone by the bridge window, viewing the top of mountain peaks passing by. "Get us lower and closer Deek," asks Burke. Deek with his right hand already stationary on a lighted panel, slowly moves his hand and through the bridge window, their flight path takes them lower and closer to the mountains. Rose now stands and leans on the bridge window, looking for the temple of Kattarus.

In the middle of a snow covered mountain pass, the sky is clear as can be and a brilliant blue, as a light wind softly brushes the top of glistening snow drifts. Suddenly Burke's UFO streaks by at mach one speed, clouding the entire view with snow dust.

Returning to the cockpit of Rhim Baynyu's fighter, he too proceeds towards the same mountain region as Burke's UFO. A communication on his com link comes through from one of his crew, "My lord Baynyu! We are under heavy attack! Our engines still offline!" The sound of a huge explosion is suddenly heard, then followed by total silence.

Baynyu's face grows incredibly angered, as he continues to push forward with determination to find Burke and the Akkinuu.

  Back above the city of Terathis, Baynyu's starship explodes all throughout, as it falls to the streets below, with one last great explosion. A moment later, residents of Terathis exit their dwellings and look upon the remains of it and cheer loudly. The remaining Cathellion and Silustrian craft perform a victory fly by over the wreckage and residents.

  Back inside the temple of Kattarus, Pete removes his jacket, now much drier, and carefully places it over lady Lorrian and her newborn baby girl Hope. She smiles and says, "Thank you." Pete smiles and replies, "No problem."
"No problem? What is this Earth meaning?"
"You know, you're welcome."
"Oh, much thanks Pete." Suddenly the sound of people running closes in, as a familiar voice, Azzar's, echoes loudly throughout the temple, "Lorrian! My Lorrian!" Lady Lorrian shouts back to his voice, "Here Azzar!" Azzar still carrying his son on his

shoulders, and the rest of the Akkinuu now enter the ancient domed hall. Azzar seeing lady Lorrian holding their newborn baby Hope, smiles with relief and happiness. He runs faster to her side and carefully sets down their son, gets on his knees and kisses her. The rest of the Akkinuu also filled with joy to see she and newborn baby Hope are safe. Azzar then gazes upon his new beautiful baby girl. He instantly smiles with tears of joy, as he cradles her head and kisses her forehead. Their son also gets on his knees next to them and smiling, then says, "Wow. Am I gonna have a baby when I grow up too?" He then looks down at his stomach and places his hands on it. Everyone then laughs briefly, and lady Lorrian replies, "Not exactly Januu." Pete instantly looks surprised to hear his name and asks, "Did you just say Januu, as in Januu Yasuun?" Everyone looks at Pete as Azzar stands up with excitement and replies, "Yes, my grandfather's name. Do you know of him, and where he might be?" Pete knowing of Januu's passing and not wanting to ruin the precious moment of their child's birth, shrugs it off by saying, "Um, not exactly. Professor Burke spoke of him once. Yeah, that's it." Azzar's face quickly dims of hope as he says, "Oh, I see."

Azzar approaches Pete and hugs him while saying, "Thank you all powerful one! I'm eternally grateful for what you have done!" At this point, Pete remains speechless, as Azzar remains hugging him for a moment. Azzar then draws away and humbly bows with praying hands, and returns to lady Lorrian's side. Pete then turns and looks in the direction of Kattarus' tomb.

Returning to the bridge aboard Burke's UFO, Rose and him stand leaning on the edge of the bridge window, looking out at the snow covered mountain tops and valleys, hopeful to find the great temple of Kattarus. Burke suddenly points and says, "There!" Rose looks in the same direction as Burke and says, "Yes, that's it!" Burke turns to Deek and says, "Turn us twenty degrees port side and slow us down to pulse power!" Deek nods and adjusts the flight controls.

At the front of the temple looking out towards the sky over the valley, Burke's UFO descends towards it. After a moment, it lands safely with ease. The entrance ramp opens and extends downward to the ground. Back aboard on the bridge, Burke and Rose begin to walk away to exit the UFO, as a communication from another crewman on a Silustrian UFO is heard on the communication monitor. Burke and Rose stop to listen. "Chancellor Burke! Korrinion destroyed! Won we have!" Burke, Rose, Deek and the rest of the crew all appearing happy at the news. Burke says to Deek, "Tell them wonderful job! And have them rendezvous with us here." Deek nods and gets on the com link, as Burke and Rose walk away to exit the ship.

Chapter Nine
Tomb Of Kattarus

Back in the temple, all the Akkinuu surround lady Lorrian and newborn baby Hope, Azzar and their son Januu, as Pete grabs a torch located on the wall next to the dark entrance leading to Kattarus' tomb. He pulls a lighter out of his pant pocket and lights the torch. He looks back at everyone, and notices lady Lorrian watching him. She nods, then Pete turns and enters the dark mysterious entrance. A moment later, Burke and Rose enter the temple and walk up to lady Lorrian's location…everyone smiling at the sight of them. Azzar stands with excitement and says to Burke, "Landin! A beautiful baby girl I have!" "Oh? That's wonderful!" Burke looks at lady Lorrian and baby Hope. "She's beautiful indeed. Good to see you both ok, "says Burke. "Thank you, and thanks to Pete." Burke then looks around for Pete, noticing him not present, he then asks her, "Speaking of which, where is he?"
"Where none may enter but him, the tomb of Kattarus."
"Kattarus? Where might that be?" Lady Lorrian looks in the direction of the entrance to Kattarus' tomb and replies, "There." Burke also looks in the same direction and asks her, "Tis safe, for him to enter?"

"Indeed it is. For only the Zensmittorith may enter safely," says Azzar. Burke nods then says, "I see." Burke then gets on one knee and says to lady Lorrian, "We best tend to you my lady." She smiles and nods as Burke takes out his communicator and speaks to Deek, "Deek, bring me the emergency medical kit." Deek's voice replies, "Yes professor."

Back in the dark mysterious tunnel that leads to the tomb of Kattarus, Pete continues slowly and cautiously down the narrow carved passage. The walls consist of a roughly carved stone, and interestingly have ancient painted hieroglyphics about them…human, animal, and constellation looking in nature somewhat that of ancient American cultures. Pete studies them as he continues. He soon comes to a large stone door at the tunnels end, and about its face are more carved looking hieroglyphics, but sophisticated as compared to the walls. In the center of the door, four chiseled looking hieroglyphics present…a crescent symbol, a figure looking like ancient man, star symbols, and a carved out shape of an average size human hand. Pete speaks to himself while staring at the hand, "I've seen this before, ten years ago." Yes, the same four carved stones that lay on the floor in the ancient Mayan looking temple in south America. Pete places his hand on the hand and pushes, and the carved hand glows white, then the entire door swiftly slides open to the left, revealing a set of steps leading down into more unknown charted territory. Pete proceeds down the steps, and the door swiftly closes behind him. He looks back at the door, then forward, continuing his journey to Kattarus' tomb.

  Back outside in front of the temple, Deek exits the UFO and carries in his hand a small emergency medical kit. As he gets just forty or so feet away from the UFO, he stops walking on account of the sound of something in the sky approaching. He turns and looks at the horizon behind the UFO and notices Rhim Baynyu's fighter closing in on the UFO's position. Baynyu begins firing his lasers at the UFO, and Deek quickly turns and begins to run towards the temple as fast as possible. The UFO suddenly explodes and Deek is hurled through the air from the blast wave, landing on the ground several feet away, hitting his head on a rock and being knocked unconscious or killed. The remaining crew sadly perished in the explosion.

Back inside the temple, everyone now looks in the direction of the entrance with wonder, and complete silence fills the hall. Azzar and Burke both look at each other and Burke quickly rises to his feet and says to him and Rose, "Make sure no one leaves here. I'll be right back." Azzar nods and Burke turns and runs towards the entrance to the temple. After a moment he arrives at the entrance and stops, looking around cautiously, and seeing what's left of his UFO smoldering in the near distance, and none of his crew present, including Deek. Baynyu's ship not visible anywhere either. Outside the entrance from the left side, Baynyu suddenly steps in front of Burke, facing him. Burke startled yet very angry says, "Damn you to hell! Who are you?" Baynyu grins and replies, "The last one you want to cross paths with, I assure you. And whom might I have the pleasure knowing are you?" Burke begins to back up very slowly, and secretly reaching for his laser pistol replies, "Chancellor Burke. You do realize, you're remaining fleet have been defeated, and you now stand out numbered quite so?" Baynyu stalks Burke's every footstep, as Burke continues walking backwards and hand now on his laser pistol, ready to draw on Baynyu at any given second.

Baynyu's face now grows angry, as he stops walking, staring at Burke with fierce anger in his eyes. Burke quickly draws on him but only reaches the halfway point when Baynyu waves his hand at Burke, and Burke is hurled through the air backwards, landing close to the Akkinuu and Rose. Burke not seriously injured moans in pain, as Azzar and Rose race to his side and help him sit up. Everyone else staring at Baynyu in fear, as he walks into the hall. He then looks at lady Lorrian. "Ahh, lady Lorrian…last member of the Akkinuu council to speak upon the denial of what is rightfully mine."

"The right of passage was never yours to begin with Rhim Baynyu! You aren't, and never will be the Zensmittorith! You are exactly just the opposite, evil!" Baynyu begins laughing aloud and claps his hands. He then walks up to lady Lorrian, looking at baby Hope and says, "Well well, what have we here?" Lady Lorrian holds Hope tightly and draws away from him. Burke, Rose, Azzar and everyone else remains calm and staring at Baynyu.

  Back in the deep dark tunnel leading to the tomb of the great Kattarus, Pete walks into a chamber measuring twenty five foot across by sixteen feet high. And in the center of the chamber, the tomb of the great Kattarus rests. The tomb itself being composed of a bright polished marble, gold and black in color…and interestingly, one hand symbol is present in the center side facing Pete. Pete marvels at the tomb, and looks all around the chamber with the torch, seeing that nothing but the tomb of Kattarus is present. After a moment, Pete approaches Kattarus' tomb, and slowly places his hand on the hand symbol. The symbol lights up and Pete backs away, as the lid on the tomb slides away towards the backside, and stops three quarters open. A light source from within the tomb becomes present, and Pete walks up to the tomb and looks down in it, and is amazed to see a clear casket, and the mummified remains of the great Kattarus himself. Resting in Kattarus' hands, is the strange looking crescent weapon as in the hands on the statue of Kattarus. Suddenly the lid to the casket opens up till it's fully open, and a hologram appears in the middle of the chamber above Kattarus' tomb, it being a recording of Kattarus himself. "Welcome. You are my successor, the next Zensmittorith. I wish you well being with wisdom and knowledge in your path of life. You are now the greatest hope for peace and tranquility in the Universe. Take the Lascittor from my hands, and may you wield its power with true virtuous intentions." The hologram of Kattarus fades out, and Pete reaches in and gently pries away the Lascittor from Kattarus' hands. Pete's eyes suddenly glow bright white.

   Back in the hall where Baynyu now poses threat to Burke, Rose and all Akkinuu present, he stands over lady Lorrian, and leans down to grab baby Hope. Azzar quickly stands and runs towards Baynyu and shouts, "No!" Baynyu looks at Azzar and waves his hand, and Azzar is hurled backwards, hitting the far wall of the hall and being knocked unconscious. Rose and everyone else remains still as Burke quickly races to Azzar's aid. "You piece of filth," lady Lorrian shouts at Baynyu. He just smiles evilly and continues to grab baby Hope from lady Lorrian's clutches. "No," she shouts as Baynyu takes baby Hope and holds her up, staring at her. Baby Hope looks at Baynyu with fright in her eyes, and quiet. "Don't harm her, filthy traitor," says lady Lorrian. "Such a small thing she is," says Baynyu as he continues to hold her up. Burke stands up and says, "For heaven's sake man! Give her back the child!"

"When I get what I came here for…then, and only then shall I return the child!" Baynyu then looks at lady Lorrian and says, "Now…you will tell me how I can gain entrance to the tomb of Kattarus. Or else, you shall never see your precious child ever again woman. Do I make myself clear?" Lady Lorrian now with a look of helplessness, looks over at Burke, then her people, then back at Baynyu, "Let my child and the rest of us go, and I shall tell you."
"You are in no position to make demands upon me. I will make the demands! And you will abide by them! Now tell me, how do I gain passage? The Lascittor awaits me."
"The Lascittor awaits only for the true Zensmittorith. And surely you are the furthest thing from it!" Baynyu suddenly grows angry and makes a fist at lady Lorrian and grits through his teeth and says, "Why I could crush you right now. Do not tempt me!" Baby Hope begins to cry, and lady Lorrian holds out her hands, "Please, give her to me? I will tell you."
"I know you will. Now tell me."
"And you will honor your word?"
"You have no choice in the matter."
"Very well then." Just as she begins to tell Baynyu

how to gain passage to the tomb of Kattarus, Pete himself has just now returned from there, and lurks in the shadows of the entrance watching and listening. Pete tucks the Lascittor behind his back between his waist and pants. Lady Lorrian continues, "The passage remains a secret, even kept from us remaining Akkinuu. Kattarus himself constructed this temple, and all of his knowledge and secrets perished with him. None have ever attempted to gain access to his tomb, for the sake of his curse, warning of all that try to enter besides the Zensmittorith, shall meet certain death." Baynyu now looks at lady Lorrian with doubt in his gaze. Pete sneaks up to the back of Kattarus' statue and signals Burke by waving. Burke sees Pete and quickly signals back with a quick wink. "Fables! Myths! All lies to scare away the week minded, such as all of you," shouts Baynyu.

Chapter Ten
Final Judgment

Pete quickly steps out from behind the statue of Kattarus, facing Baynyu and holds out his hands towards baby Hope. Baynyu looks at Pete with puzzlement, as baby Hope flies out of Baynyu's hands and safely into Pete's. Baby hope looks at Pete and smiles. Everyone but Baynyu now displaying a look of confidence at Pete's reappearance, as Baynyu looks at Pete fiercely and asks, "So, you must think you're the next worthy candidate to wield the Lascittor?"
"I don't think I am, I know I am," replies Pete. "And just might whom you be? You are but a child," Baynyu says with a doubtful grin. "The Name's Pete, and you're gonna wish like hell you didn't cause the people of this planet any trouble. And that's not a threat, it's a promise." Baynyu instantly wears a fierce look and says, "We shall see man child, we shall see!" Baynyu suddenly waves his hand at Pete, and Pete reacts quickly enough to counter Baynyu's power, putting his own hand up and over powering Baynyu and tossing him backwards, sending him to the ground. Baynyu sits up with a furious look, as Pete says to everyone else, "Come, take her and leave this place now!" Lady Lorrian and Azzar quickly walk up to Pete and take baby Hope, then

quickly head toward the temple entrance. Everyone else quickly follows Azzar and lady Lorrian's lead, except for Burke, who walks up to Pete and says, "Be careful Pete. He is interestingly powerful as well." Pete looks at Burke while Baynyu gets to his feet and replies, "Not to worry, gramps. Oh, and you're gonna have a lot of explaining to do when we get back home, to mom and dad mind you." Burke raises a brow and says, "Yes, explaining."
"Go now. I've got this." Burke nods and quickly walks away toward the temple entrance, Rose waits for him halfway. Everyone now out of the temple except for Pete and Baynyu, and Baynyu says aloud, "You are no match for me boy! I will have you begging for mercy before I am finished with you!" Pete grins and crosses his arms then replies, "Sounds to me like you're imagination's got the best of you! Bring it!" As Pete and Baynyu now face off from about twenty five yards apart of each other, and the pool of water center of them, Baynyu makes the first move by quickly directing his hands at the statue of Kattarus, and hurling it at Pete. Pete easily uses one hand and deflects it towards Baynyu, but Baynyu ducks and avoids it, as the statue crashes into the wall, shattering into pieces. "Not bad, not bad at all,"

says Baynyu. "You're gonna have to do a lot better than that to impress me," says Pete while grinning again and crossing his arms. Baynyu suddenly slices the air with his hand in Pete's direction, and Pete is swept off his own feet falling to the ground, but quickly stands back up and says, "Still not impressed." Pete holds out his hands towards the pool of water where lady Lorrian just moments ago gave birth to her beautiful baby girl Hope, and his eyes glow brilliant white again…Baynyu suddenly with a look of doubtfulness upon his face, as Pete makes a swirling motion with his hands, and all the water in the pool incredibly turns into a powerful whirlpool. Pete then quickly motions the whirlpool in Baynyu's direction, Baynyu putting his hands up and covering his face, as the whirlpool hits Baynyu and spins him like a top into the temple wall. Pete's eyes still glowing and he says, "More like that!" Baynyu now soaking wet, in a bit of pain and displaying some light bruising about his face and hands, slowly rises to his feet and replies, "So you wish to play rough? I can oblige you there." Baynyu grits his teeth and quickly motions a large temple column to break free and fall on Pete, Pete just barely able to jump back and deflect the column in the nick of time. "If that's the best you've got, you're in a world of hurt dude! Tell ya what I'm gonna do for you...I'm gonna give you this one and only chance to surrender to the Cathellion authorities, or we'll continue here, and I can promise you, it's not gonna end in your favor chump." "Never will I surrender! And never will any other than I wield the Lascittor! Never!" Pete takes the Lascittor out from behind his back and holds it out. "You mean this?" Baynyu's eyes grow wild with anger from the sight of the Lascittor in Pete's hands. Baynyu quickly raises both of his hands towards the ceiling of the temple, and the ceiling above Pete begins to crumble into large pieces and fall towards Pete. Pete quickly turns and begins to run away from the large pieces of falling ceiling debris, but isn't fastest enough to escape its wrath. Pete is quickly submerged in the pile of ceiling rubble, his presence nor his voice present whatsoever. "Ah hu hu hu hu," Baynyu laughs manically, then briefly claps his hands. "Foolish boy!" Suddenly the entire temple and ground beneath it begins to rumble and shake, so much that Baynyu himself can barely contain his own balance. A brief moment later, all the rubble from the ceiling that lay on top of Pete, miraculously flies up and away from Pete, him not appearing to have suffered any injury from the debris, as he himself rises up like a phoenix from the ashes of a fire. Baynyu stands still with astonishment at the sight of Pete, as Pete holds the Lascittor with both hands…the points of the mysterious weapon towards the ground. "No more chances," says Pete, as he suddenly raises the Lascittor high in the air, then quickly stabs the ground with it while staring at Baynyu with his glowing white eyes. The incredible effects from the Lascittor in the ground, agitate the earth all around Baynyu in a way that resembles seismic earthquake activity. Within seconds, Baynyu is swallowed up by the loose shaking ground, him screaming with fear for a brief moment, as Pete removes the Lascittor from the ground…and the entire ground stops shaking and returns to its normal hardened state. Pete stands up and his eyes stop glowing as he says while looking down where Baynyu last stood, "That'll hold ya." Pete takes one last look all around at what's left of the once great Kattarus' temple, then turns and walks away.

Back outside the temple, Burke, Rose and a few more Akkinuu men walk towards the scattered debris from the remains of Burke's UFO. Burke holds up a little light device the shape of a pen, searching all around for any signs of survivors from the destruction, compliments of the late great evil Rhim Baynyu. Suddenly a brief faint moan is heard just some ten or so yards away. Burke walks quickly towards the sound, Rose and the others fallow.

  From behind a large boulder near the scattered debris, Deek slowly walks out, appearing to have several lacerations and bruises from the devastation. He walks towards Burke and the others with a limp. Burke sees him and shouts his name. Deek stops walking and looks at him, as everyone else walks up quickly to notice Deek being the sole survivor of the devastation. Burke shines his light on him and asks, "The others?" Deek shakes his head with great sadness to the loss of his friends and crew. Burke and Rose walk up to Deek and assist him. A moment later, Pete, Azzar, lady Lorrian, their son Januu and the rest of the Akkinuu enter the scene. Burke turns to Pete who is standing right beside him, and hugs him. Pete smiles as Burke says, "Thank goodness you're ok!" Burke pulls away and asks Pete, "What of Baynyu?"

"Don't think we'll have to worry about him ever again. He's tucked away in a safe place." Burke displays a look of relief and says, "Pete, I am terribly sorry for all the years of keeping the truth from you. I believed for the most part I was doing the right thing…but I was wrong in doing so. Can you find it in your heart to forgive me?" Pete rests his hand on Burke's shoulder and replies, "Hmm…ok. But mom and dad, I don't know."

"Yes, I can only begin to imagine what they'll think." Everyone now stands still looking at Burke and Pete, then Rose walks up next to Burke and Pete and clears her throat. Burke looks at her with a smile and says, "Pete, may I reintroduce you, to your grandmother?"

Pete looks at Rose and they both smile, then hug. Tears of joy begin to roll down Rose's cheeks. Pete then looks at Burke and Rose with question. Rose answers, "Your father." Pete nods with a smile. Deek then addresses Burke, "Professor, contacting the fleet? Helpless we are." Burke turns to Deek and replies, "Yes…it appears we have that one small dilemma." Pete steps in and says, "Not to worry. I'll take care of that." He then looks at Burke and asks, "How can we make it back in time now, before mom and dad notice anything? Your time converter is destroyed."

"Yes, that does present a problem. But not to worry…We'll do our best to return at a feasible time, once we've joined with the fleet again. And I do believe it's in the best interest, that all of us return to Earth." All the Akkinuu celebrate upon hearing Burke's speech. Pete then pulls out the Lascittor from behind his back and hands it to Burke. Burke takes it with question as Pete says, "Hold on to this…wouldn't want it falling in to the wrong hands." Pete then turns and runs away super fast in the direction of Terathis.

Returning to Earth at the Lowery's residence, it is now night time. Inside, James and Debbie sit on the couch as we last seen them, holding each other and looking down at the floor with sadness upon Pete's remaining disappearance. Suddenly they both hear Pete's voice, "Hey mom, dad." They both quickly turn to see Pete standing behind them, accompanied by Burke. They quickly stand up and run over and hug Pete. "Where have you been," asks Debbie as tears of joy flow down her cheeks. "Just for a little trip mom. Everything's fine." Debbie then looks at

Burke with anger and says, "You! You have a lot of explaining to do mister!" Burke rolls his eyes and replies, "Yes…as a matter of fact I do." Rose now enters and stands behind Burke, smiling at James. James and Debbie briefly look at her. Burke then winks at Pete, and Pete winks back. James does a double take upon Pete's wink. Burke then places his hand on James' shoulder and smiles with fatherly love. Pete then pulls away from hugging and begins to walk towards the staircase to his room and says, "I've gotta give my friend Lynn a call. You all have a lot to discuss anyway. Oh, Lynn said Happy Birthday mom. See ya's!" Pete jogs up the stairs out of site, then Burke says to James and Debbie, "Let's see…where to begin?"

  Outside in front of the Lowery's house, James is suddenly heard shouting, "What? My father? My Mother?"

This book is dedicated to the loving memory of my beloved mother Paulette Francis Croley 12/31/43 - 12/10/16, and all others whom we have lost we greatly loved…

ALIENS BELIEVE TOO! PROJECT SILUS

Written by
Brian Hiller

Introduction:

It all began long ago, when the unknown mysterious crafts made their presence known to mankind...many different races of extraterrestrials visiting Earth, shocking mankind with their amazing abilities of mechanics and flight. And the obvious questions on everyone's mind, "Who and what are they? What is their interest with Earth?"

The further we discover more mysterious evidence of the possibility of extraterrestrial life existing throughout our Universe, the more we shall continue to learn, of what may truly be, and have been existing among us for a very long time! Perhaps, longer than we'll ever know?

Brian Hiller

ALIENS
BELIEVE TOO!
PROJECT SILUS

In Outer Space viewing Earth in the distance, the year is 1970, and Earth's atmosphere glows ever so abundantly. A satellite in the near distance glides by slowly but steadily, at a speed of six thousand five hundred miles per hour. Suddenly and fast, a shiny metallic circular object jets by the satellite narrowly missing it headed towards Earth, possibly at an approximate speed of forty thousand miles per hour, dwarfing that of the satellite's speed…followed by an eerie noise from the mysterious object trailing behind it. Within seconds the mysterious object is out of sight and sound.

It's three o'clock in the afternoon inside a University laboratory located somewhere in the state of California, as a young man in his mid thirties, professor Landin Burke, English descendant, dressed in a lab coat and wearing goggles, tinkers with a science experiment. The usual glass vials filled with chemicals roasting over Bunsen burners. He reaches into the pocket of his lab coat and pulls out a small gold coin, with ancient inscriptions upon its face. He then retrieves a pair of hemostat pliers from the table and clenches the coin firmly, next very cautiously and slowly dipping the gold coin into a vial filled with a strange red substance brewing over a burner. As the coin touches the red substance, it begins to glow brilliantly, as if a light bulb ready to burst. Someone knocks on the door startling him and causing the coin to drop into the vial, "Oh crap," says Landin as he quickly grabs the vial and throws it across the room…the vial and coin exploding loudly upon a chalkboard, leaving a very large gaping hole. He looks in the direction of the door and hears an older man's voice, "Professor! What is going on in there? Dean Gates here! Open up!" Landin quickly replies, "Everything is just fine! Just had a little spill is all!" Landin jogs over to the chalkboard and grabs a sheet off a table adjacent to it and quickly covers it, then walks over to the door. Dean Gates knocks again as Landin opens the door, and there stands your usual looking University Dean, wearing glasses and a snooty look. "Professor, the university will not tolerate your insubordinate behavior any further! Do I make myself perfectly clear?"

"Certainly Sir, perfectly clear." Gates looks into the lab briefly, then nods and finishes, "Very well. Your class will be arriving an hour earlier than the usual in the morning. So I suggest you prepare, and get a good night's rest."

Gates smiles, then turns and walks away. "Will do sir! Will do," replies Landin. He closes the door then says, "Damn…I was so close." He removes the goggles and his lab coat and exchanges them with a brown tweed coat on a coat rack and puts it on. He walks over to his desk and grabs his briefcase, then walks over to the table where he previously conducted his last experiment and pushes a button turning off the Bunsen burners. "There's always tomorrow," he says with a hopeful tone, as he turns and walks away.

Four hours later on an old country road just outside of Landin's town, the sun has just finished setting, as he drives down the road in an old sixties pickup, with the radio playing opera music. He tries his best to sing along as well. A moment later, a strange bright light appears on the road just ahead of him in the distance. He notices it immediately and turns off the radio while slowing down, curious as to what the strange light source could be. After just a moment more of driving, Landin notices two black sedans with four men dressed in black suits, wearing hats blocking the road way, facing his direction. Landin slows down and stops just thirty or so feet from them, puts his truck in park, then bravely steps out and looks at them. One of the men walks up to Landin and says with an American accent, "Professor Landin Burke I presume?"

"Who in heavens are you," replies Landin.

"Please just answer the question sir. Are you professor Landin Burke?" Landin gives the strange man a curious glance then replies, "And what if I am? Who are you gentlemen, and what does this concern?"

"Are you professor Landin Burke or not," the strange man now demands with authority.

"Yes! Now tell me what this concerns, the meaning of this!" The remaining three men also walk up and stop next to Landin's side, and the strange man continues, "A matter of the utmost importance and secrecy professor. I'm afraid you'll have to come with us sir." Landin looks at the other men, then the stranger in charge and replies, "By who's authority?"

"The highest authority sir, I assure you." Landin agrees to cooperate and walks with the strange men to their vehicles. He gets in with them, and they peel away into the darkness of the night, his old truck with the engine left running just sitting in the middle of the road.

Two hours later at what appears to be a secret government airfield, an un-marked air liner taxies down a dark runway, headed towards some enormous buildings. Spot lights from several manned watch towers around the buildings, routinely search the entire area for any intruders trespassing. The un-marked air liner slowly makes its way towards one of the buildings, and two enormous doors begin to slide open. The air liner briefly stops in wait for the doors to fully open. A moment later, the doors are fully opened as the air liner slowly and cautiously makes its way into the building. Once inside, several military soldiers carrying machine guns run towards the entrance of the building and form a line, guarding it as the doors begin to close. On the opposite side of the building, many freshly constructed rooms are visible, with a few distinguished looking men and women wearing white lab coats, entering and exiting the rooms. The air liner's engines begin to throttle down, as its entrance door opens. A stair truck quickly arrives at the entrance door, as Landin walks up and stops at it accompanied by two of the strange men from earlier. He stares all around, especially at the rooms with the men and women dressed in the lab coats working.

"I assume you'll be telling me now what this is all about," says Landin. "Soon enough Mr. Burke, you will know. After you," implying Landin to exit the air liner replies one of the strange men.

   Once exited from the jet, Landin is escorted by the strange men in the direction of the lab rooms. A moment later, one of the doors open and a military General accompanied by a lovely young woman dressed in a blue, tight elegant outfit holding an odd looking notepad, walk up to Landin and the strange men then stop. The general holds out his hand to greet Landin, "Hello professor Burke. I'm General Slater." Landin holds out his hand with no haste. They shake and Landin replies, "Slater huh? Heard of you once before." They finish shaking and Slater introduces the lovely woman, "This is Rose. She will be briefing you as to why you are here, and why she, we'll be needing your assistance concerning a very important top secret issue. And professor, one more thing…she's not your ordinary woman. " Landin looks at Rose, and her him. They both stair into each other's eyes, instant attraction occurring.
"You could say that again," says Landin. They both smile as Landin takes her hand and gently

Kisses it, "My pleasure Rose."
"Thank you," Rose replies as the general adds, "We'll be seeing you later professor."
"General." Slater and the strange men walk away as Landin and Rose continue staring at each other, smiling. She pulls her hand away and says, "My, you Earth "hm hm", I mean you are quite over bearing." Landin briefly looks at her with puzzlement and replies, "Just to a certain degree my good lady. Am I missing something here?" Rose turns and begins walking towards the lab rooms and replies, "And very inquisitive I might add."
"Well, given the situation, it's only human to be curious." They both reach one of the lab rooms and stop. Its door still closed, and Rose turns to Landin, "What I'm about to show, is completely confidential. I must have your sworn promise you will tell no one of this."
"For you my lovely lady, you have my sworn promise. I'm ever so eager to see what this is all about."
"Very well then…but I warn you, you are about to see something that only I, and a few others here from Earth have ever seen. And you may be frightened."

"Not to worry…I've seen many things that would frighten the dickens out of most!" Rose grins and replies, "Oh? For your sake professor, I hope your right?" She then turns and opens the door to the lab.

There in the room under several bright examination lights, three bluish grey short aliens sit in chairs conversing with other people in lab coats taking notes. The look on Landin's face is somewhat of a shocking look. He then smiles and says, "I knew it! All this time it's been covered up, the truth!" All the aliens then glance over at him as Rose replies, "For many good reasons it has been." She takes his arm and asks, "Would you like to meet them? Come." She leads him over ever so slowly to greet the aliens. They arrive just feet away and the aliens all bow briefly and smile at him. Landin briefly smiles and waves his hand, then looks at Rose and says in undertone, "Do they speak English by chance?" Rose chuckles and replies, "Yes, enough to understand." The smallest of the three aliens stands and walks over to Landin and extends his hand, and Landin slowly grasps his hand to shake. "Jeet I am. Silus my home, far away," Jeet's voice sounding that of a four year old on a sugar high.
"Professor Landin Burke at your service, Jeet." Jeet smiles and nods, then walks back to his chair and sits again. "That wasn't so bad. Maybe you are

fearless as you say you are," says Rose.
"Well, there are some things I'm fearful of. And I tend not to speak of them. So, now maybe you will tell me why I've been pulled away from my average everyday normal life, and escorted here to a room full of aliens under armed military personnel, in the middle of God knows where?" Rose looks at Landin with a serious look, "Yes…we need your help. Your scientific formulas are highly noted, especially on bio engineering chemistry."
"Wow, it would seem the government's been keeping tabs on me for quite some time. Wonder what else they know about me. So what is it exactly you need, from me… and more importantly, why?"
"First, I must level with you. I'm not from here…your world." Landin's eyes grow wild full of curiosity, and he immediately asks Rose, "Where is it exactly you're from?"
"Twenty light years away, planet Cathelle in the Lexium galaxy. It is a world similar that of your Earth." Landin briefly scratches the back of his neck and says, "Heavens, I'm speechless."
"Thought you might be. Another reason your government and I believed it be best to skip formalities." Landin chuckles and adds, "And that you've done very well I might add." Rose pulls out a syringe and suddenly sticks it in Landin's arm, "Ow," he shouts and asks, "What on heavens Earth are you doing to me?" Rose draws blood and replies, "Just a small sample of your blood."

She finishes quickly and Landin asks, "My blood? What does my blood have to do with anything I'm getting myself involved with here?" Landin rubs his arm while Rose removes the needle on the syringe, then places it back in her pocket and replies, "A man of your genius, possibly a rare genetic coding."
"My genetic coding? Please do explain?"
"Have you ever wondered why you are so intelligent? Know so many things?" Landin smiles and replies, "My dear lady, I was born with it. Sure I'm gifted in certain areas, and I assure you it's only natural." Rose smiles and places a bandage on Landin's arm, then holds her hands together, "We shall soon see. Now to get to the nature of our business…I need your help to get me and my Silustrian friends here back to my world. From there, they can safely return home." Landin looking extremely inquisitive now asks, "Let me guess, you and your friends here crash landed, and need my as you put it "genius" ability to repair your ship? Yes?"
"Something like that, a little more complicated."
"Oh, how so?"
"A day ago, my friends here and I were attending a meeting between the Cathellion Council and their Chancellor, Jeet, whom you just met. Several assassins suddenly appeared out of nowhere at the council hall, shooting and killing several of our people. We were ever fortunate enough to escape with our lives."

"Sorry to hear that. So why Earth, the connection?"
"The Silustrians, my friends there, have been in contact with your people for a great time…and believed it would be wisest to find safe exile here. Upon our arrival, your Earth's atmosphere for some reason played havoc with the shielding systems on our craft. So we fortunately were able to make a safe landing here at this facility, but our shielding systems now in-operable."
"So you need my assistance to repair your shielding systems?" Rose looks at Landin with a yes, and he adds, "I've never worked on anything like that before, much less something of alien origin."
"Will you please at least try professor? We need to return and find out what is happening now." Landin remains staring at Rose's plea for his assistance, thinking to himself if his assistance will be applicable enough to help repair her craft. After a moment, he agrees and says, "On one condition."
"What is your condition professor, replies Rose. "That you address me as Landin." Rose smiles and says, "Ok, Landin." Landin smiles and adds, "That's more like it. Ok, take me to your craft, Rose." "Right this way," says Rose as she turns and walks away, Landin following on her heels.

Moments later located outside behind the large hanger, two armed military men stand guard, as the door opens and Landin and Rose exit. They continue walking under several piercing search lights in the night. After a moment, they reach what definitely appears to be a large silver disk shaped UFO, resting on the ground supported by three footed landing gear legs. An access ramp from the UFO suddenly lowers down, and Landin stops walking, staring with great intrigue. Rose stops walking as well and looks at Landin as he says, "My word…I never imagined the day I would actually see one, much less ever board one for that matter." Rose smiles and replies, "This should be quite interesting for you then."

"Oh…you could say that alright." Another Silustrian alien present on the UFO, walks up to the entrance and stops while greeting with a smile. Landin smiles back and continues to walk up the entrance with Rose into the UFO. Once inside, they continue to walk up another ramp that spirals upward to the main bridge…Landin ever so intrigued now. "Incredible," says Landin. Once all the way up the ramp, they arrive on the bridge, and Rose walks up to the main control console touching an indicator screen, bringing up the UFOs diagnostics information. Landin walks up and stops next to her, looking at the screen and says, "Amazing! I still can't believe this is really happening. Your ships central computer," he asks. "Yes. If you're able to understand the diagnostics it is revealing, you will see the main shielding system is insufficient." Landin looks closely at the screen, then after a moment says, "Yes, I see. What sort of projection array does it use?" Rose looks dead at him and replies, "See? You are very intelligent, perhaps more so than any other Earthlings?" Landin smiles and modestly says, "Well, maybe not the most intelligent, but able to make do when it comes to certain things." Rose smiles and adds, "Yes." Landin continues to study the diagnostics on the screen.

Meanwhile back in the hanger, alien Jeet exits the examining room and walks towards a room located near the end of the hanger. He suddenly stops just feet away from the door, on account of hearing General Slater speaking to someone else in the room. Jeet eavesdrops ever so quietly.
Slater's voice," This must be kept secret. They must not learn of our plans to detain them. Another man's voice replies, "Don't worry about a thing sir. These aliens won't suspect a thing. And when we have them finally detained at zero station, we can begin our research." "Good. I'm glad the pulse beam your men created was able to take out their shielding system. And to think, they actually think professor Burke will succeed in fixing it." Slater and the other man begin to laugh, and Jeet quietly but quickly walks away un-noticed. He quickly walks back to where his other Silustrian companions sit in the room. He reaches the door and it suddenly swings open. There, an armed soldier holding a machine gun points it at Jeet, him freezing in his tracks. "Where do you think you're going," says the soldier.

The soldier then motions Jeet with his gun to walk back towards the room where Slater is present. Jeet complies. After a moment they reach the room. The soldier opens the door and forces Jeet to enter. "Sir, I believe we have a problem," the soldier says to Slater. Jeet looks up at Slater and Slater replies, "Is that so?"

  Back inside the UFO, Landin and Rose both help each other disassemble one side of the main control console. Landin laying on his back and prying on a panel, as Rose holds a tray of strange looking hand tools. Landin suddenly pulls his right hand away in pain from a sharp corner of the panel, "Ahh," he shouts. He briefly shakes his hand, then Rose holds his injured hand. "Let me see it," she asks. Landin says, "Oh it's nothing." He then looks up at her, staring deeply into her eyes in a trance. Rose rubs his hand briefly then while still holding it, looks at Landin staring into her eyes. She smiles then releases his hand while saying, "Shall we continue?" Landin smiles and replies, "You're a tough one to crack. Yes, let us continue."

  Back inside the Hanger at the rear entrance door, another Silustrian alien opens the door and stops, looking in the direction of Slater's location, seeing the armed soldier holding his gun pointed…but cannot see who he has it held on. The alien quietly and slowly approaches the door to Slater's location, then stops just fifteen or so feet away…seeing that it is Jeet being held at gun point. The alien listens in on the conversation. "What is it you've heard," Slater demands from Jeet. Jeet shakes his head and replies, "Heard? Assure of nothing I heard." Slater takes a seat behind a makeshift office desk, leans in on his elbows and says, "Assure me huh? I think you're lying to me. Looks like we're gonna have to do this the hard way." Slater then signals the soldier to shove Jeet into the room and closes the door. The alien quickly turns and runs away to the entrance which he entered. He makes it there and exits calmly due to the fact of the two armed soldiers standing guard on each side of the entrance outside.

Back at the door leading to Slater's room, the door opens, and out walks a strange looking man dressed all in black and wearing shades. He looks around very briefly, then closes the door and walks away towards the main entrance in the Hanger.

Returning inside the UFO, Landin and Rose continue their work at the main control console…trying to fix the shielding system. Landin pulls out an odd looking fuse filled with a red substance and says, "I believe this could be the problem. It appears to be shall I say, baked?" Landin hands the fuse to Rose and she says, "You mean no longer of use?" Landin chuckles and replies, "Yes. What are those contents, liquid composed of?" "Trimonium hydrochlorinite."

"Hmm? Never heard of that before. Do you have a spare one anywhere aboard your ship?" Rose tightens her lips and shakes her head, then replies, "But its contents may be obtained here on your Earth."
"Oh? And where might we find it?"
"You do have a laboratory?"
"Well yes, I do. You think I might have its identical compound there?"
"Yes, you may." Suddenly the alien that witnessed Jeet's detainment arrives and says, "Hurry we must! Danger we are in! Jeet captured! Slater man!" Rose and Landin both looking shocked. "Where is Jeet," asks Rose. "Room with Slater man and gun!" Rose quickly rises to her feet, the same for Landin, and she reaches into her pocket and pulls out a very small laser gun. "You stay here with the professor! I'll be back soon. In the event I don't return, take off for Silus!"
"Wait a minute," says Landin. Rose looks at him and he continues, "I'm coming with you, and not voyaging off to god knows where with your friends here!"
"No, it's too dangerous!"
"I've lived my whole life in danger! I am coming with you, whether you like it or not. Let's go." Rose grins then nods for him to follow, as they both leave the bridge. Outside the UFO, Rose and Landin exit calmly, on account of the two armed soldiers present at the entrance door. Rose and Landin walk up to

the door, Rose smiles and the soldiers smile back. Suddenly the voice of another soldier speaking on one of the soldiers hand radios, "Attention! All personal commence detainment of the visitors!" The smiles between the soldiers and Rose quickly transform to intense stares. The soldiers raise their machine guns, but are countered by Rose drawing her laser gun and firing at one, hitting him in the shoulder, and Landin punching out the other. Both soldiers down and out for the count, Landin and Rose look at each other and nod, then continue through the entrance. A siren now begins to scream in the dark night air.

Once inside, Landin and Rose quietly and cautiously run up to a corner of one of the walls, where Jeet is detained. They peek around the corner to see several soldiers running around, searching for them. The door to the first lab room where the other Silustrians are present suddenly opens, and out walks the remaining two Silustrians held at gunpoint, being escorted towards Slater's office. Rose and Landin both look at each other again and nod. When the soldiers and captive Silustrians get near the door to Slater's office, Rose jumps out and shoots at both of the soldiers, hitting them and sending them quickly to the floor. "My, quite the aim you have," says Landin. The two Silustrians smile and walk quickly to Rose and Landin. "Get to the ship. Hurry," says Rose, and the two jog away very quickly towards the entrance. Rose and Landin both walk up quickly to Slater's door, while the alarm continues to blare throughout the entire complex…and several lab technicians and soldiers scurry about. Rose still with her laser gun drawn, looks at Landin as he implies he'll open the door on three. They both nod and Landin grabs the door knob and counts to three quietly. He opens the door all the way and Rose jumps in the room with her laser gun aimed dead at Slater's head. Slater doesn't so move a muscle, while the soldier quickly aims his machine gun at Rose, and Jeet standing in between everyone. Landin ever so slowly enters the room and stops behind Rose. "Don't think for a moment I won't end you General," says Rose. Slater slowly looks at the soldier and says, son, put down your weapon." The soldier hesitates, and Slater adds, "That's an order!" The soldier still hesitating, "Now," shouts Slater, and the soldier finally complies, slowly setting his machine gun on the floor. Rose kicks it away from his feet then says, "Why General? Explain the reason for your actions?"

"You won't get out of here alive," replies Slater. "That's where you're wrong General. Consider your relations between the Silustrians, and my people over!" She then signals Jeet to exit the room. The soldier's machine gun at Landin's feet, he picks it up and asks Slater, "Yes, why General? Why have you done this?" Slater remains silent and shrugs his neck with no reply. "What do we do with them," asks

Landin. Rose signals Landin to exit the room and he does so. Rose then slowly backs up, her laser gun still aimed at Slater, and when fully out of the room, quickly closes the door and aims her laser gun at the steel construction door frame. She fires several times, welding the door shut. She then turns to Landin and Jeet, "Hurry," as they all run away towards the rear entrance. "Over there," a soldier shouts, as machine gun fire is heard, and bullets ricocheting all around them. They all safely reach the entrance and exit. Rose once again closing the door and sealing it shut with laser fire. Everyone quickly returns to the safety of the UFO, the entrance ramp closing quickly behind them.

Once inside, Rose, Landin and all Silustrian aliens occupy the main bridge…Rose and Jeet immediately assuming control at the control console. "Are you doing what I think you're doing," Landin asks Rose. The UFO begins to make a strange humming noise, as Rose replies, "Yes. You better take a seat over there and strap yourself in!" Landin takes her advice and hurry's over to a row of four seats located near what appears to be a window. He straps himself in the left center seat and says aloud, "Where are we going?" Rose ignores Landin's question, as she and Jeet continue with the controls. Three of the other Silustrians also hurry over and sit next to Landin, they too strapping themselves in. They look at Landin and smile, then he smiles back and nods.

Outside the UFO, The landing gear retracts and the UFO remains stationary, defying all gravity. Suddenly, several military soldiers riding in trucks race towards the UFO, and search lights focus intensely on it as well.

Back inside Slater's office, he and the soldier are both trying to bust the door open free, compliments of Roses handy work. Slater stops and shouts, "Damn aliens!"

Returning to the view of the UFO hovering off the ground, it suddenly launches upward at an incredible speed, just in the nick of time as the armed soldiers aim their guns at it.

Inside the UFO, Landin holds his seat firmly, "WOO," he shouts. Through the bridge window, the Earth seen getting further and further away…seemingly at a rate of thousands of miles per hour. Landin viewing it says aloud, "Where are you going?" Rose replies, "Not to worry. All will be fine soon." Landin turns and looks at Rose, "Fine soon? What do you mean fine? I would hardly say this is fine." Rose looks at him and says, "My apologies, but we must return to Cathelle." Landin quickly displays a look of shock and says, "You're taking me to your home world? Where's my say in all of this?" "It's the only choice we have now. Besides, your people will be looking for you now…and that itself can't be safe. Would you agree?" Landin thinks for a moment and replies with reluctant tone, "Yes, that could very well be the case now. But what of your shielding systems? Will the atmosphere of your planet play havoc on the ship? Burn us to a cinder? And what of foreign space debris?"

"A chance we'll have to take. When we arrive, we'll enter the atmosphere at an accelerated velocity. Our atmosphere is much different then that of your Earth."

"How so," asks Landin. "Its density is less greater than of Earth's. Therefore we won't heat up as much as we would from your Earth's atmosphere." Landin raises a brow and says, "Hmm, that sounds logical enough. So, how long before we reach your planet? And just how far away is it might I add?" "Twenty cycles…as your people say light-years. And we shall be there in a matter as your people say, two hours." Landin now looking surprised by Rose's reply, "Good heavens! I would've never imagined that possible! This is all so incredible!" Rose smiles and adds, "You will surely enjoy seeing my world for the first time as well." Landin also smiles and replies, "And that I am certain you are right my dear." Rose looks at Landin curiously from his reply, smiles, then turns to Jeet. "The coordinates are set." Jeet nods, as Rose leaves the control console and walks over to Landin and sits next to him. Landin stares at Rose while smiling ear to ear and says, "I am very intrigued, as well as excited at the same time, to be amongst you and your companions here."

"I am pleased as well, and thankful for your assistance, Landin." He smiles again and asks, "Tell me Rose…why do you suppose General Slater did what he did? Have you any idea?"
"Truthfully, from the moment we arrived, I felt insecure…something out of place. What through me off, was the fact that he insisted upon providing us with some help."
"And that's where I came into the picture. Yes, I see. All a trick, to take you and your friends here hostage, and to do God knows whatever with you all." Rose nods and adds, "And steal our ship, for themselves."
"Rose, on behalf of all us good, descent and peaceful Earthlings, I'm terribly sorry this had to happen. Not all people of Earth are as Slater is. There is a lot of good in us, and a lot of us would rather be on good terms with you and your friends here." "Yes, I see that quality in you…and for that, there may still be some hope for peaceful relations with us?" Landin and Rose both smile, as they stare into each other's eyes.

  Back on Earth at the hanger where General Slater tried his best to abduct our friends Rose and the Silustrian aliens, the alarms have stopped and soldiers reloading into trucks. Slater exits the rear entrance where our friends last exited and stops, looking around with anger and disgust. From behind him, the strange man wearing a black suit and dark shades exits the entrance and stops just behind

Slater. "You imbecile. You let them escape," says the strange man with angered tone. Slater quickly turns facing him and angrily shouts, "Who are you calling imbecile? Do you know who you're addressing runt?" The strange man slowly puts his head down with a smile, then pulls his dark shades off and looks at Slater dead in the eyes, "It is you that does not know who you are addressing!" The strange man's eyes suddenly light up bright red, as if red flash light beams. Slater's expression is quickly as if totally shocked, and froze at the sight of it. Slater then suddenly passes out, falling lifeless to the ground. The strange man's eyes return to normal. He puts his dark shades back on and walks away into the darkness.

   Back aboard the UFO somewhere in deep space light-years away, Landin and Rose still remain seated next to one another conversing, while Jeet and crew continue piloting the UFO towards planet Cathelle. Through the bridge window, light speed is visible…stars, planets, nebulas all streaking by as if tiny specs of light. Landin turns his head to look at the amazing view through the bridge window, "So incredible! It never dawned on me, that one day I would be traveling through outer space…yet as a child I always dreamed of what it would be like. And now, that dream has become a reality." Rose smiles and also looks at the amazing view through the bridge window and adds, "So it would seem."

Landin looks at Rose and her him. They both look into each other's eyes, intense romantic attraction pulling them both in closer. As they lean in to kiss, a brief alarm sounds. Rose pulls away from Landin and looks over at Jeet, "Arrived the Lexium Galaxy we have! One cycle away from Cathelle we are," says Jeet. Rose stands up and says to Landin, "Better strap yourself in again and hang on." Landin immediately straps himself again as Rose returns to the main controls next to Jeet. Through the bridge window, light speed suddenly begins to slow down rapidly, until the UFO's speed is only traveling at a velocity of a thousand or so miles per hour. Also through the bridge window, several planets and a sun begin to show in the distance, getting larger with every passing second. Landin staring through the bridge window at the amazing new sight of the Lexium Galaxy and its planets and says, "Heavens, such a magnificent sight!" Rose smiles to Landin's complementary words and adds, "Yes, magnificent it is." Rose lightly touches a strange looking symbol on her control console screen then speaks, "We're in need of emergency landing support! Terathis control, do you read?" Landin quickly turns to Rose with concern. A man's voice then replies to Rose's request, "Yes, we read you! Sending emergency assistance now! You'll be escorted to landing port 1-A after re-entry!" Rose replies, "Thank you! Understood!" Landin asks Rose, "Is there still something you haven't told me, that I should be aware of?"

"Just precautionary measures, replies Rose. "Oh? I see," says Landin.

Just above the beautiful Earth like, radiant planet Cathelle's upper atmosphere, our friends UFO streaks by and towards Cathelle, still traveling at a rate of approximately one thousand miles per hour…easily piercing its way through the atmosphere without sustaining damage.

Back aboard the UFO, the look on everyone's face, especially Landin's is tense. The entire UFO begins to shake and shutter from the atmospheric conditions. Rose and Jeet hang on to the edges of the main control console, while maintaining control as well. Suddenly an alarm sounds throughout the bridge. "What is it," shouts Landin, as Rose, Jeet and crew continue to do their best to control the UFO. "Just a minor hull breach in the lower half," replies Rose. "How minor is minor," asks Landin. Viewing the outer lower level of the UFO's hull, a small portion of what appears to be a seam, begins to tear apart from the atmosphere's turbulent conditions. Suddenly just in the distance, two stealthy type Cathellion fighter craft are drawing nearer to the UFO.

Back on the bridge of the UFO, a man's voice from one of the fighters is heard on the coms speaker, "This is squadron leader E-1! Follow us in!"

Through the bridge window, the two Cathellion fighters become visible, and assume a position directly in front of the UFO. Landin now displays a look of relief, as the turbulent effects from re-entry begin to subside. After a brief moment of traveling through heavy clouds, the surface of planet Cathelle now reveals itself…indeed resembling Earth's beautiful land masses and oceans. Landin completely intrigued, un-belts himself and stands in front of the bridge window for a better view. "My, if my eyes don't deceive me, I'd say it looks like Earth." Landin turns to Rose with a grin and she smiles.

As the Cathellion fighters give safe escort to our friends, the surface of Cathelle draws much nearer, revealing an enormous city coming into view…Terathis, the Capital of Cathelle. Mile high skyscrapers fashioned with various amazing shapes and materials adorn the entire sky over Terathis. Enormous holographic images of advertisements adorn the exteriors of the buildings, while various craft fly everywhere on sky highways.

Back aboard the UFO, Landin continues staring in awe at the amazing sight of Terathis. "Good heavens…no words can describe this. How many years, centuries for you and your people to advance such as this," asks Landin. Rose smile and replies, "In Earth years, ten thousand. Cathellion years, eight thousand." Landin looks at Rose curiously and asks, "So, one Earth year is approximately a quarter greater than that of yours?" Rose smiles and nods, "Correct." Landin turns back to the sight of Terathis and adds, "Goodness…and to know we Earthlings are still but children in comparison."

"Not all Earthlings," says Rose. Landin looks back at Rose with an inquisitive stare.

  High above the Terathis skyline, atop one of the tallest buildings exists a landing port. Several centuries dressed in royal attire, and armed with laser rifles stand guard around the perimeter. Our friends UFO and the two Cathellion fighters begin to descend towards the landing port. After a moment, all ships land, and a few of the centuries run up and stand guard near the entrance of the UFO, as the entrance begins to open. Once fully opened, the Silustrian crew first exit, followed by Jeet, Rose and Landin. Landin wears a look of intrigue, as they make their way to the bottom of the entrance ramp, and set foot on the roof of the building. One of the centuries approaches Rose and says, "My lady Rose, your father is aware of your return and requests your presence."

"What of the assassins? Have they been caught," asks Rose. "No, but we've managed to find their location, and a team of scout soldiers are on route now as we speak, to infiltrate their base." Rose nods and says, "Good to hear." Rose then turns to Landin with a smile and gestures with a nod to follow her, as she and Jeet walk away towards what appears to be an odd looking octagon shaped elevator in the near distance. Landin follows promptly, while gazing all around at the magnificent new world. When everyone reaches the elevator, a door swiftly opens, then everyone enters, and the door swiftly closes.

   Inside the elevator, Landin asks Rose, "So, were on our way to see your father, who is as well fortunate to have survived the attack from the assassins?" "Yes. And please, whatever you do, don't tell him of our previous encounter with your people. It would not at all go pleasant on his behalf." Landin smiles and says, "Not to worry Rose…keeping a secret is one of my specialties." Rose smiles at Landin and the elevator door swiftly opens again. Everyone exits into a large hallway composed of smooth walls and floors, with more armed soldiers stationed at all entrances…Rose and Jeet turn right, Landin follows. After a brief moment of walking, an older man, Roses father Aiden Vanstrom dressed in formal attire, exits quickly from a large adjacent hallway entrance in our friends direction. His eyes light up with joy upon seeing Rose. He immediately shouts her name and jogs up to her. Rose and Aiden hug. "So very happy to know my little princess is ok," says Aiden. "And happy to know you are too Father." Landin remains still to the side, awaiting introductions. Rose pulls away from Aiden and introduces Landin to him, "This is professor Landin

Burke from Earth Father." Aiden looks at Landin very curiously, as any father would with great interest where their daughters are concerned. Aiden extends his hand to Landin, and Landin accepts. "My father, Aiden Vanstrom, Supreme lead councilman of Cathelle," says Rose with pride flowing in her words. "Tis quite an honor to meet you sir," says Landin. "A professor you say," asks Aiden. They finish shaking hands and Landin replies, "Yes. And from what I've seen here on your world already, I am most intrigued indeed!" Aiden looks at Jeet and says, "Chancellor…good to see you are ok." Jeet nods and smiles in return. Aiden then addresses everyone, "Enough with formalities. You all must be starving! Come, we shall eat." Aiden then looks at Landin and adds, "And you can tell me how it came to pass, you coming here to Cathelle." Rose and Landin look at each other briefly, as Aiden places his arm around Rose and leads the way. Landin thinks to himself, *"Oh brother, this is going to be interesting."*

In a baron area of canyons far away from the city of Terathis, hidden away from any wondering eyes, exists a secret stronghold. What appears to look like an average hundred foot high and wide wall of rock, suddenly disappears, as if a hologram shield, revealing an opening to the inside. A strange, dark but shiny looking pear shaped craft, with wings that resemble that of a jet aircraft's, fly's into the entrance and out of sight…followed by the fake hologram wall of rock reappearing. Inside the well hidden fortress landing bay, several Cathellion men are present, dressed in dark soldier attire…carrying laser rifles and standing guard, as the mysterious looking craft finishes its landing cycle. A ramp extends out and down to the ground from the craft, followed by one man dressed in what appears to be a Terathis century's outfit. He displays a serious look as he walks down the ramp with determination in his stride. Another soldier quickly approaches him and both stop in their tracks. "Is it true of scout troops knowing our location, and on their way as we speak," asks the soldier. "Yes! Prepare your men for battle captain! We've very little time!" The captain nods and jogs away, as the what appears now to be traitorous century, continues to walk away quickly towards a large entrance at the other end of the bay.

  Returning to the Terathis Council building inside the main Council hall, all of our friends are present and sitting at a long table and eating. Rose's father sits at the end, and Rose herself sits next to Landin, and Jeet across from him. "So Professor, how is it you came to be present with us here today mind my asking," asks Aiden. Landin and Rose briefly glance at each other and Landin quickly replies, "Well, it being so that my government back on Earth asked for my assistance, in trying to repair the shielding systems aboard the craft we arrived here in…and which we were unable to, due to the need for your daughter to eagerly return home as soon as possible." Aiden smiles at Rose and holds her hand, then looks at Landin with curiosity and says, "So kind of your assistance professor, but it still doesn't explain your being here now." Rose interrupts, "I asked him to come with us father, in case of any further assistance on the way here. He's a very intelligent man." Aiden looks at Rose and adds, "I see." He then addresses Landin, "Well, as long as you're here with us, please do enjoy your stay." "Thank you. Already am quite a bit." Landin takes a bite of food then looks at Rose and winks. "The current threat of the assassins is no longer a major concern, as our best scout troops are in route this very moment, to engage them and end their evil schemes, and get to the bottom of the reason behind it all," says Aiden. Jeet looks at Aiden and asks, "Completely sure you are of this Councilor, safe we are now?" Aiden quickly replies, "Yes Chancellor, completely." Jeet smiles and nods, then stands up and says, "Return to the ship I will now, and begin preparations for the shields…our journey home." Aiden stands and briefly bows to Jeet and says, "Of course Chancellor. Again, my apologies for all the horrible mishaps here." Jeet nods then walks away, as the rest of our friends continue with their dinner.

   Returning to the inside of the well hidden mysterious fortress, located in a baron region of mountains, several soldiers run around in preparations for the Terathis scout troops to arrive. The traitorous century from earlier enters the landing bay, this time while carrying a medium size black box, resembling a tool box. He quickly walks to the mysterious craft he arrived in earlier and enters. The captain watches him with concern as to why he chooses to leave on the eve of battle. He shouts, "Where are you going?" The traitorous century ignores him and continues into his craft. The mysterious craft then begins its take off cycle, the holographic wall of rock disappears, and the craft jets out and away from the bay. The captain turns to his men and shouts, "Ready with the laser cannons!"

  All around the outer perimeter of the fortress, multiple laser cannons suddenly pop out of hidden holes, ready for the in-coming scout troop's arrival. Meanwhile, in the distance the traitorous century's craft is visible but for a brief second, as it disappears at sonic speed.

  Located high up on a balcony of the Council building, Landin and Rose stand next to each other…gazing at the distant sun strangely setting in an Eastern direction. "Truly a magnificent site," says Landin. "Yes, it is, isn't it," replies Rose while smiling. Landin inches his way closer to her then says, "So...your father suspects nothing?"
"A bit early it may be for us to draw a conclusion."
"Hmm, about us…I must confess, never have I ever

felt as you would say, overwhelmed by a women before, as I am with you Rose." Rose turns to him and gently caresses his face, then wraps her arms around him, gazing into his eyes. They both quickly kiss passionately, as if nothing else in life matters at the moment.

On the top of another building just across the street from the Council building, the traitorous century's craft lands. Inside the cockpit of the craft, he touches his monitor and an image of the mysterious man from Earth, whom angrily inflicted harm to General Slater appears. "If you intend to see your sister ever again, I suggest you finish the job," says the mysterious man. The century nods and replies while gritting his teeth, "Yes, I will. You Tre'toan are scum!" The Tre'toan man smiles and shakes his finger while replying, "Now now, that is not a wise choice of words, Lieutenant Krendal. You have till tomorrow." The Tre'toan man's image fades out, and Krendal stands up and grabs the odd looking black box, then exits the craft.

Back at Krendal's hidden fortress located in a baron area of mountain region, several scout troop craft decked out with military style laser cannons, approach the fortress head on. Laser fire begins immediately between them. The scout crafts concentrating fire power on the fortress laser cannons, and after a moment begin to prevail upon doing so. Several more scout craft arrive and land just below the fortress entrance. Exit ramps quickly lower, as dozens of scout troops packing laser rifles emerge and proceed in the direction of the fortress entrance.

In a luxurious room dimly lit by candle light, Landin and Rose lay next to each other on a plush rug, while both holding a glass of red wine. Landin leans in to kiss her, and Rose obliges willingly. They both set their glasses of wine down and kiss passionately, as a swift wind enters the room from a window and dowses the candle's flames. The faint sound of a wine glass tipping over is heard, followed by the sounds of two bodies wrestling in the heat of passion.

Back on the roof top located across from the Council building, Krendal now wearing a mask walks over to the edge of roof adjacent to it and carrying the black box. He stops at its edge, where a three foot high retaining wall exists, then opens the box, it revealing four individual parts of what appears to be a laser rifle. He sets it on the ground and begins assembling it. After a moment the rifle is fully assembled, it also containing a scope, and he rests the rifle in hand pointing towards the Council building roof. Through the scope, reveals digital read out of the entire Council building roof top. He focuses in on the Silustrian UFO.

Returning to the battle at Krendal's fortress, the scout troops have managed to make their way to the hidden holographic entrance, while laser fire still remains constant between both parties. One of the scouts takes out a digital scanner and holds it in the direction of the hidden entrance. He then turns to his team, "It's shielded! We need some EC charges!" Another scout carrying a bag, quickly runs up to the entrance and pulls out three small square charges and places them just centimeters from the entrance wall. Everyone then clears the area, as the scout pulls out a flip lever switch and says aloud, "Fire in the hole!" He flips the switch and an enormous explosion of electricity rapidly devours the entire holographic entrance. With the entrance now completely accessible, all ground troops then run towards and into the entrance, firing their lasers as they go.

Inside the fortress entrance, several if not most of Krendal's men are quickly killed or severely injured during the battle...proving to be no match for the scout troops. The remainder of Krendal's men quickly surrender, dropping their weapons with hands raised high...the battle ending in just a matter of seconds. The scout troops cheer loudly, yet unaware the assassin's leader Lieutenant Krendal still remains at large. The scout troop in charge pulls out a communicator and speaks into it, "Sir, we've managed to force the assassins to surrender."

Back in the capital city Terathis, just beneath the Council building in a military control room, several soldiers sitting at consoles, and standing look at the Captain in charge of the assault on the assassins, as complete silence fills the air. He finishes speaking with the scout on the communicator, "Well done! Report back to base with the prisoners, as soon as a full sweep of the area is complete." Everyone in the room cheers loudly after hearing the good news.

   Back atop the Council building, the distant sun begins to rise as Rose's father Aiden walks towards the Silustrian craft, where Jeet now exits to greet him upon the news of the assault and capture of the assassins. Jeet takes a few steps and stops, then bows briefly to Aiden. Aiden walks up to Jeet and also bows briefly. "Great news I bare Chancellor. Our scout troops have caught the remaining assassins. There is no longer a threat," says Aiden with assured tone. Jeet smiles and replies, "This news, good it is to hear." Just a ways behind Aiden and Jeet, Landin and Rose now exit the elevator and walk in their direction, both slightly grooming themselves upon their recent actions.

   Just across from the Council building roof top on the building adjacent to it, Krendal still lay in wait, and aims his laser rifle. Through the scope, he aims at Jeet. As Landin and Rose walk towards Aiden and Jeet, the glare from the scope's glass gets Landin's attention. He stops in his tracks and peers over looking to see what it is and immediately sees Krendal aimed and ready to fire. Rose stops and also looks to see Krendal aimed on Aiden and Jeet's position. Both Landin and Rose run in Aiden and Jeet's direction while shouting to get in the ship. Aiden and Jeet both turn towards Landin and Rose with wonder. Krendal takes a quick breath, then pulls his trigger. A laser pierces its way through Jeet's chest. He looks down at his chest and notices he's been shot. He slowly wipes blood from his chest, looking at it, then Aiden. Aiden looking at Jeet shouts with anger, "NO!" Aiden then grabs Jeet as Jeet falls lifeless towards the ground. Landin and Rose arrive, Rose on a communicator and looking across the roof tops at Krendal now getting into his ship to flee the scene. "The Profit's building! Hurry, Rose says aloud in her communicator. Jeet now resting in Aiden's arms for his final moments looks up at Aiden, "End this way…do not." Jeet exhales his last breath. Aiden and Rose now shedding tears.

Krendal's ship takes to the sky and jets away, but is quickly subdued by several scout craft firing at him. Jeet's fellow Silustrians quickly exit the ship with disbelief upon their faces, and surround Jeet. After a moment, they gently pick him up and carry him into the ship with great sadness in their eyes. Aiden looks at Rose and says, "How can we explain this horrific tragedy to their Queen, how?"

Landin and Rose remain quiet, as Aiden stares with anger at the ground. "I thought we had rid ourselves of those ruthless, merciless killers! It's all my fault!" Aiden then looks at Rose with disgust. Rose quickly replies, "Father, it was not at all any of your doing! Do not blame yourself for this horrific act!" Rose holds Aiden's shoulders, as he then looks her in the eyes with grief, while both shedding tears. "I will go to Silus and explain to their Queen what has happened, and apologize on behalf of Cathelle for Chancellor Jeet's misfortune." Landin asks, "Have you a clue who that assassin was, and why kill the Chancellor?" Aiden still looking at Rose replies, "No…but we are soon going to get to the bottom of it!" Aiden quickly turns and walks away. Rose wipes her tears and looks at Landin.

Almost to the outskirts of the city, Krendal continues his escape, trying to out maneuver the scout ships, but they are as fast and maneuverable as his. He descends quickly into a route filled with many other craft flying in both directions, in a final attempt to evade them. A large square craft suddenly crosses Krendal's path, his craft smashing directly into and through the large craft, exiting through the other side…on fire and falling straight to the ground below. Pedestrians on the city streets below look up and see Krendal's ship falling. Everyone screams and runs away from the area of impact. Krendal's ship crashes to the ground, up ended, but does not explode. Amazingly, the entrance ramp opens, and a moment later, Krendal badly bruised and lacerated while still wearing a mask, crawls out of the smoldering wreckage. The scout craft arrive and land in the streets on both sides of Krendal, their guns aimed directly at him, as he struggles to his feet. "Do not move! Place your hands on your head now," says one of the scout pilots through his loud speaker. Krendal complies and slowly begins raising his hands. After a moment, he quickly turns and tries to run, and is shot with a greenish laser beam from one of the scout craft, sending him to the ground, but only immobilizing him. Two scout pilots hop out of their craft and quickly jog up to Krendal with laser guns drawn on him.

  Atop a building just a few buildings away, the strange Tre'toan man hovers in his own mysterious dark looking craft, it resembling a sleek sports car with wings. He glares at the sight of Krendal's capture, then jets away quickly towards Krendal's location on the street below. The Tre'toan man then fires intense red laser beams on Krendal and the scout pilots entire location, blowing up the scout craft and killing Krendal and the scouts…in an attempt of erasing any knowledge of Krendal's, or his own involvement in the assassination of Chancellor Jeet. The Tre'toan man then shifts his craft directly upward and jets away at light speed.

Back in the military command post located deep beneath the Council building, the commander and all his personal still remain at their posts. Aiden enters and everyone stands to attention. Aiden walks up to the commander, and the commander orders everyone as they were. "Sir, we managed to get some truth from one of the assassins, in return for a lighter sentence." Rose and Landin now enter as well, and stop to listen. "Go on," says Aiden. "Well, it turns out to be one of our own who led the assassination attempts."
"One of our own Commander?"
"Yes sir…a lieutenant Krendal, third scout recon."
"And now the Silustrian Chancellor is dead. Why him a target I can only imagine."
"We just received word that the assassin who killed the Chancellor has also been killed, along with four of my men sir." Aiden's face grows angry and he replies, "By the gods! My condolences Commander. Inform their family's at once, and send them my deepest sympathies." 'Yes sir, right away." Aiden turns away and stops at the sight of Rose standing in front of him. "Father, how are we to find out who's really behind it all now, with the lead assassin assassinated himself? Surely someone else is at the bottom of this."
"I don't know Rose. And we might never know either. When do you intend to leave for Silus?"
"Right away." Landin steps in and adds, "I'll be

joining you." Aiden gives Landin a great look of curiosity and says, "It would seem you've taken a very fond interest in my daughter professor. Not that I disapprove…just knowing what I've been told of you Earth men. Please do not bring, or allow any harm to her whatsoever."

"No harm shall come of it. That you have my solemn word on sir," replies Landin with a smile of integrity. Aiden nods, then leans in and holds Roses shoulders, kisses her on the cheek and says, "Please do be careful on your journey. You're all I have left Rose."

"Don't worry father, I'll be extra careful." Aiden kisses Rose's cheek once more, then walks away as Rose and Landin look at each other. Landin raises a brow.

  Back on the bridge of the Silustrian UFO, Rose, Landin, and the rest of the Silustrian crew are present, as Rose and Landin finish placing a panel on the main control console. "This is the part where we cross are fingers," says Landin. Rose looks at Landin unknowingly of his words, while one of the Silustrian crew walks up to the console and lays his hand on the control screen. The ship's engines begin to hum, as Rose then places her hand on another control screen, it being the ship's shielding systems. After a moment, Rose smiles and says, "Yes! The shields are working!" She then looks at Landin, him smiling ear to ear upon the good news, and he winks. Rose looks at the Silustrian crewman and says, "All is well…set your course for Silus." The crewman smiles then raises a fist with joy, and the remaining crewman smile and raise a fist as well.

  On the roof of the Council building, Aiden exits the roof elevator just in time to see Rose, Landin and the Silustrians take to the sky and zip away. He continues looking up and says, "Please do return safely my child.

  Returning to the bridge of the Silustrian craft a few moments later, Rose and Landin now sit near the bridge window, light speed travel present through the window. Rose pulls out the vile containing the sample of Landin's blood she took from him back on Earth. She slowly twirls it between her fingers, staring at it. Landin ever so curiously looks at it as well. "I wonder what we'll find, once we test this," says Rose. "Hopefully nothing frightening," Landin replies while smiling. Rose places the vial back in her pocket and says, "When we arrive on Silus, it might be best if you stay aboard for a short while."
"Yes, I understand…breaking the news to their Queen of the Chancellor's horrible misfortune, will surely be a matter of the utmost importance." The Silustrian crewman controlling the craft at the control console says aloud, "Silus very soon!" After a moment, looking through the bridge window, the craft arrives out of light speed, and in the distance a beautiful new world, Silus, of which almost looks

identical to that of Earth lay before them. Landin stands and leans on the window's ledge and says, "My goodness, it's magnificent!" Rose joins him, gently clenching his hand and replies, "Yes...it is." They both then turn and gaze into each other's eyes, then kiss passionately. The Silustrian crewman all smile at the site of them kissing.

It is daytime high above a beautiful Silustrian city, Capital City, thriving with incredibly constructed towering buildings that gleam upon the skyline, and many other strange craft never seen before, as our friends craft begins to land atop a large landing port...and many dozens more of the same craft are present. A large vacant area on the platform suddenly flashes with circular lights, indicating area of available landing.

Aboard on the bridge, Landin remains looking out the window in utter amazement at the sight of Silus for the very first time. The Silustrian crewman begin walking away to exit the craft along with Rose, her briefly stopping next to Landin, "I'll try not to be too long. Just make yourself comfortable till I return, ok?" Landin smiles and replies, "Yes, I can manage that." Rose kisses his cheek quickly then walks away, as Landin continues his observation of the amazing new world that lay before his eyes.

Outside of the craft, the Silustrian crewman exit along with their now deceased fellow Silustrian Chancellor Jeet, wrapped in cloth. Rose follows right behind them, as they are all greeted by two other Silustrian officers dressed in a sort of silvery type military attire, and carrying laser rifles. The officers quickly escort everyone away onward to the Queen's palace.

Located in the center of Capital City, is the Queen's palace, towering amongst others and adorned with beautiful Silustrian architecture…large pearl looking rings and metallic columns fastened together setting the tone. And resting on the highest column, a statue of what appears to resemble an alien like Dragon made of stone. Our friends Rose, the Silustrian crewman and the two officers arrive and enter through a large entrance. Once inside, they enter into what appears to be a very large hall, the ceilings an approximate height of thirty or more feet…they too adorned with Silustrian architecture, paintings and statues. Everyone keeps walking until they arrive at a very long dinner table. The Silustrian crewman gently rest Jeet's body on the table, all of them with great sadness about them. At the other end of the hall, a beautiful young Silustrian woman that appears to be half human looking, with large blue eyes, wearing a shimmering form fitted one piece and a platinum tiara, Queen Mirla of Silus, walks in our friend's direction with curiosity in her stare.

Back aboard the Silustrian craft, Landin remains standing with arms crossed and looking out the bridge window. Something behind him suddenly catches his attention. He quickly turns and sees another younger Silustrian alien…the alien curiously staring and smiling at him. "Earth man you are. Deek I am," says Deek with pleasure in his tone. Landin smiles and replies, "Pleasure meeting you Deek. I am Landin, professor Landin Burke." Landin extends his hand to Deek and they briefly shake. Deek nods and replies, "Know Jeet, my brother?" Landin clears his throat and replies, "Well…um…yes, I did make his acquaintance." Where Jeet, professor," asks Deek curiously. Landin under the assumption he has to be the bearer of bad news, tries to muster an easy way of breaking the news of his brother's demise somehow. "Deek…I don't know how to put this easily…your brother…he…well." Deek instantly senses something terribly wrong upon seeing and hearing Landin's attempt to tell him. "Where Jeet," Deek now demands. "Your Queen's palace." Deek quickly turns and runs his fastest towards the exit of the craft. "Deek! Wait," shouts Landin as he quickly follows Deek.

Outside the craft, Deek runs his fastest down the entrance ramp and towards Queen Mirla's palace. Landin also runs down the entrance ramp, trying to keep up with him…already panting heavily. "Deek!

Wait," shouts Landin, as Deek continues running his fastest. After a couple moments of running, Landin stops for a breather and says, "Too many burgers and shakes." He then continues on his trek after Deek.

  Back in Queen Mirla's palace, she herself briefly views Jeet's body, then looks at Rose and asks, "How may I ask did this happen?" Rose replies, "An assassin. Why the Chancellor, we do not know…but we have captured several of the assassin's followers. They will be forced to tell why, or hang for treason!" Mirla slightly tilts her head and nods. Suddenly the doors to the hall slam open, and Deek runs up towards the table where his lone brother lay dead. Everyone clears away to the side as Deek finally arrives and stops, looking at Jeet with total disbelief. Deek embraces Jeet and begins crying. Landin jogs up and stops. Everyone looks at him briefly, then Deek. Deek looks at Rose and everyone else, "How? Why my brother?" Mirla gently embraces Deek, giving him comfort.

  Located in an interrogation room in the capital city Terathis on Cathelle, five of Krendal's followers stand handcuffed to the wall, while a soldier stands guard. Aiden enters with another fellow Councilor and stands in front of them. "The first of you that make the right decision by telling me why Lieutenant Krendal assassinated the Chancellor of Silus, will receive a lighter sentence…life imprisonment. Otherwise…the lot of you shall hang for treason! Now who will be first?" All the followers briefly look at each other, then straight forward away from Aiden. Aiden then continues, "Ok, maybe this shall change your minds?" Aiden turns away from the followers and points at a large monitor on the opposite wall. A display of five more men, hanging from the neck dead becomes visible. All the followers suddenly look worried and begin to say, "Ok, ok! I'll tell!"

  Back on Silus in Queen Mirla's palace, everyone still remain standing as Deek and Jeet's fellow Silustrian crewman carry Jeet's body away…Deek's head hung low. Mirla looks at Rose and asks, "You mentioned they. Who may you be referring to?" "One of our Lieutenants, Lieutenant Krendal was in league with someone we do not know of yet. Unfortunately he too was assassinated after Chancellor Jeet. We will find out who's responsible and why."
"I see, very well. I wish to continue our relations with your people miss Vanstrom. However, the news of Chancellor Jeet's misfortune may result in a negative opinion of your people amongst mine."
"Let us hope that doesn't happen your majesty." Mirla then looks at Landin and asks, "And who might be the pleasure are you my good sir?" Landin smiles and replies, "Professor Landin Burke

of Earth your majesty." Mirla wears a curious look, briefly looking at Rose, then at Landin again. She asks him, "Pardon my asking sir…but how and why are you amongst us today?"

"Quite a long an unbelievable story your majesty. One that I still find hard to believe myself I might add. And it is of my own choice to be here among us today, even under the current circumstances. You and your people have my full respect and support your majesty. Tis an honor meeting you." Mirla smiles and replies, "Thank you Mr. Burke." She then looks at both Rose and Landin, "Come, we have much discuss." She then turns and begins walking away towards the entrance she arrived by…Rose and Landin both look at each other then following Mirla. Rose suddenly stops walking and clenches her stomach, as if a minor pain bearing down on her. Landin stops as well and holds her shoulders. "What is it," he asks. "Nothing, don't worry. You go on ahead. I'll catch up with you later." She quickly kisses him then turns and walks away quickly. Landin left ever so puzzled as Rose walks away towards the exit of the palace. "Rose, where are you going," shouts Landin. Rose turns briefly and replies, "It's a woman thing!" Landin nods and remains watching her for a moment, then continues to follow Mirla to wherever she leads him.

 Moments later, in what appears to be a sophisticated Silustrian laboratory filled with super advanced medial analysis equipment, Rose lay on a table as a Silustrian medical officer walks up to her and stops. In his hands he holds a clear type of medical chart, displaying holographic readings. "Here is the data you require. Specimen analysis complete." He then hands Rose the chart and adds while smiling, "Congratulations in order." He then exits the laboratory. Rose with all curiosity looks at the chart, and after doing so instantly wears a look of fear. She quickly sits up and holds her stomach, then looks forward and says, "Oh no. This can't be." She remains staring forward with a look of disbelief.

Back on Cathelle in the Council member's hall, Aiden and several other members sit across from one another. "Tre'toans! Filthy Tre'toan scum are the reason for the attacks," says Aiden aloud, as he slams his fist on the table. He continues, "I hereby declare war on any Tre'toan that sets foot on Cathelle! They will not manage again whatsoever to infiltrate or sway anymore Cathellion! Not as long as I myself have anything to say about it!" All council members nod in agreement.

Returning to Queen Mirla's palace, in her personal quarters, her and Landin sit on luxurious couches across from one another. "Yes, I study and experiment with many things of great interest back home," says Landin. One of Mirla's servants enters, a Female Silustrian, and pours drinks for them.

"Science has always intrigued me, but not a passion of my own," replies Mirla. Landin takes a sip of his drink as the servant exits the quarters. "Your majesty, pardon my ever so curious mind…but how is it, well, you became to be different then other Silustrians mind my asking?" Mirla smiles and replies, "Exactly, I only remember that of having a human father, and my mother being Silustrian. How I came to be is still of a mystery professor." Landin nods and adds, "A good enough, and amazing explanation your majesty." Rose suddenly enters the quarters and stops, looking at Landin with concern. Landin stands and asks her, "Are you ok now?" Rose then wears a fake smile and replies, "Yes, yes. I'm fine now." Landin still looking at Rose asks, "Something troubles you?" Rose smiles again and replies, "I'll tell you later." She then walks over to Landin and takes a seat next to him. "So, what are we talking about," Rose asks of Landin and Mirla.

   Several hours go by, as the mysterious distant sun now rests below the horizon, of this beautiful new world Silus. Capital City still thriving with illuminated buildings, strange craft of various shapes and sizes flying around…and amazingly, many different alien species besides that of Silustrian nature tour its streets and shops.

Located just outside the city at an approximate distance of only an eighth of a mile away, exists an enormous mausoleum. Several Silustrians are present holding lighted staffs and carrying Chancellor Jeet's coffin towards the inside. Jeet's coffin also appearing to be illuminated as well. His brother Deek walks behind with a great look of sadness. At the entrance ahead, Queen Mirla, Rose, Landin and all Jeet's fellow crewman stand awaiting with comfort at this very sad time for Deek and everyone else. As Jeet's coffin passes by into the entrance, everyone looks at Deek with great empathy. He nods at everyone with thankfulness in his time of need.

Moments later, everyone exits from the mausoleum, Landin and Rose right behind Deek. Landin briefly looks at Rose then walks up behind Deek and rests his hand on his shoulder, stopping Deek, and Deek turning around facing Landin. "Your brother, a great individual he was. Him and his endeavors will never be forgotten, or go un-avenged. That you have my word on Deek." Deek smiles just a little and nods, then turns and continues walking…Queen Mirla looking at Landin ever so curious while smiling.

Back at the Queen's palace, Landin and Rose present in their own chambers sitting down on a luxurious couch, compliments of Mirla.

Landin looks at Rose with question and asks, "So my dear, will you tell me now of what it is that may be troubling you?" Rose does a double take, then replies, "What I'm about to tell you, may be a bit too much for you to believe, or handle." "Try me. Certainly can't be no more of surprise than the way things have been so far." He chuckles then Rose continues, "Ok, but don't say I didn't forewarn you. I'm going to have your child." Upon Landin hearing Rose's words, he stares at her for a moment just speechless with shock. "Really? How do you know this? I mean, doesn't it take longer than just two days for you to find out?" Rose smiles and replies, "Not with us Cathellion women." Landin smiles and says with joy, "That's wonderful! So soon and unexpected too."

"Yes, soon." Landin kisses Rose, then hugs her, she now displaying worry and wonder about her face. "I'm gonna be a father," Landin says with complete joy. Rose then looks at Landin with serious intention, "I must have our child here, on Silus." Landin now looking ever curious asks, "Here, why so?" Rose takes a deep breath, exhales and replies, "Something you wouldn't understand."

"Again, try me. I'm very good at understanding my dear." Rose explains, "Two good words can explain it all…my father. He would not at all be able to accept this news."

"And why so, do explain?"

"Just trust me on what I'm saying, he never would.

And someday I'll explain to you why. Now isn't the time." Landin tightens his lips and nods, as Rose leans in and kisses him. Just outside the entrance, Mirla turns and walks away quietly with grace in her stride...also ever so curious upon Rose's words with Landin.

  Six months have passed, as a new sunrise now pierces its way through the curtains of Landin and Rose's bedroom. A strange but brief clanking noise awakens Landin. He sits up and yawns, then gets out of the bed wearing but only a sheet. The strange but brief clanking noise continues, Landin walking in the direction of its origin. Once out of the room, he stops and looks in the distance across the living room, and to his surprise sees Deek, preparing him breakfast on a large servant's tray. Deek notices Landin and smiles. Landin smiles and says, "Well I'll be a monkey's uncle, if my eyes don't deceive me? I'd say looks as if you've been quite so kind as to bring me breakfast my good friend." Landin gestures and bows to Deek. Deek smiles again and asks, "Uncle, monkey?"
"Just some old Earth humor is all." Landin walks over and takes a seat on the couch in front of the tray. He grabs what looks like a biscuit and takes a bite. He quickly but very briefly displays distaste, then humors Deek by saying, "Mm, tasty. Reminds me of one of my mother's old recipes. Deek nods with thanks. Rose now walks out of the room in a

shear nightgown, and looking as if full term already. She sits down next to Landin and smiles at Deek. "Good morning Deek," she says. "Good morning," replies Deek. "Biscuits and tea my love," Landin asks of Rose. She looks at Landin, then Deek, him smiling, then picks up a biscuit and bites. She too briefly displays distaste and places it back on the tray. "Don't think it's gonna agree with us this morning," she says as she rubs her stomach. Landin looks at Deek and says, "Thank you so kindly for the wonderful breakfast Deek." He discretely winks at him, then Deek smiles and exits the chambers. Rose leans back on the couch and suddenly exhales in pain. She holds her stomach firmly as Landin asks, "What is it love?" She begins panting heavily, and her water breaks. "This is it," she says loudly. "Oh my," says Landin as he wraps his arms around her and helps her to her feet.

   Somewhere in a Silustrian medical facility, Rose lay on an operating table, and Landin also present holding her hand. "Everything's going to be fine love," says Landin. Rose looks at him with furious eyes while in heavy labor pain. Amazingly, a human looking doctor enters the room accompanied by a Silustrian nurse. "Hello. I am doctor Novi. We can now proceed." Landin looks at him and asks, "Have you done this before, delivered, pardon my asking?" "Yes, many times. All will be well, I assure you. But I'm afraid you'll have to wait outside sir."

Landin nods then looks at Rose, "I'll be right outside the door love, ok?" She nods then Landin leans in and kisses her. He walks away and stops facing doctor Novi, "I have your word…everything will be fine," asks Landin. "Yes, you have my word." Landin then takes one last look at Rose, winks then exits the room.

An hour has passed, since Landin left Rose in the operating room, and he now stands pacing in the hallway just outside the room with worry about his face. Mirla and Deek also present, sit on a bench next to the door. "Do not worry professor. I'm quite certain all will be ok," says Mirla. "I do hope you are right your majesty," replies Landin. Suddenly the familiar sound of a baby's first cry is heard. Landin freezes for a moment while staring at the operating room door. He smiles widely then races to the door, opening it and running in. Inside the room, Rose now holds her and Landin's healthy baby boy. Tears of joy run down her cheeks as Landin walks over to her bedside, joining Rose and their new edition to the family. Landin also begins to shed tears of joy, as he cradles his new son's head. Mirla and Deek also now enter the room. Landin looks at doctor Novi and says, "Thank you so much!" Doctor Novi smiles and leaves the room. Rose looks at Landin and asks, "What are we gonna call him?" Landin still smiles with tears of joy and replies, "James, after my father." Rose smiles and says, "James it is."

One month has passed since Landin and Rose's new born baby James safely arrived, as baby James lay asleep in bed between Landin and Rose, still on planet Silus. Rose's eyes suddenly open, and she stares at Landin and Baby James for a moment. She then quietly and cautiously kisses baby James, then Landin. Tears begin to run down her cheeks. She quietly then gets out of bed wearing a night gown and walks over to a dresser, then begins pulling out clothes, as if ready to pack.

A few moments later, Rose now fully dressed and carrying a small shoulder bag, stands at the foot of the bed, watching Landin and baby James. Tears still inch their way down her cheeks. After a moment, she whispers ever so softly, "Bye my loves." She then turns and walks away towards the chambers entrance. A few seconds later, Landin's eyes open and he notices Rose no longer in bed. He gets up wearing pajamas and walks out of the room looking everywhere for her, but nowhere in sight. He then jogs to the entrance door, opens it and looks out, seeing Rose walking with her bag. "Rose, what are you doing love," he shouts. Rose stops in her tracks, puts her head down, then turns to him. Landin jogs up to her and stops then asks, "What is the meaning of this? Why are you dressed and carrying a bag in the middle of the night?" She looks at the ground again, then him and replies, "I can't stay here. I have to go. I was gonna tell you, but thought it best to just leave."

"Leave, why? What's going on," he asks with nervous tone. Rose looks at the ground again briefly, then at Landin and replies, "It isn't possible for me, none of this! My father would drop dead if he knew! And I would never have a seat at the council either!" Landin now wearing a look of disgust loudly says, "Father, the council? You mean to tell me that your father and the council mean more to you than our beautiful new son, or me?" Rose now stares at the ground as Landin continues, "I don't know what to think at this moment. How could you do this?" Rose replies, "It's only the half of it."

"Half of it? What do you mean by that?"

"Who you, and our son are."

"Me, our son? This better be good." Rose takes a deep breath, exhales and explains, "Your actual being." Landin now looking clueless as to what Rose is trying to imply replies, "Being…being human you mean?"

"No…being Akkinuu as well." Landin stares into Rose's eyes and asks, "Akkinuu? What is this, Akkinuu you speak of?"

"Remember the blood sample I took from you? Well, I tested it…and it came up with positive Akkinuu DNA." Landin now looking ever curious asks, "You're saying, that I, and our son are part of some other race of beings?"

"Yes…ancestral."

"This is all beginning to sound crazy! So even if our

son, and I are part of this Akkinuu ancestral race you speak of, how can that be such a bad thing, enough to make you abandon your own son?"

"They, the Akkinuu are very disliked by my father, and several other council members, for reasons I will not speak of here."

"So for that, you truly are just gonna walk away from your son, and our love? And there's nothing I can say to change your mind?" Rose looks at Landin with sadness and gently kisses his lips, then replies, "No. Goodbye." She turns and walks away. Landin struck with heartbreak and in total disbelief, continues to watch her walk away out of his and his son's lives…wishing it was all only a nightmare. Rose turns a corner, now out of sight and sound. Landin turns and sees Queen Mirla standing at the other end of the hall, with tears in her eyes of this grave happening. She remains completely speechless, as Landin returns to his chambers.

The next day has arrived, as Landin sits at the table in Mirla's dinner hall, holding his baby James and singing to him. "Campptown ladies sing this song, Doo-da, Doo-da. The Camptown racetrack's five miles long, Oh doo-da day." Baby James smiles and giggles, still unaware of Rose's absence. Mirla and Deek enter the dinner hall and take a seat as well, admiring Landin and baby James. "Good morning professor," says Mirla. "Good morning your majesty. We did manage to somehow get some rest last night, in light of current events." Mirla smiles briefly, then leans in and asks, "So…what are your plans now professor?"

"Plans…yes. The first thing that comes to mind, is my son here living a normal life. And that is something he will have." Mirla looks at Landin curiously and says, "You and your son are more than welcome to stay here with us, as long as you desire. There are others like you here as well, Akkinuu." Landin smiles and replies, "Why thank you so graciously your majesty. I may very well take you up on the offer…but first, I must return home, Earth. A most important matter I need to take care of." Mirla nods and replies, "Deek here shall assist you on your journey. For his age, he excels among most navigators." Deek smiles at Mirla, while Landin replies, "Thank you so graciously again your majesty." Mirla smiles and nods.

It is broad daylight in a large city Back on Earth, where in front of a church Landin stands with baby James wrapped in a blanket. He walks up to the church doors and is greeted by a nun. She says, "Are you sure this is what you want?" Landin hands baby James to her and replies, "Yes, I am sure. I want him to go to a good honest home. A normal life is all I want for him. And I will be checking up on him from time to time." Landin leans in and kisses baby James one last time, then looks at the nun and says, "Thank you sister." She smiles, as Landin turns and walks away with a tear rolling down his cheek.

  The year is 2007, thirty seven years since Landin Burke said goodbye to his baby boy James. In front of a small town paper somewhere in Arizona, The Dailey Chronicle, a man walks out dressed in a suede sports jacket, jeans and snake skin boots, James Lowery, newspaper reporter, Landin Burke's son. James walks up to a beat up looking minivan and enters, while just across the street in the shadows of a building entrance lurks his father professor Landin Burke, dressed in a dark drifter and dark cartwheel style hat, watching James. He smiles at the sight of him and says, "Proud of you my boy." He then puts on a pair of dark sunglasses, turns and walks away into a small crowd of afternoon shoppers.

The beginning…